CLAN N

BRUJAH

GHERBOD FLEMING

author	gherbod fleming
cover artist	john van fleet
series editors	john h. steele and stewart wieck
copyeditor	anna branscome
graphic designer	ron thompson
cover designer	ron thompson
art director	richard thomas

More information and previews available at white-wolf.com/clannovels

White Wolf Publishing
735 Park North Boulevard, Suite 128
Clarkston, GA 30021
www.white-wolf.com

First Edition: April 2000

10 9 8 7 6 5 4 3 2 1

Printed in Canada.

For my parents.

*(You can read this one;
it's a sweet, nonviolent, love story.
I promise.)*

BRUJAH

part one:

smoke and mirrors

Thursday, 14 October 1999, 1:47 AM
Dockside, *U.S.S. Apollo*, the Inner Harbor
Baltimore, Maryland

He'll never go for it.

As he walked along the waterfront, Theo had no illusions that his current task was anything but doomed to failure. There was little chance for gain, and presumably much risk of loss. The feeble breeze blowing in off the Northwest Branch of the Patapsco River shared Theo's lack of enthusiasm. The night was unseasonably warm, but the Brujah archon still wore his heavy leather jacket, as well as the omnipresent black baseball cap.

The Sabbat's breathing down our necks, and I'm playing diplomat, he thought, shaking his head.

The Inner Harbor area was quiet. The museums, shops, restaurants, the aquarium—all of them catered to the tourist dollar, and tourists generally went to bed early. This "revitalized" part of the city was Prince Garlotte's pride and joy.

Theo didn't understand it. He could only take so much "quaint" before he gagged. He preferred other parts of the city, *real* parts of the city, where real honest-to-God people lived and died. The trickle-down economics of the uptown developers didn't ever seem to trickle that far. But those real neighborhoods weren't where the prince and his refined, financier buddies spent their time, so what did they care? They were already the kings of the mountain. They had everything they wanted at the top, and not much was left for anybody else. It didn't have to be that way. Money and influence were like water—left to themselves, they flowed downhill. Problem was, they never were left to themselves. Some greedy, button-down motherfucker was always building a dam, so the thirsty bastards at the bottom of the hill were left with jack shit.

What the world needed was somebody to bust some fucking dams.

But Theo couldn't honestly say that he lived up to that philosophy. Not all the time, anyway. Not most of the time. Times like tonight, he felt more like a damned houseboy. *Yes, sir. No, sir.* The pisser was that he could run roughshod over Garlotte. Theo could *make* the prince see things his way—or at least agree to go along. But nothing was ever that simple. Too heavy a hand now caused more problems later. Restraint was the difference between an archon and a thug.

Maybe a thug has the better deal, Theo thought. Bust heads now, ask questions later, if at all. The idea wasn't completely foreign to an archon's job description, but it wasn't the way to go when a prince was involved. Especially a Ventrue prince. The blue bloods were just too damn tight. Too many friends, or if not friends, flunkies, in high places. Threaten a Ventrue and he might give in rather than take a punch, but the next thing you knew, Interpol was on your ass, and your haven was condemned by the local housing authority and bulldozed, and all your credit cards were cancelled. Bad mistake. So on went the kid gloves.

Like I got time for it.

It wouldn't matter whose feelings were hurt when the Sabbat rolled into town. But Theo played the game anyway.

He stopped about a hundred yards from Garlotte's boat—Garlotte's fucking *schooner*, rather. A sterile reproduction of a nineteenth-century merchant ship. The thing reminded Theo of a slave ship. The period was off by at least several decades, but that was the first thought that came to his mind every time he saw it. Lord knew that Garlotte got his kicks from playing lord and master. But what prince didn't?

Theo had it on good authority that, before the prince's Embrace, Garlotte had been nothing more than a bankrupt petty noble in England, that unlife had treated him a hell of a lot better than real life. Still, Garlotte was prince of Baltimore, had been for a couple of centuries. That said something about the man. He might be an impulsive and arrogant son of a bitch, but he had something going for him. Even if that something was only luck.

"I'd take luck over brains any night," Theo muttered to himself.

He reached into his jacket and pulled out a pack of unfiltered cigarettes and a small box of matches. Cancer wasn't too big a worry, all things considered. He struck a match on his jacket zipper, lit up, and drew in a big carcinogenic breath. The smoke crept along the back of his throat until he breathed two swirling gray pillars from his nose. Some Kindred—those who went in for things coy—played at smoking in the winter, so mortals wouldn't notice their lack of breath in the cold air. Theo just liked the taste.

He liked old burnt coffee too, and on occasion a sip of blood from a week-dead body.

A gray cloud trailing along behind him, Theo continued on toward the prince's play ship.

He'll never go for it, Theo thought again. He knew it; Jan knew it. But they had at least to make a polite attempt to convince the prince that Jan's plan would work. Garlotte would balk, then they'd play hardball. That was what it was going to come down to. No doubt about it. Political cover bullshit. That's all this visit was about. Ass-Covering 101. Theo hated it, and he hated even more the fact that he played along with it. But here he was. Never mind that the Sabbat were snaking their way north from Washington. Never mind that there were a hundred thousand more productive things that he should be doing. This visit, the whole plan, Theo reminded himself, did have something to do with the Sabbat, but that thought did little to lighten his mood.

As he approached the prince's ship, a dark silhouette appeared at the top of the gangplank. The figure paused for only a second before stepping out of the darkest shadows. Katrina, childe of Prince Garlotte, moved smoothly and confidently with a feline predatory grace as she disembarked from the ship. She, too, wore a black leather jacket and a black baseball cap, although with a short pony tail sticking out the back.

Theo almost smiled as he and his shapelier double met near the edge of the dock. With their similar dress, he could have been looking in a mirror—a funhouse mirror, where the reflection was a foot and at least a hundred pounds smaller, and pale white instead of dark brown. "Your mama always dress you that funny?" he asked in a deep, serious rumble.

"You gotta appointment?" Katrina asked in return.

Now Theo did smile slightly. He folded his arms. "I think he'll see me."

Katrina folded her arms also. "I wouldn't go in just yet."

"And why's that?"

The sudden explosion that answered Theo's question blasted him and Katrina off their feet. For a drawn-out instant as he sailed airborne away from the water, Theo caught sight of the giant fireball that, seconds before, had been Prince Garlotte's ship. Then the Brujah archon landed with all the concussive force of the explosion that had launched him. The impact sent the world spinning.

When he finally came to rest, Theo lay on his back for a few more seconds. A smaller eruption of fire and lumber sent another tremor through the dock and sprayed him with a shower of flaming debris. Instinctively he covered his face, his only exposed skin other than his hands.

When most of the fragments of the U.S.S. *Apollo* had stopped landing all around him, Theo sat up. He was a dozen yards from where he'd been standing. A large section of the ship's hull was sinking beneath the water with an impressive hiss of smoke, and then the ship—aside from the smoldering pieces that lay scattered on the dock or floating on the water—was gone.

"Shit." Theo climbed to his feet, not bothering to brush himself off. He sighed deeply. Garlotte had—

or *had* had—enough clout with the city fathers that the cops left him alone. But this…this was going to draw attention.

Theo spared a few more seconds to survey the wreckage—and saw Katrina lying not far away on the dock. He shook his head. "Shit."

As he ambled over toward Katrina, she groaned and raised up on her elbow. Her hat was gone, her hair and clothes disheveled. The pale, once-perfect skin of her face was abraded, although her blood had already begun to repair the worst damage. She looked at Theo but seemed too dazed to flee.

He stood above her and planted his fists squarely on his hips. "Get up."

Katrina just nodded at first. Then the words seemed to sink in. Favoring one leg, she climbed painfully to her feet. Theo still glowered down at her. Sirens were sounding, in the distance but drawing closer.

"You know," he said, "if I'd seen you here, I'd have to break your fuckin' head."

Katrina stared at him, blinked, twice. Some of the fog of confusion began to clear from her eyes. She regarded him warily. She wasn't foolish enough to try to run away, or maybe she was just too shaken by the explosion. "Yeah?" She was skeptical, not hopeful.

"Yeah." There was no question that he could do it—he could reach out and snap her in two. There was no question that he *should* do it. "This city ain't where you want to be," he said instead.

Katrina nodded again, only slowly catching his meaning. She seemed to become aware of the approaching sirens now too and began to edge away from Theo, cautiously testing her weight on her injured leg at first, but more obviously hurrying after the first few steps.

"Hey," Theo called.

She cringed at the sound of his voice, but stopped and turned back to face him.

"There's two of the prince's lookouts on those two buildings back there," Theo said, pointing back over his shoulder like he was thumbing a ride. "Unless you want witnesses."

"Yeah. I know," Katrina said. "I'll take care of it." She limped away from that charred portion of the dock as quickly as she could.

Theo shook his head. "Shit," he muttered to himself again. By the time the fire trucks and ambulances showed up, he was long gone.

Thursday, 14 October 1999, 2:51 AM
Babcox Industrial Park
Green Haven, Maryland

"Do you see them?"

"No, I don't see them. Just shut up," Clyde said testily.

"I don't know how you can lose a *Chevette*, for God's sake," Maurice said anyway.

"Just *shut up*." Clyde gripped the steering wheel tightly. He made a hard turn between two old warehouses. Beyond the throw of the headlights, the night seemed ominously quiet and empty.

Tense silence—for a moment, then, "It's not even a real car."

"*Look*," Clyde strained to keep from yelling, "they hung a U-turn, they were coming right at us…. What'd you want me to do, plow right into them?"

"Don't yell at *me* about it," said Maurice.

"I'm not yelling!" Clyde yelled.

"*Sounds* a lot like yelling," Maurice said, growing angrier himself.

"Maybe Reggie and Eustace have found them."

"I doubt it," Maurice said. "And how come *they* get the pick-up? I bet nobody in a Chevette would've run us off the road if we'd been in the pick-up."

"Will you *please* forget about the pick-up!"

"You're yelling again."

"I am not ye… Look. Did you see how many there were?"

"It was a Chevette, for God's sake. There couldn't have been more than two or three."

"Maybe Reggie and Eustace have found them," Clyde said again without much hope.

"I doubt it."

The various warehouses, especially in the dark, were indistinguishable from one another. Clyde spurred their own car past a long row of bay doors and aluminum siding. He turned left between two buildings.

"Haven't we been this way already?" Maurice asked.

"No," said Clyde. He wasn't sure if they'd been that way already or not, but he wasn't going to give Maurice the satisfaction.

"Where are Reggie and Eustace when we need them? They ought to be here. Not that they'd be much help. But they've got the truck."

"A-ha!"

Clyde jerked the car to a stop, killed the headlights. Ahead, pulled up to one of the warehouse doors, was an unoccupied Chevette. Clyde and Maurice both sat and stared at it for a moment. Clyde's mouth was suddenly very dry. He could feel his fangs sliding down like they did when he was excited or nervous. He looked over at Maurice, but Maurice was still staring at the empty Chevette.

"You got your gun?" Clyde asked.

"Yeah. For whatever good it might do."

"Right." Clyde reached behind the seat. He had a baseball bat. He wasn't a very good shot, and he liked the feel and weight of the bat anyway.

The car doors creaked when they got out. The two Kindred eased closer to the Chevette, bent down, looked underneath. They peeked through the side windows, through the hatchback window. There was blood on the carpet in the back. Clyde licked his lips, wasn't sure if it was in response to the blood or just to wet his parched lips.

As they edged toward the warehouse, Clyde started to have second thoughts, and third thoughts, and fourth…. Maybe those hadn't been Sabbat vampires that had run him off the road. Maybe he'd just *thought* he'd seen a red-eyed, fang-baring maniac behind the wheel of the Chevette. Maybe the blood in the back of that car was there for some perfectly ordinary reason, like…like…

Maurice tapped him on the shoulder and whispered, *"You go first."*

"Thanks."

Clyde reached for the doorknob with his left hand, shifted the bat in his right. The door was unlocked. Inside was black. Lasombra black, Clyde thought. Just inside the door, he smelled blood—just a few drops, a dribble on the cement floor. Slowly, his eyes started to adjust and Clyde could make out tall metal racks full of large boxes on wooden pallets filling the dark space. There was a light switch near the door, but maybe the Sabbat—or whoever it was—didn't yet know he and Maurice were there. Clyde found a piece of broken wood and, as quietly as possible, propped open the door. Maurice followed him more deeply into the darkness.

They kept to the aisle along the wall, glancing down each perpendicular row between the racks that extended beyond vision. The blood kept to that aisle also. Every few yards, Clyde's nose would twitch, and he would smell the droplets on the floor. He thought that maybe he could just make them out as he tried to step over them, but he wasn't sure. He and Maurice had moved beyond the scant light from the propped door, and the gloom deepened with every step. All was silent, except for the shuffling of their feet along the cement.

One of the next rows—the center row?—was wider, and Clyde could see the far wall of the warehouse, maybe fifty yards distant. A bay door was open there, and although it was dark outside, it wasn't *as* dark, and a long, distorted rectangle of the warehouse was slightly illuminated. Near the center of that patch lay a woman, a girl really. She was hog-tied, and gray duct tape covered her mouth. Even from that distance, Clyde thought he could smell the bloody abrasions on her wrists and ankles, where she'd struggled against the rope. Or maybe it was the gash on the side of her face, or the smeared blood she lay in, or the intermittent trail that led from her to Clyde's feet.

"*Oh, Jesus…*" Maurice whispered; then, "*It's a trap.*"

Clyde nodded. It probably was a trap. But the girl's eyes were open. She didn't see Clyde and Maurice, but she was still alive, conscious, struggling weakly.

In all his years of feeding, Clyde had never had to beat someone. He'd never so much as left an open wound…but these monsters of the Sabbat seemed to revel in pain and torment. So even if it was a trap, he was seized by a sense of resolution. He gripped the baseball bat more tightly.

"Come on."

"Um…don't you mean this way? Clyde?" Maurice faltered, but fell in behind before Clyde got too far down the center row.

Clyde couldn't take his eyes from the girl. She was alive. She was bleeding, but he could see now that she was aware, that the wounds seemed largely superficial. Facial lacerations tended to bleed freely. He and Maurice could scoop her up and make a break for it out the bay door. They could save her.

Except that was when Clyde heard the muffled sounds of struggle behind him. He turned just as a big, muscled figure, wrestling with Maurice from behind, slit Maurice's throat. That wasn't going to finish Maurice, but the natural instinct when one's throat is slit is to freak out. And Maurice did. His attacker ripped away Maurice's pistol, held it to Maurice's temple, pulled the trigger.

Clyde flinched. The gunshot didn't seem real, couldn't be real. The contents of Maurice's skull, spread out for all to see, couldn't be real. The blood-splattered grin of his attacker couldn't be real.

Maurice's limp body slid down to the floor. His killer was covered from neck to toe in skin-tight black rubber, interrupted here and there by zippers and metal studs. His head was shaved and tattooed. In one hand, he held Maurice's gun; in a second, a knife; in a third, a machete.

Clyde blinked, horrified. *Third hand?*

He—*it*—had a third arm attached near the center of his chest.

Clyde turned and ran. *Get the girl. Get out.* That was all he could think. He couldn't acknowledge the madness he was fleeing, couldn't think about it right now. *Get the girl. Get out.*

But the girl wasn't alone anymore. Two more of the bondage-clad Sabbat were standing over her, both grinning like the other. But something else was wrong...unnatural. Clyde glanced behind him. The three-armed, tattooed thing that had killed Maurice was coming closer. The third hand waved daintily. Clyde looked back at the girl, at the two rubber bodysuits. The two thugs were the same as the first one. They didn't just *look* the same—same clothes, same shave, same tattoos—they had the same *face*, like they were made from the same mold. Clyde looked back and forth again. He stumbled. The darkness seemed to close in. He wondered what kind of hellish nightmare he'd fallen into.

But, no, there was a difference among the three, he realized. Arms. The two Sabbat ahead by the girl didn't have three—or they *did* have three arms, but only between them. One had two arms, the other only had one. Clyde looked at his own hands, his own two. That *was* the right number, yes? The image of the three-armed monstrosity slitting Maurice's throat was so indelibly seared into Clyde's mind, three somehow seemed right.

No matter. The demons must have read his mind and were willing to accommodate him somewhat. As Clyde looked on in disbelief, the one's only arm began to wither away, and a third arm sprouted from the chest of his compatriot, bulging and then bursting through the taut rubber of his bodysuit.

In that instant, Clyde was overcome by a revulsion for these creatures that dwarfed the most severe loathing he'd ever felt for himself, for what he'd become. His own petty angst was a sign of awareness, a milepost of humanity that these creatures had left far behind. He stepped forward and raised the bat—

—And it was snatched from his grasp from behind. A flurry of blows forced him to his knees as the three-armed beasts converged on him. At the feet of the armless Sabbat, the girl's desperate, bulging eyes beseeched Clyde, asked the impossible of him.

The no-arm literally danced, jumping gleefully. "Here kitty, kitty," it said in a high twittery voice, the words interrupted by squeaking giggles. "Some milk for kitty, kitty…" it said, and then began kicking the girl, stomping her head, smashing its boot into her face.

Clyde could not help her. He cowered under the blows of the demons, his own bat turned against him, fists, the machete. He was relieved slightly when one of the first kicks to the girl's head drove consciousness from her. It was a small mercy. Clyde hoped to escape the madness as well. He wished for a quick end.

He was not to be so lucky.

Thursday, 14 October 1999, 11:48 PM
Telegraph Road
South of Baltimore, Maryland

Something about the delivery truck caught
Theo's eye. There was no specific give-away, no tell-
tale sign that he could put his finger on. The truck
was unmarked, but it wasn't unusually old, dirty or
beaten up. There were plenty of places a delivery truck
might be going. The real estate between Baltimore
and D.C. was a continuous stretch of suburb, office
and commercial space, after all. And a lot of these
guys worked at night—to beat the traffic. The truck
was going just a few miles per hour over the speed
limit. Maybe that was what got Theo's attention.

These guys usually drive like NASCAR on crack.

Whatever the reason, Mr. Maryland State
Trooper evidently had a similar idea. Theo was hanging well back from the truck when he noticed the
cop car easing up behind him. At first he assumed
the cop was interested in him—racial profiling, black
guy on a motorcycle. Police, to Theo's thinking,
weren't an out-and-out threat, but they were a complication to be avoided. Business tended to be ugly
enough as it was, without adding gun-toting mortal
paramilitaries to the mix. Sure, the local prince had
some of the middle and maybe upper command
wrapped around his little finger, but that often didn't
translate to shit with the patrolman who stopped you
on the street. This particular trooper caught up and
began pacing Theo.

Theo was already going slow enough not to gain
on the delivery truck. He eased off the gas even

more—slowed to the speed limit, three miles per hour under, five under. The cop was riding his tailpipe now. The cop pulled left, cruised on past, and caught up with the truck in just a few seconds. Theo maintained his distance.

The trooper paced the delivery truck for maybe half a mile before the lights atop the patrol car flashed to life and added whirling blue patterns to the monochromatic yellow of the street lamps. Theo slowed and dropped farther behind.

The driver of the truck slowed too, then turned into the next office-park side street. The patrol car followed. Theo turned the corner just as the police cruiser disappeared around another turn to the left. The blue lights were still visible and came to rest in what Theo could just make out as a parking lot on the other side of a row of landscaped trees and shrubbery.

The Brujah pulled up to the curb and killed his engine. As he stepped over the foot-wide strip of manicured turf and into the cover of the shrubs and trees, shadows stretched out to greet him. No twig, leaf, or pine needle snapped or made any sound at all beneath his size-thirteen boots.

Theo watched from the shadows as the trooper, out of his car, approached the truck from behind. The cops were bound to be on edge. There had been so much "gang violence" over the past few months. Drug warfare, the papers and TV news called it. A violent realignment as King Crack lost its novelty and newer, deadlier forms of cocaine and heroin—and their dealers—vied for ascendancy. All bullshit, of course. But that didn't change the basic fact that a lot of shots

were being fired—by somebody, for some reason—
and innocent bystanders were paying a heavy price.
The cops knew that much only too well. This trooper
approached the truck with a hand on his gun.

Theo waited. If it turned out to be a routine traffic stop, he was back on his bike and nobody knew
he was ever here. That's what he was thinking when
the hand that offered a license to the trooper also
took hold of the cop's wrist and yanked him up off
the ground and through the open window into the
truck.

"Shit."

Theo stepped out of the brush and jogged toward the truck, keeping out of the lines of sight of
the driver's window, the side-view mirror, and the
video camera on the inside of the trooper's windshield. *The dead trooper,* Theo thought.

As he got into position, Theo reached under his
jacket and unclipped his baby: a Franchi SPAS 12,
twelve-gauge combat shotgun. With familiar ease, he
unfolded and secured the metal stock, then clicked
off the double safeties. He was in single-shot, which
was fine with him.

The delivery truck's engine rumbled to life. Not
wasting any time, Theo pumped and fired. The nearly
simultaneous blasts of the shotgun and of the front
left tire exploding shook the night.

The driver, leaning out the window to look at
the tire, realized too late the cause of the blowout.
Theo was already switched over to semi-automatic.
From closer than twenty yards, his first burst caught
the driver square in the face, neck, and shoulder. Four
shells, forty-eight lead slugs, tore through flesh and

bone. The driver's head was gone. His left arm fell to the pavement.

Before the report of the shots had faded to silence, Theo had circled wide behind the police car and come around to the passenger's side of the truck—just as the passenger, splattered with blood, jumped down from that door. He wore a generic deliveryman uniform—tan, with a green-trimmed patch that read "Wallace." To Theo's eyes, though, there was no disguising the lifeless flesh, lifeless as his own, running only on borrowed blood.

Wallace was anxiously watching back in the direction of Theo's first two shots and never knew, even when the next burst hit and ripped his chest open, what happened.

Theo stepped closer to the bloody mess that had been Wallace and took a quick glance in the cab of the truck. The state trooper, covered with more blood and bodily matter than Wallace had been, was crumpled into a heap. His neck was broken—with the angle of his head to his body, it had to be—but his eyes were open. Perhaps he still clung to life.

No time for sympathy. Theo didn't know if the trooper had called for backup, but more importantly, the Brujah heard movement from the back of the truck. Less than a minute had passed since he'd blown out the tire. In the space of a few more seconds, he reached into a pocket, took seven more shells—solid tungsten slugs this time—and reloaded. His long and nimble fingers, given the speed of blood, were a blur even to him.

Theo took a few steps away from the truck. He loosed a burst at the side wall of the cargo section.

The slugs, designed to penetrate light armor, ripped through the thin metal. Alarmed screams rang out from within. Theo could hear bodies diving for cover. He slid around to the rear of the truck and plugged another burst through the cargo door. More shouts of pain and panic.

That should keep 'em on the floor for a second.

With that extra bit of time, Theo reloaded again. The shells were in before he finished pulling back another ten yards. As one member of the Sabbat cargo grew brave and threw open the rear door, and as Theo backed quickly away, he fired two bursts at the fuel tank.

The cacophonous roar of flame and metal rattled the windows of the nearby office buildings. The explosion spun the patrol car back several feet. Theo stood and surveyed his handiwork for just a few seconds. The truck chassis was blackened and burning. Plumes of black, acrid smoke billowed into the night sky. No more Sabbat. Not much in the way of bodies for anyone to find—some dust among the ashes, and an unfortunate state trooper.

Theo wondered for a moment if the officer had already been dead or if the explosion had finished him. Not much difference really, at this point. Finally, Theo went to the patrol car, opened the door. He ripped the video camera from the windshield, cracked open the casing with his hands, and tossed the device into the fire.

That was that. He was little more than a breeze through the darkness. Weapon holstered, back to his motorcycle. He'd been away from his bike fewer than ten minutes. He was gone before the cleaning crew in one of the offices was able to report the explosion.

Holy shit!

Octavia swung the hatchet—there was hardly enough room; the steering wheel seemed to press right up in her face—and somebody's hand flopped into the passenger's seat next to her. The rest of the arm jerked back out the window damn fast. She didn't have time to gloat.

Something hard—a fist—smashed the window just a few inches from her face. She lunged over, cheek against the severed hand in the seat, to get away from the grasping fingers from the other direction. She swung the hatchet across her body, smashed her forearm against the steering wheel, but the blade still managed to slip between fingers and separate knuckles. Another bloody hand jerked back.

She and Jenkins had stopped to check out an abandoned auto. Like they were supposed to do. Fuck if these *things* didn't swarm their car as soon as she'd cut the engine. And fast too. One of them had slammed a metal rod *through* the fucking engine block. That was before the things had pulled Jenkins, kicking and screaming, through the window.

Now everything was all hands and flying glass and blood. The back window was gone. They were squirming in that way. Others were beating the windshield. That'd be gone in a few seconds, and then they'd be coming that way too.

Octavia swung again. The hatchet lodged in somebody's forehead but then was wrenched from her grasp. She heard screams and laughter.

Crash!

There went the front windshield. And the impact set off the fucking air bag, knocking her senseless, pinning her to the seat. Hands grasping, and then her own hatchet...

Friday, 15 October 1999, 3:27 AM
Pendulum Avenue
Baltimore, Maryland

"Right this way, sir," said the butler, when it became apparent that the guest was not about to give up his jacket.

Despite the open, spacious foyer, Theo felt hemmed in. The impeccable decor, the precise placement of every vase, every bauble, contributed flawlessly to the design and conveyed an impression of restrained elegance. Not gaudy or ostentatious. Rather tasteful, cultured. Theo could recognize all this. After all, Don Cerro had spent a good portion of the late nineteenth century escorting him around from one of the finest Kindred courts of Europe to another. Theo was well acquainted with the refinement of patrician tastes. He just didn't like it.

A younger Brujah might have made a point of tracking mud in on the sparkling tile and the Oriental runner, or of knocking something over, or slapping the butler on the back and breaking his ribs. Theo still felt the destructive urges—just not those coy, little, petty ones. Why spit in the man's face when you could break his nose instead? No, the anger was never far below the surface. That came with the blood. Maybe Theo had just acted on enough of his anger and seen enough over the years to know that Robert Gainesmil was not the enemy. He was just a symptom.

So Theo followed the butler through the wide halls with their high ceilings. Normally, the Brujah archon would have ignored this invitation from

Gainesmil. But tonight wasn't normal—because last night Theo had seen the former prince of Baltimore blown to bits. Theo had seen it, he'd seen who'd done it, and he'd let her go. It was worth his while to keep an ear to the ground when normally he wouldn't care what the locals thought. So when he'd gotten back from his sweep south of the city—and reamed out the perimeter patrol that had missed the delivery truck, even though there was no real way they could've known—and received a message from Gainesmil, Theo had decided to respond.

They reached the study—or whatever the hell the room was—after a few minutes. It was far enough from the front door to give an impression of the size of the estate, but not so far as to belabor the point. The butler turned the knobs and, with a gentle push, the double doors swung open quietly and easily.

"Mr. Theo Bell."

"Thank you, Langford," said the Toreador host.

Gainesmil sat in a straight-backed chair, his posture perfectly erect, knees together, slippered feet flat on the deep brown carpet. He wore a smoking jacket, red with ermine trim, and beneath it a silk shirt with his signature frilled jabot. Behind him burned a small fire. Gas logs, Theo noticed. A gas line into a Kindred's haven could be a bad idea.

Ballsy to keep it on, Theo thought, *after last night*.

"Refreshment?" Gainesmil asked, gesturing toward a decanter on a table nearby.

"No thanks," said Theo. *Bottled blood. No thanks*.

"That will be all, Langford."

"Yes, sir." The butler backed out of the room, pulling the doors closed as he went.

"Please, sit." Gainesmil indicated the matching chair across from his own. Theo sat and folded his arms.

"I appreciate your agreeing to see me, Archon Bell," Gainesmil began. "I know you keep a busy schedule."

"Not a problem…as long as the Sabbat don't attack."

Gainesmil laughed politely at the presumed joke, then realized that Theo's expression was, as very nearly always, unchanged. The Toreador elder cleared his throat. "Well, then. Let me be brief." As if not fully resigned to his declared brevity, Gainesmil paused for a long moment. He was obviously choosing his words carefully, approaching, perhaps, a subject about which he didn't wish to be completely forthright.

"Sheriff Goldwin," Gainesmil said, "has suggested that last night's attack upon the prince…upon the *late* prince, was most likely the first phase of the Sabbat offensive against our city." He paused, as if expecting comment from his guest, but Theo said nothing.

"Prince Garlotte, of course, is no longer with us…" Gainesmil said, but then he faltered slightly, the slightest tremor of emotion evident in his voice.

Theo noticed but did not react. Genuine regret at the loss of a long-time friend and ally, or merely a display to imply such tender feelings? Gainesmil had not done the deed himself, but had he contributed? Theo turned that possibility over in his mind. Had Gainesmil goaded Katrina into the Kindred equivalent of patricide?

"Several members of the prince's security detail were lost in the explosion," Gainesmil went on. "And two sentries on buildings near the ship were found dead. More importantly than the ghouls, however," he dismissed the ghouls' deaths with a wave of his hand, "Malachi and Katrina are unaccounted for." He paused again, but Theo still only looked at him. "They are presumed destroyed."

Theo waited. *Whatever you've got to say, go ahead and say it.*

"You arrived at the scene ten or fifteen minutes after the explosion."

Theo nodded.

"You were patrolling in the area."

"Coming back from patrolling farther out," Theo said evenly. "The Inner Harbor's been pretty safe."

"'Pretty safe,' as you say," Gainesmil agreed. He raised a finger and tapped his lips, slowly, three times. "There was, however, an instance…oh, three months back, when the Inner Harbor was not so safe."

Again, Theo waited impassively. He could see where this was headed, but wasn't about to help Gainesmil along. *Spit it out.*

"The attack on Mr. Pieterzoon. I believe you are aware that it occurred?"

Theo nodded. This could be ticklish. He'd followed Pieterzoon that night because he didn't trust the bastard and wanted to find out a little more about how the Ventrue spent his nights. Dumb luck that that Sabbat hit squad had wandered in that night— bad luck for them, good luck for Jan, and for the Camarilla, Theo had come to decide.

But if Gainesmil knew Theo was around for the

attack on Pieterzoon *and* was closer than he'd claimed when the *U.S.S. Apollo* went sky high... Even though there was no real connection, it wouldn't look good. It might be enough to stir up trouble, if that's what the Toreador was after.

"Why did you keep silent about the attack on Mr. Pieterzoon?" Gainesmil asked.

"Same reason Prince Garlotte and Mr. Pieterzoon kept quiet about it," Theo responded. "Same reason you kept quiet about it, I 'spect. Kind of embarrassing for the prince to have a guest attacked in the heart of the city. I didn't have any reason to embarrass Garlotte."

Gainesmil contemplated this. He seemed to accept it. Or maybe it just wasn't what he was most interested in. "At the scene of the attack...of the explosion," he asked, "did you notice anything...anything that would lead you to question Sheriff Goldwin's supposition that the Sabbat were behind it?"

"Watcha got in mind?"

"Anything at all. Anything that might point toward...*other* involvement."

Theo stared at him flatly. "I ain't a detective, you know. I didn't go over the crime scene for clues."

"Of course not. Of course not. But you still might have noticed something...something amiss?"

Theo thought on that for a minute. He tapped his lip three times for good measure. Then, "Nope."

Gainesmil's expectant expression drooped noticeably. "I don't mean to hurry you. Take your time to—"

"Nope. Didn't notice nothing."

Several seconds passed before Gainesmil realized that his mouth was still open. He closed it. "You see," he continued in somewhat strained but still pleasant tones, "certain associates of Sheriff Goldwin did inspect the scene, and—"

"And you don't trust 'em," Theo said.

Gainesmil again consciously closed his mouth and spoke with a viper's smile: "It is always worthwhile, as I'm sure you would agree, Archon Bell, to solicit as many perspectives as possible."

"I generally stick to my own perspective," Theo said. "That is, unless Jaroslav tells me different. Then I usually go with his perspective."

"I see." Mention of the Brujah justicar seemed to unnerve Gainesmil slightly.

Remember who you're talkin' to, Toady-boy. Theo didn't mind being underestimated. Let them think he was big and dumb if they wanted. But he had little patience for being patronized. Amazing what a little name-dropping could do—just a not-so-subtle reminder that Theo had been hand-picked as archon by one of the most ruthless, fanatical, and just plain mean sons-of-bitches to come down the Camarilla pike in a fucking long time.

"I see."

"So you think Goldwin's people fucked up, or that he's shading what he really found," Theo said.

"It certainly is reasonable to suspect that the Sabbat are responsible," said Gainesmil, backpedaling as fast as his little semantic legs would carry him from his intimation of a moment before. "But the sheriff produced little if any hard evidence, and there are...other possibilities."

"What evidence do you want—other than a lot of fuckin' little pieces of boat all over the harbor?"

"Well…of course we may never find definitive proof. But other possibilities should not be ruled out, not yet, even if they can't be proven. After all, Sabbat involvement, though not unlikely, is merely supposition as well."

"Other possibilities," said Theo. "Like what?"

"As I said, Malachi and Katrina are *presumed* destroyed."

"*Garlotte* is just *presumed* destroyed," Theo pointed out.

"I met with the prince—*on the ship*—just less than an hour before the explosion. He did not have plans to go elsewhere."

"Would he have told you?"

"There were few secrets between Prince Garlotte and myself."

"Few that you know of."

Gainesmil shot a fierce glare, but then his expression softened. "True enough."

"You think Malachi and Katrina were involved," Theo said.

Gainesmil frowned. He rose from his chair and began to walk slowly around the room.

If this is brief, Theo thought, *I'd hate to get the long version.*

"No doubt it *was* the Sabbat…" said Gainesmil, "*but*," he raised a finger in emphasis, "without proof to that effect, speculation that parties unaccounted for could have been involved, and with nefarious intent, is not particularly wild or outlandish."

"Wild or not," said Theo, "it's speculation. I don't see the difference."

"It is *possible*," Gainesmil insisted.

"Look," Theo said. "Do you, without any proof, want to go tell Xaviar that the only Gangrel on Garlotte's payroll is who you *think* blew him up?"

"This has nothing to do with Xaviar!"

"It's got everything to do with Xaviar, or somebody like him. You go casting aspersions like that, and some offended Gangrel is going to come looking for you. He's not gonna want to discuss what you *think*, and he's not just going to piss on your mailbox. No. He's gonna make your insides your outsides."

Gainesmil was still pacing—until the mention of rearranging his anatomy. The thought did not play well with him, apparently. He pursed his lips, retook his seat.

"Besides," Theo added, "do you think explosives were Malachi's style? I mean, the guy was happy if you tossed him a raw bone."

Gainesmil chuckled wryly at that, but he was only momentarily cheered.

"Katrina?" Theo mused aloud. "I never thought she had enough…"

"Direction?" Gainesmil offered.

"Yeah," Theo agreed. "That works." It was true, as far as it went.

"But she was spiteful. Heavens was she spiteful."

"Show me a chick that ain't."

Gainesmil laughed quietly again, but mostly he was absorbed in his own thoughts.

"Anyway," said Theo, rising, "whoever the hell it was, if they blew themselves up, it don't really matter. If we find out somebody's still kickin', then we got something to talk about. Until then, I got things to do."

"Of course. Of course." Gainesmil was jolted from his reverie. He stood with Theo, then reached and pulled a nearby tassel. Not too far away, Theo heard a bell ring—a bell that mortal ears would not have noticed. Within seconds, the butler was opening the study doors.

"Langford," said Gainesmil.

"Sir?"

"Archon Bell has been more than gracious. Kindly see him to the door."

"Yes, sir."

Theo nodded in parting to Gainesmil and then followed the butler back through the hallways of the Toreador's haven. On the way, Theo smoked half a cigarette and tossed the butt into a flower vase near the front door. Sometimes, he decided, the little things were enough.

Friday, 15 October 1999, 4:11 AM
Little Patuxent Parkway
Near Columbia, Maryland

The Dodge pickup eased onto the shoulder and stopped a full twenty yards behind the trashed Crown Victoria. The truck's engine kept running. The headlights washed over the dents and shattered windows ahead.

"That Octavia's car?" Reggie asked.

Eustace studied the other vehicle for a long minute. He rolled down his window and spat onto the gravel. "Fuck, yeah."

"Thought so."

They sat and watched the car. Eustace reached forward and changed the station on the radio. There was a pleasant breeze coming through the window.

"Think anybody's still in it?" Reggie asked.

"Dunno," Eustace said. He reached behind his seat, retrieved his sawed-off, double-barreled, twelve-gauge shotgun and double checked that it was loaded. "I let you know." He spat again before getting out, wiped his mouth on his sleeve.

As Eustace approached the other car, Reggie watched carefully, only looking away for a second to change the radio back. Eustace stopped by the Crown Victoria and studied it carefully. He scratched his head and spat. Before too long, he walked back to the truck.

"Somebody done fucked it up," Eustace said.

"Don't say."

"Best call Slick. We don't want the po-lice tripping over this one."

"Well all right then."

Reggie reached for the cell phone, while Eustace changed the radio station.

Saturday, 16 October 1999, 11:20 PM
McHenry Auditorium, Lord Baltimore Inn
Baltimore, Maryland

"Theo! Thank God…." Lydia met him in the hallway leading to the auditorium. From behind her came the sounds of heated shouting. The corridor, expensively carpeted, was lined with impassive ghouls—those of Garlotte's security team that hadn't been on the ship three nights ago and gotten themselves blown to Kingdom Come. Malachi, the Gangrel scourge and usual guardian of the conference room, was conspicuously absent as well.

The shouting from the auditorium continued unabated. Theo instantly recognized one of the voices—the loudest—that kept shouting down those that rose in opposition.

"Lladislas," Theo said.

"Yep," Lydia said. She had rushed forward to meet Theo, but he'd kept on walking, so she was forced to change directions and head back toward the double doors to keep up with her elder. "He wants to be the new prince. He's demanding a vote of support."

Theo stopped in his tracks. Lydia kept going, realized he'd stopped, and reversed direction again. "*Vote?*" Theo growled. "What does he want to be— prince or fuckin' prom queen?" The archon started forward again without warning, just as Lydia got to his side, and left her behind. She scrambled after him.

He didn't slam the double doors open. He wasn't angry or disgruntled, not any more so than he usually was; he didn't need to make a dramatic entrance. The showmanship he left to others. Yet the instant he entered the auditorium and began down the side aisle, the debate died away. The Kindred at the head of the sloped room didn't regard him with fear or awe, at least not all of them did; the argument didn't end so much as pause. Theo was not their arbiter extraordinaire. Yet his presence cast the previous "discussion" in a whole new light.

He could feel the change in those first few seconds—not a lessening of tension, but more the tension coming to a head. He sensed something else as well, something Theo suspected was a direct result of Garlotte's destruction—a dangerous lack of restraint in the argument.

Then again, he thought, *maybe that's just Lladislas.*

"*Theo Bell.*" Lladislas's voice boomed and filled the entire auditorium. "Just the man we needed to see."

No one else spoke. The others—Jan, Vitel, Gainesmil, Isaac among them—watched in silence as Theo continued down the aisle toward the conference table—a *new* conference table, he noticed. Somebody had replaced the one that Xaviar had dug his claws into. That had been a touch-and-go night. Garlotte and the Gangrel justicar both had egos big enough that they'd barely fit in this room. How things changed. Garlotte was fish food, and Xaviar, his pride wounded, was supposedly leading his clan out of the Camarilla. Theo shook his head and frowned.

Lladislas apparently thought the gesture was directed at him. His brow furrowed deeply beneath his slightly receding hairline. "This city is under siege, for God's sake," the exiled prince of Buffalo continued. "It needs a new prince, and it needs a new prince *now*. I'm a man of experience. I've run a city. Actually run it—not played second fiddle." He shot a pointed glare at Isaac and at Robert Gainesmil. Each leveled a cold stare at Lladislas in return. "I've made the tough calls, the life and death decisions," he added.

"And the latest entry on your résumé," spoke Marcus Vitel, formerly of Washington, D.C., "is that your city fell to the Sabbat."

Lladislas's eyes slowly grew wide. His face, always ruddy-cheeked—quite unnatural for a vampire—darkened noticeably.

"Your city fell to the Sabbat," Vitel went on, suddenly seeming very weary, "as did mine." He held his hands, palms raised, out to his side, as if to disavow any malicious intent in his words.

The conciliatory gesture may have given Lladislas brief pause and served to prevent him from springing to violent attack, but he was far from soothed. Vitel's barb struck deeply and took hold.

"I wouldn't expect you, of all Kindred, a rival and a *Ventrue*, to support me," Lladislas snarled.

Vitel maintained his calm demeanor and even allowed a slightly bemused smile to creep onto his face. "I am certainly Ventrue…but rival?" His eyebrows rose inquisitively. "You have nothing that I want, Lladislas, and I without my city possess nothing for you to covet." Then Vitel's smile faded. His manner turned hard, perhaps pained. "As for *this* city, it is nothing more to me than refuge. Consider yourself suitor without rival. Busy yourself with trinkets, if you will. I shall content myself with nothing less than recovering the pearl that is trodden under the cloven hooves of swine."

Lladslas, like everyone else around the table, remained silent. Theo found that he had stopped short of the table to listen to Vitel and the words that resonated with such a deep sense of loss. The Brujah archon now took his place, and Lydia sat beside him.

This brief oratory was the most that Theo could remember Vitel saying publicly since the deposed prince had fled Washington. Vitel had attended most of the leadership conferences and offered his opinion, occasionally. He had even used his contacts in the nation's capital to help bring about a temporary curfew in that city—admittedly not a cure-all, but an obstacle for the Sabbat to work around at a crucial time while the Camarilla refugees streaming into Baltimore were being molded into a passable defensive force. Vitel had contributed to the cause, but he had spent most of the past months in seclusion. Whatever games he was playing—he was Ventrue; he had to be up to *something*—were behind the scenes. Pieterzoon had attempted several times to break through the wall of solitude, and Victoria, before she was shipped off to Atlanta, had undoubtedly tried to co-opt Vitel. Jan had even mentioned to Theo that Vitel seemed a broken man, that the loss of his city and his childer were a millstone around his neck.

Like I give a rat's ass, Theo thought. The blue bloods' little personal dramas weren't going to keep the Sabbat from rolling into the city. And at the moment, Lladislas, even though he was a Brujah himself, wasn't helping matters by agitating to become prince.

"If you've gotta ask permission," Theo said, break-ing the silence, "you're not the prince." He folded his arms and stared directly at Lladislas, daring his clanmate to cross him.

To his credit, Lladislas held his peace—just barely. His face reddened again, and his hands curled into white-knuckled fists, but he kept his mouth shut. Theo took this as a hopeful sign for Lladislas's future. Evidently Lladislas also recognized what was obvious to Theo and probably to several of the others, cer-tainly to Jan and Vitel: Lladislas had no constituency in Baltimore. He had few loyal supporters, there were too many Kindred of age present for him to bully his way to the top, and, unlike in his own city, there was nobody who owed him favors.

Even so, Lladislas wasn't a fool—blunt, yes; fool-ish, no. In normal circumstances, he never would have made his bid. But these were not normal cir-cumstances, not with Garlotte destroyed and the Sabbat edging northward from Washington every night. Conventional politics were thrown on their head. Even lacking a power base, Lladislas still could have become prince—if this council of elders had supported him. And that likely would have happened if Theo had pushed for his clanmate. But Theo knew things that Lladislas did not.

So Lladislas fumed, but he said nothing. There was no case to press without Theo's endorsement.

"It is absolutely true," said Jan Pieterzoon, filling the awkward silence, "that every city needs a prince. Our sense of order is what separates us from those monsters to the south."

Pieterzoon, slight of build, with wire-rimmed glasses and short, spiky blond hair, was unassuming— in a dangerous way. He brought to the table a canniness born of centuries of practice and a pedigree that caused many Kindred to blanch at the mention of his name. If after the fall of Hartford to the Sabbat others held him in lesser regard, that was because they, like Lladislas, were not privy to details that Theo was.

Now that Theo had cowed Lladislas, the archon could tell that this was a turn of events for which Jan was quite prepared.

"Considering that Prince Garlotte himself named this body as an *ad hoc* council of primogen, of sorts, in addition to its role coordinating the regional defense efforts against the Sabbat," Jan continued, "it is entirely appropriate for us to propose a candidate to assume the responsibilities of prince."

Theo gave no sign of approval or disapproval, although he suspected where Jan was going. *Good move*, Theo thought. *Just suggesting somebody. Not claiming too much authority, even though nobody in the city is gonna buck the folks in this room. Now he's gonna pick a local....*

"I'm sure we would all agree," Pieterzoon said, "that in such perilous times, stability among our own leadership is beneficial, even crucial. The way we can ensure the stability and skilled leadership that Baltimore enjoyed under the stewardship of Prince Garlotte is to set forth an individual who is intimately familiar with the city."

Theo didn't have to look around the table to know the two possible candidates, one of which Jan undoubtedly had in mind. Process of elimination: Lydia, though a bright kid, was present only as a place-holder until Theo had arrived. Lladislas had shot his wad and come up short. Vitel had opted out. Marston Colchester, the Nosferatu liaison, wasn't even here—at least not officially. Neither of the Malkavians, Roughneck and Quaker, were of the stature, not to mention temperament, to command a city.

That left only Robert Gainesmil, Garlotte's confidant of many years, and Isaac Goldwin, the former prince's sheriff and childe.

But the Malkavian, Roughneck, had a different idea. "What you say is all well and good, Mr. Pieterzoon. I'm not arguing, mind you…." His hair and long beard were wild and unkempt. As he spoke, Roughneck constantly pulled his fingers through his thick whiskers. His eyes gazed fixedly at some inde-terminate spot on the table. "But Theo would make a hell of a prince. Nobody gonna fuss with him in a time of trouble. Any other time, for that matter."

"Hell of a prince," echoed Quaker, who spent his nights among the homeless and looked the part.

Theo felt all eyes in the room shift toward him. When he looked, fiercely, at the two Malkavians, Roughneck seemed to wilt under Theo's gaze, even though the Malkavian himself hadn't looked up from the table. Meanwhile Quaker, true to his name, be-gan to tremble ever so slightly and cast shifty, worried glances at everyone else around the table—except Theo.

"I already got a job," Theo said at last.

"Indeed," Jan chimed in, reclaiming the agenda, much to the relief of the Malkavians. "Although the suggestion is well taken." Theo turned humorlessly toward Jan, but the Ventrue merely smiled politely in return and added, "Justicar Pascek would never willingly part with the services of his most esteemed archon." Jan paused. "That would leave Mr. Gainesmil and Sheriff Goldwin as the most likely successors to Prince Garlotte. Would you care to comment, Archon Bell?"

Theo held in a sigh. Was Jan for some reason enjoying this? He had to know damn well that Theo didn't give a shit about these political charades. This stuff wasn't supposed to be done by committee. King-making was a diversion for the backroom crowd. This stuff was all show anyway. Theo turned to look at them: Goldwin the Ventrue and Gainesmil the Toreador. He regarded them coolly for a long moment, then turned away.

"Flip a coin or whatever."

Isaac bristled slightly at the comment. Gainesmil took it more stoically. The Toreador, in speaking with Theo the night after Garlotte's demise, had certainly been trying to seed doubt in the Brujah's mind about Isaac's credibility—and loyalty, despite the fact that Gainesmil had not directly tried to link the sheriff to the explosion. Theo hadn't given Gainesmil any reason to expect support, so the less-than-shining non-endorsement, though a disappointment, had come as no surprise. An uncomfortable silence again fell over the auditorium.

"As I was saying," Jan said, picking up where he'd left off before the Malkavian's interruption and not allowing Theo's caustic words to linger too long, "to ensure a smooth transition of power..."

Theo tuned out much of Jan's spiel. Like most members of that clan, Pieterzoon had a way of using a hundred words to say what could easily be said with one. Some Kindred assumed that, by talking more, they asserted their importance. Jan probably didn't buy into that shtick, but even if the flowery language was just a cover for whatever he really had going on, at times like these, Theo still had to sit through it all.

"...the late prince's own childe and long-serving sheriff, Isaac Goldwin, would serve ably as the new prince of Baltimore," Jan wound down at last.

During the verbose ramble, Theo had shifted in his seat slightly so that he could see the reactions of both Isaac and Gainesmil. That way, once Jan finally got to his point, the archon didn't obviously have to show the least interest, not even so much as to turn or raise his head. Isaac or Gainesmil, whichever wasn't chosen, would be the one likely to protest.

Isaac, flattered and more than a little relieved, attempted to cast his grin in a magnanimous light and sat noticeably taller in his seat. Gainesmil, interestingly enough, merely nodded in agreement with Jan's pronouncement.

I wonder what Pieterzoon promised him? Theo mused. It was telling that Jan, unlike Lladislas, had lined up support for his horse *before* the meeting that would decide the matter. Then again, Lladislas had not been forced to deal with much difference of opinion while ruling over Buffalo—not that people hadn't disagreed with him, and probably often, but they hadn't ever said so to his face.

"I'm honored," Isaac began, "to be supported by such an august group…."

Theo's thoughts again drifted away. Now it was Isaac's turn to run his mouth, to pucker up to the elders who, for all practical purposes, had just made him prince. Nobody was going to make too much noise about what was decided by the childe of Hardestadt the Elder, the last Camarilla princes of Washington and Buffalo, and a Brujah archon. Gainesmil and the Malkavians, as well as the choice of Goldwin, gave the decision a veneer of provincial legitimacy. Anyway, who else was going to be prince? Nobody else—if Gainesmil gave in, as he seemed to have—was available. None of the out-of-towners was going to support another, and Garlotte had spent a good deal of energy discouraging competition to his rule, so none of the other locals were politically con-nected enough to stand on their own. Theo sure as hell didn't want the job. There was, of course, a lot of Kindred manpower in and around the city these nights, but most of it was devoted to preparing for the seemingly inevitable assault that the Sabbat was going to launch sooner or later.

"…And I plan to continue the tradition of tough but fair governance practiced for so long by my sire…."

The Sabbat. Now *that* was something worth wor-rying about. *That* was something deserving of a lot of attention. The raids north were coming more fre-quently and in greater force. The bastards were testing the defenses, getting ready for the big push. Theo had, over the past two nights, already pulled most of his patrols from the outer perimeter near Fort Mead and strengthened the second line at the airport. It was a ploy he'd known for some time that he'd undertake. He and Jan had talked about it months ago, back in August when Buffalo had fallen and they had made their plans. Jan didn't have his head stuck as far up his own ass as it seemed sometimes, but the time and energy wasted with these councils was still aggravating. If it weren't for the fact that every once in a while—a very long while—something important happened at these stuffed-shirt gatherings, Theo wouldn't bother with them at all.

"...Because Baltimore has become a city of hope for the Kindred...."

But of course, since Theo himself had taken such a personal interest in securing the city, that left Jan and now Isaac, and Garlotte and Victoria before them, free to play their parlor games. Just leave it to the Brujah to do the heavy lifting.

That's the only way the real work ever gets done, Theo thought. *Speaking of which...*

As Isaac droned on about a prince's obligations to his fellow Kindred, Theo reached into his pocket and took out his pager. He gave it a good long look, stuck it back into his pocket, and stood to leave.

"Gotta go," he said without further explanation when Isaac paused in his oration. Theo tapped Lydia on the shoulder. She followed him from the auditorium and past the security ghouls. Theo didn't bother waiting for the elevator. He used the stairs instead. He wasn't rushing, but he was so much taller than Lydia that she had to hurry to keep up as they made their way across the ornate lobby.

"Sabbat raid?" Lydia asked, almost expectantly.

"Uh-uh."

"Problem with one of the patrols?"

"Nope."

She continued along beside him as they left the Lord Baltimore Inn. "Then who the hell paged you?"

"Nobody," Theo said. "I just had to get out of there."

"So you're not in a hurry to get somewhere?" Lydia asked.

"Not right at the moment."

"Give me a ride up to Slick's? I don't feel like stealing another car just now."

"Sure," Theo said. "Where's your boys?"

"Probably there already."

Theo wasn't parked far from the inn. He waited until Lydia climbed onto the bike behind him and then cranked the engine. "Hold on."

"I *am* holding on."

Theo looked down, and damned if she wasn't. Her arms didn't reach all the way around his torso, but her white hands were latched onto folds of his jacket. Any jacket that fit Theo was bulky. This one was thicker than regular leather would have been— reinforced to deflect at least small-caliber fire or a glancing blade. The little bit of blood required to heal a pesky wound could make a big difference in a close fight. Theo knew.

Even after they'd started off crosstown, Theo wouldn't have felt Lydia sitting behind him if he hadn't know she was there. She was small and light like a feather, but Theo had seen the effect that her words and actions had on her peers—the Anarch crowd. Many of them were Brujah. The majority were also among the youngest of Kindred. An Anarch's relative youth was both a cause and an effect of his or her being an Anarch: a cause because he was low man on the totem pole and had no patience for the powers that be; an effect because only rarely did an Anarch, without the protection of some prince or other influential patron, outlive his own era. There were few old Anarchs.

Theo himself had been fortunate enough to be Embraced by a sire who was willing to spend many years instructing and educating his protégé. For whatever reason, few sires were so patient in the modern nights. Either that or the childer, independent in mortal life, demanded the same independence in unlife. The Anarch wanted freedom, and he wanted it *now*, if not before. That didn't sit well with a sire who considered "the Curse of Caine" to be, in fact, a gift, and who also expected slavish devotion from his new charge. A lot of Kindred never survived a sire's discipline.

Theo glanced over his shoulder at Lydia. The archon didn't normally play taxi for his foot soldiers, but this one had potential. She seemed the more reasonable sort, the pragmatist. She might avoid the pitfalls and make it somewhere. Or not. Time would tell for sure. Best not to get too attached.

She noticed him looking back and leaned forward, closer to his ear so that she could shout and be heard over the engine. "Before you got there, to the meeting," she said into the wind, "they were talking about Garlotte, about the explosion."

"Is that so?" Theo said evenly.

"They said it couldn't have been an accident. Too big."

Theo nodded. He kept his face turned partially to the side and watched the road out of the corner of his eye.

"Must've been Sabbat," Lydia continued. "Assamites wouldn't have been so sloppy."

Theo nodded again and turned away from her. Lydia wasn't going to say anything that he didn't know, and with her few comments, she'd already communicated to him what he'd wanted to find out. She was a good gauge of the Anarchs' mood, of sentiment on the street. Lydia believed what she was telling him. That the Sabbat would have sneaked into the city and blown up the prince seemed perfectly reasonable to her. And why not? That was the explanation that Theo had helped sell.

After the explosion, he'd gotten the hell away from the docks, circled to the west, and returned ten minutes later to watch with concern as the mortal authorities cordoned the scene of the "accident." That's what it was being called in the mortal press. Gainesmil, even if he was unhappy with Isaac's handling of the matter, was familiar with Garlotte's connections in the city government and in the media. He'd seen to it that the investigation went no further than that. Gainesmil might not believe that Garlotte's destruction was the work of the Sabbat, but the Toreador was toeing the party line.

Good for him, Theo thought. The whole Garlotte thing was just a distraction anyway. Theo avoided considering the fact that he'd had the opportunity to put an end to the matter, but had not.

The two Brujah rumbled northward, the motorcycle tearing a ragged swath through the relative quiet of the night. It didn't take them long to leave behind the sanitized Inner Harbor. The blocks beyond were a mix of offices, antique stores, restaurants, and gentrified row houses. The street parking was an unbroken line of luxury cars: BMW, Mercedes, SUV, SUV, SUV… Theo half wondered if these people had convinced themselves that they needed four-wheel drive to navigate the potholes of the city streets.

These enclaves of privilege soon gave way to areas of less polish. The paint wasn't fresh. Not every remnant of graffiti had been washed away. The shops and homes had bars over the windows. More of the cars had dents, or mismatched panels, or a missing hubcap.

As Theo rode, he now thought not about Lydia but about another pale, female Kindred: Katrina. A troubling question kept bubbling up in his mind, a question about her, and about what he had done—or not done. Over the past few nights, as he'd ridden on patrol, even as he'd tried to make sure that Gainesmil didn't have any real idea of what had happened, Theo, as was his habit, had ignored the question. There were just too many niggling details that arose over the course of eternity. Theo had decided that much after not quite two hundred years. Too many details to pay attention to them all. He liked to let them sit for a while, percolate. Most of them simmered away of their own accord until there was nothing left. Time and inattention worked at them, caused them to deteriorate and then disappear altogether. The important details, on the other hand, stood the test of time. They held solid. Those were the questions that demanded a decision, that required action.

Three nights was not long enough to determine anything. Not really. But events were moving quickly these nights. The world was a completely different place now than it had been when Theo had joined the ranks of the undead. Computer technology and communications advancements were doing all over and exponentially what the Industrial Revolution had done. Life was growing faster and faster every night. And so was death.

Theo had adjusted better than some; better than a lot, in fact. He'd never closed himself away from the world like so many Kindred had. He had contact of some sort with somebody, Kindred or kine or both, most nights. A lot of the crusty old-timers he had business with might go years without speaking to another soul. Theo shook his head. Too much time for thinking, that way. Too much introspection.

"Something wrong?" Lydia yelled at him over the roar of the engine.

"Nah."

Too much thinking, Theo thought. *Maybe that's what's happening to me. Maybe I'm getting too old.*

But whether he was getting too old or not, and whether three nights was too short a period of time to ignore the niggling thought, the question about Katrina was still hovering close enough to distract him—and distraction, especially in the face of Sabbat raids practically every night, could get his ass blown apart.

The sound of the engine surrounded Theo. He was not dangerously removed from the city around him—he stopped at a red light, he wove his way around potholes—but the bike's purr enveloped him in his own world of inner truth and consequences. It was a world with which he still was not completely comfortable, a world where fists and blood were not always the right answer. He had existed all his years as a mortal and many as Kindred without knowing of this place. Don Cerro had needed many years to teach him of it. Theo's first inclination had always been anger, violence.

But he hadn't reacted that way to Katrina. He could see her, in his mind's eye. She stood atop the gangplank, first in the shadows, then stepping out. She was dressed very similarly to him. Amusing but inconsequential enough. In Baltimore, overpopulated with Kindred as it was at the moment, it was difficult to throw a brick without hitting a vampire wearing black leather. What else?

She had stopped him from going onto the ship. She could just as easily have slipped away, and he would have climbed on board and—boom, archon fish food. But she'd warned him away and almost gotten herself blown up in the process. Was that why he'd let her go? Because that was what was bothering him—not what she'd done, but what he'd done. Letting her walk away was stupid. It was a complication he didn't need, one that still might come back to bite him on the ass. Was that why he'd spared her, because she'd spared him?

Not bloody likely, he decided at once. He might have cooled a degree or two from the firebrand of his youth, but sentimental he was not. He wasn't going to so much as sniffle if somebody snuffed Garlotte's kid—yet *something* had kept him from breaking her skull, even though that was what the situation and his office had demanded of him. What, then?

Self-interest? In a way, Katrina had made Theo's job easier. Considering what he and Jan had planned, Garlotte would have been a major pain in the ass. Now Isaac was prince, and it just didn't seem possible that he could kick up as much of a fuss as his predecessor could have.

This, too, Theo dismissed almost out of hand. He was well used to dealing with obstacles. That was his job. Plus, no matter how aggravating Garlotte might have been, the Camarilla, in the long run, was worse off without him. He was a figure of stability, and that above all else was what the Camarilla stood for.

What the hell? Theo wondered in disgust. He hadn't calculated algorithms when he'd decided to let Katrina go. He hadn't even really *decided* to do it. He'd just done it. It was instinct. Like knowing that something wasn't quite right about that damned delivery truck that was doubling as a Sabbat transport. That was what his gut told him. That was what he *did*, and he did a damn good job of it. He'd tried countless times to explain to Don Cerro that trusting his gut was what he did best.

Trusting instinct uncritically, Don Cerro had always responded, *is the first step toward conquest for the Beast.*

"Yeah, whatever."

"*What?*" Lydia yelled over the engine.

"Nothin'."

Theo scowled and accelerated suddenly through a yellow light. Lydia had to grab tightly to stay on. The archon didn't want to think about Katrina. He sure as hell didn't want to talk about her. A few more blocks and they were at Slick's, and Theo had more immediate concerns to occupy his mind. He pulled over to the curb.

In this part of the city, graffiti was the norm, the rule, not the exception. Some of it was colorful and artistic, some profane and violent, but it was ever-present. The row houses, those that weren't abandoned and boarded up, had chipped and peeling paint, if any at all. Pawn shops outnumbered groceries two to one. The few cars parked on the street were either junkers or new SUVs—the drug dealers liked to have lots of room for their stash and for weapons.

Slick's place, from the outside, was nothing more than one battered row house among many. A scruffy white guy in a jean jacket, with a black skullcap, sat on the stoop. He watched Theo and Lydia as they approached.

"Watch my bike, Jeb," said Theo.

"Sure thing," Jeb said, then, "Hey there, sweet thing," to Lydia.

She gave him the finger. "Watch the bike, hot shot."

Inside was both less and more than it appeared from the street. The front room was a wreck of old furniture with torn plaid upholstery. Crumpled newspapers littered the floor as well as the couches and chairs. Around the room were a handful of make-shift ashtrays—plastic cups, bottle lids, a sardine can with a few sardines in it—all overflowing with ashes and cigarette butts. Beyond the front room—there was no more house. Same with the two houses to the right, and the three to the left. The very end units on the block were intact, but the six inner houses were basically one-room facades.

The central portion of the block, surrounded by the facades to the front, the two full-length houses to the sides, and a tall brick wall with two large gates to the rear, was crammed full of cars in various stages of repair and transformation. To the right, a make-shift grease pit had been constructed. In the center of the workspace, ten cars were parked very closely together. Most sported sizeable dents. Some were riddled with bullet holes. Windshields were cracked or completely shattered. To the left of the work area, several men were attending to bodywork and spray-painting. Theo stood for a moment and watched the assortment of Kindred and ghouls at work.

With so many patrols on the street every night, and with so many clashes against the Sabbat—all violent and most involving gunfire—a quick change of wheels was more than a mere convenience. In the first weeks, when the Sabbat had just rolled up the East Coast from Atlanta to D.C., Theo and his troops had been running south every night, probing the disorganized Sabbat forces in the nation's capital, often striking deep within the Beltway. Getting in as far as possible meant not driving the same car every damned time. A little paint and a new license plate went a long way, but sometimes the vehicle was shot up a bit too. Bullet holes were a dead giveaway, and were a red flag for the cops as well as the enemy. There were always more cars to steal, of course, and the Camarilla was constantly augmenting its "gunship fleet" to replace vehicles that were just too badly damaged, but the grand theft auto rate had already tripled in the past months. Something as mundane as stolen cars, on that large of a scale, could still be a threat to the Masquerade. So Theo's boys recycled, and Slick was the master.

"Theo, my man!" The old black man grinned beneath his upraised welder's mask. The hissing blowtorch he held cast blue-orange reflections from his gold tooth. "You here to tell me I ain't going fast enough?" His grin just got bigger, revealing several empty spaces around his glowing tooth. "Try not bustin' up so many cars!"

"I was just in the neighborhood," Theo said.

"Buuuullshe-it."

Theo walked slowly toward the grease monkey. Slick was hunched over slightly. He always was. He had a large knot on his back—crooked spine, injury, something like that. Theo didn't know for sure, and he'd never had a reason to ask. He had, however, been around once when a stupid son of a bitch had called Slick "Nossie." Word got around of Slick's reaction, and as far as Theo knew that was the only time anybody had commented on the hump—which reminded Theo...

"You mind turning that thing off," Theo said, not a question.

Slick grinned even bigger and cut the gas to the torch.

"What kinda stupid sombitch Kindred uses a blowtorch?" Theo asked shaking his head.

"You know you love me for it," Slick said. He pulled off the welder's mask and smoothed back his thin, greasy hair.

"Yeah, whatever." Theo put his arm around the much shorter man and led him away from prying ears. As they walked, Theo took note of the various cars that were being repaired and matched them to the incidents that had precipitated that need: Reggie and Eustace had driven the Dodge pickup into a cement barrier; the Camaro had taken a few hits in a firefight in Sandy Spring; Lydia had gotten the Pontiac shot up; the Pinto—*Jesus fucking God, why?*—was Roughneck's baby. Of the nearly twenty cars in the workshop, there was only one that Theo was unfamiliar with.

"You are both idiots," Theo heard Lydia's voice over the running engines and clang of hammering. Some of her gang were hanging out and watching the Grand Am get finished. The reunion seemed less than tearful.

"You and your boys are doing good," Theo told Slick and squeezed his shoulder until the older man grimaced. "How are things looking?"

Theo listened without comment as Slick gave him the rundown of which cars were ready to roll, which still had what to be repaired, and which were hopeless, good for nothing but spare parts. When the mechanic was done, Theo asked a few questions— about horsepower, about which Kindred were bringing in the cars in the worst shape—just to confirm what he already knew.

"By the way," Theo added once they'd covered the relevant details, "who the hell drives a Lexus?"

He was staring at the one car that didn't fit. There was a tarp draped over it, but Theo could read the shape. Maybe somebody had stolen it for kicks, or maybe...

Slick hesitated. "Nobody. One of the fat cats."

"Who?"

"You know...hush, hush. One of them."

Theo put his arm around Slick again but didn't squeeze at all. "Who?"

Slick hesitated again, but then quickly decided that hush hush did not apply to Theo Bell, not if he wanted to know. "Pieterzoon."

"Pieterzoon? He's already got wheels. He imported a couple of his own."

Slick shrugged. "Couldn't tell you." He felt Theo's glare turn hard. "I mean...I mean don't *know*," the mechanic clarified. "Maybe he just likes pullin' rank. You know, 'cause he can. He's getting the works: self-sealin' tires, armor, bulletproof glass...."

"When's he pickin' it up?"

"Not quite done yet. A few nights still," Slick said. "Get this. I don't call them. His man's gonna get in touch with me. Wants us to deliver the thing to *them*."

"Who'd you talk to?"

Slick ran his fingers through his hair and managed to get more grease on his scalp. "One of his asshole cronies. I don't know."

"Van Pel?"

"Yeah, I guess. That sounds right."

Theo wasn't sure what to make of this, and he wasn't sure why it bothered him. After being attacked and almost done in, Jan had imported a couple of souped-up cars of his own from Amsterdam. Why have Slick provide another now, and why try to keep it quiet?

"I tell you what," Theo said. "When you get that call, you let me know—and I mean right when you get it. Understood?"

"Sure."

"Good." Theo patted Slick on the back and started to walk away, then stopped and turned back. "Oh, one other thing."

"Yeah?"

"Up front." He pointed back over his shoulder. "Cigarettes and shit all over the place. If I hear on the local news that there was a fire, and cops and fire trucks are all over this place, I'm gonna kick your fuckin' ass." Theo turned and left.

Lydia followed Theo into Slick's. Jeb, out front, was an asshole, as usual. Lydia almost expected Theo to smack the jerk, or to buckle his knees with just that cold stare. But Theo ignored Jeb. Not that she minded. Jeb wasn't worth Theo's time. It was just that she got tired of not being able to predict what Theo would or would not do a lot of the time. Sometimes he was protective of her. Other times, like this one, he left her on her own. Lydia just wished she could predict his reactions a little better.

Being around the archon almost always made her feel like she talked too much. Like on the ride over. She never felt that way with anybody else. She was definitely not the chatty type, but somehow Theo managed to make her feel like her mouth was working overtime. Maybe it was because he seldom bothered to grunt a complete sentence. But sometimes he did. He was hard to predict that way too.

On the way over, she'd just wanted to be helpful. He'd told her to go to the damned meeting because he was going to be late. She'd figured he'd be interested to know what went on. But he wasn't, or maybe he just didn't hear her at all over the motorcycle.

Whatever.

Inside Slick's, Lydia saw her gang at once. They were the only ones not working. Slick ran a pretty tight damned ship. His guys were good at what they did, and they kept at it. Lydia's guys were morons. Two of the three, anyway. While Theo sidled off with Slick, Lydia headed for the Grand Am, which looked like it was almost done. The paint looked good. The panels were smooth. It just needed the windshield replaced and new plates.

Frankie started singing when he saw her, "Lydia, oh Lydia. She gave me chlamydia…" His partner in prickdom, Baldur, laughed hysterically.

"You are both idiots," Lydia said. "Which one of you assholes gets the brain today, or let me guess—you left it at home."

Frankie clutched at his chest and staggered back against the wall. "Oh! You *wound* me!"

"Wound this." Lydia presented the appropriate finger and stepped past them to the fourth member of her team, Christoph. His tangled red hair was pulled back. He was sitting on a crate against the wall, and his trenchcoat was spread out around him almost like a tent. Lydia could see that he was depressed—as always. He stared pensively at one of the Pontiac's hubcaps.

"What?" Lydia asked. "Did they get paint on it?"

Christoph nodded silent greeting, expression unchanged. Lydia waited with her hands on her hips, but he merely returned to his moping.

"Yeah, whatever," she said. "Why don't you sharpen your sword or something."

"Hey, Lydia," Baldur called, recovered from his fit of hilarity. "Why we gotta keep goin' out when nobody else does?"

"What the hell you talkin' about? Who ain't goin' out?"

"Everybody. I mean nobody. Nobody ain't goin' out." Baldur paused and scratched his head, having confused himself.

Lydia sighed and spoke very slowly. "Who…the hell…isn't…going…on patrol?"

"Well…Jasmine says we oughta quit."

"Jasmine says lots of things."

"Yeah, but…I mean, what's the Camarilla ever done for us anyway?"

Frankie muttered agreement with his friend.

Lydia regarded them incredulously. "Fine. Theo's right over there. You wanna go tell him?"

Baldur opened his mouth but couldn't think of anything to say.

Lydia winked at him. "That's what I thought."

"Hey, we don't owe the Camarilla nothin'," Frankie said indignantly.

"Frankie, what the hell you think's gonna happen if we don't patrol? You gonna go have a party? Find some little boys to suck? What about *after* the Sabbat rolls into town—and hangs you from a meat hook like the ugliest fuckin' I.V. bag in the world?"

"I ain't ugly."

"He's more the douche-bag type," Baldur said.

"You two *did* leave the brain at home, didn't you?" Lydia sighed and turned back to Christoph.

Frankie and Baldur grumbled quietly behind her. "Huh. Made sense when Jasmine said it."

"You better watch out, Christoph," said Lydia. "These two think too hard, they're gonna hurt somebody."

Christoph ignored her just as he'd ignored the entire conversation. Lydia picked up a grease-stained rag and threw it in his face. "Hey, you!" she yelled at him. "What the fuck? Jesus. What a waste of fuckin' blood."

"Hey, you four slack-ass bastards," came Slick's voice from across the yard. Lydia turned around and saw Theo heading out the way they'd come in. "Get your asses up front," said Slick, "and clean up all that shit. Dump the ashtrays out on the street or something."

"I look like your maid?" Frankie asked.

"Oh, excuse me," said Slick. "Robbie, go ahead and leave that Grand Am for later. We got about fifty other cars to work on first. Better yet, just clean out the goddamn ashtray, 'cause that's where this motherfucker's gonna end up."

Lydia smacked Frankie on top of the head. "We're on it, Slick." Then she turned to Frankie and smacked him again. "You feel like walkin' to Fort Meade and back, or what? Come on. Take us two minutes to pick up, you lazy bastard. That worth pissin' off the man?"

Frankie and Baldur—and even Christoph—followed with only minimal grumbling.

Sunday, 17 October 1999, 1:12 AM
A subterranean grotto
New York City, New York

The pieces were beginning to fall together, but that fact gave Calebros very little in the way of comfort. Years of work nearing fulfillment, yet he sensed extraneous factors hurtling toward him as well, needlessly, hopelessly complicating matters. Thank goodness Emmett would return soon. His task with Benito was nearly done. Perhaps the presence of Calebros's broodmate would alleviate the pressure bearing down upon him like the tons of earth above his head.

In the meantime, Calebros busied himself by easing the tension the best way he knew how—he shredded fashion magazines. Dull scissors, a razor blade, his own claws, sometimes he even pressed his face to the page and left a fang mark in a woman's shiny face or perfect, taut belly. He ignored, for the moment, the fresh batch of reports from his clanmates.

17 October 1999
re: the Prophet of Gehenna

10/16 Jeremiah reports—after weeks of
guiding Anatole, the prophet saw
Jeremiah (for who he was?) and sent him
away; Jeremiah <u>unable to resist.</u>
Anatole left at cave.

NOT suprising

Tone of report fairly frantic; does J.
need a (vacation) *Don't we all, damn it?!*

Anatole follow-up necessary.

*Ramona talking about going back to cave
perhaps Hesha could accompany?*

"Say again?"

"Monçada is destroyed."

Yep. Jan *had* said what Theo thought he'd said, and the words were no less shocking the second time for being less unexpected.

"How?"

"Assamites. Fatima."

"Shit." Theo sat down in the chair across from Jan's desk.

This suite of rooms on the seventh floor had, until recently, belonged to Prince Garlotte. He had put up Jan here in favor of the restored ship for himself—a decision that had not stood him in good stead. Jan had settled into these accommodations quite comfortably and, with Garlotte's demise, could probably stay as long as he pleased. Theo guessed that would not be much longer.

"Have you ever met her? Fatima?" Theo asked.

Jan shook his head.

"Me neither," said Theo. "And you know what? I don't know that I want to."

"I quite agree."

"Shit," Theo said again. "She did Monçada. You're sure?"

"As sure as I can be." Jan took off his glasses and set them on the desk before him. "Details are sketchy. We're not sure exactly when it happened, but the sources are reliable. Assamites don't brag about jobs they didn't really do—bad for business in the long run."

"Shit."

The name Ambrosio Luis Monçada might not mean anything to a Kindred on the street, at least not in the States, but the cardinal went back a long way in European circles. Way before Theo's time. A real badass. Monçada was probably one of the most powerful members of the Sabbat in Western Europe— or he had been, if what Jan said was true.

Theo pulled out a cigarette, struck a match and lit up. "You know who Fatima was working for?"

"No."

"Not for us?"

"I doubt we could pay her enough."

"You're probably right," Theo said. The Assamites worked for blood, the older and more potent the better. To hire somebody as top of the line as Fatima to go after a target as high profile as Monçada would take Caine's left nut. Maybe the right one too. "I guess she did it out of the goodness of her heart."

Theo couldn't tell from watching Jan if the Ventrue knew more than he was letting on. Maybe, maybe not. Jan didn't fluster easily. In facing down a hostile mob of refugee Kindred and eventually winning their acquiescence, if not their trust, he had kept his cool. In maneuvering events so that Victoria, a rival for leadership and a pain in the butt, had been hustled off to look for clues in a Sabbat city, he'd appeared collected. He'd even held together when the Sabbat hit squad had shot him all to hell and he was a heartbeat away—so to speak—from Final Death.

"Good season for assassins," said Theo. "Fatima cacks Monçada. Somebody in the Sabbat sent those bastards after you. And it wasn't even a month ago Lucita put the squeeze on Borges."

Jan's eyebrows raised, then he shrugged off the comment. "War is like that."

"Yeah. I guess so." Theo just laughed to himself. Jan wasn't about to tell him if he had or hadn't hired Lucita. Those two had some history, not all of it good. The woman, a killer whose name and reputation evoked as much fear as Fatima's, had reportedly been sighted dozens of times over the past couple of months, up and down the East Coast from Miami to Boston. Who knew which accounts were true and which were the result of overactive imaginations? She had, however, waxed several Sabbat thugs, including the former archbishop of Miami, Borges. That had put the fear of God into much of the rest of the Sabbat. Theo had been able to tell that the Sabbat he ran into were jumpy once the rumors of Lucita's activities had begun to spread. It sounded like the kind of misdirection—the "maximization of resources," as Jan sometimes said—that the Ventrue might have been behind. Jan wasn't about to say, and Theo wasn't about to ask. But there was something else that Theo wondered about, since Jan had brought up the subject.

"Monçada goin' down have any effect on us?" Theo asked.

"It might. It can only help."

Theo nodded. So Jan had some reason to believe

that Monçada had had his fingers in affairs in North America. Why else would the Ventrue mention something like this when Theo would find out about it on his own eventually? Monçada dabbling in North America. That wasn't typical.

Becoming cardinal must've given that fat bastard a helluva hard-on, Theo thought.

And Monçada's involvement might go a long way toward explaining why Vykos was slumming in the States. That Tzimisce thing by itself wouldn't have the political clout to broker a cease fire, much less an alliance, between Polonia and Borges, but if Monçada had put his weight behind the deal...

"Hmph." Theo rubbed the stubble on his chin. "Yeah. It might help us. Can't hurt."

"Are they still pushing north just as hard?" Jan asked.

"Harder."

"How long before they're pressuring the second perimeter enough to justify our pulling back farther?"

Theo shrugged. "A week, maybe."

Jan thought about that for a moment, compared it to his own calculations, and finally nodded.

"After that," Theo continued, "I'd guess...another week. Maybe two. Gonna be enough?"

Jan rose from the desk and moved distractedly toward a nearby table with a crystal decanter. Strangely enough, the decanter was not full of blood. Jan removed the stopper and almost instantly Theo could smell the aroma of strong whiskey, scotch. Jan poured himself a glass, then raised it to his mouth, just enough to wet his lips. Still holding the glass before his face and gently swishing the liquid, he closed his eyes and took a deep breath.

"Two weeks," he said, eyes still closed. "I need two weeks from that point. Can you guarantee me that?"

Theo paused before speaking. He wasn't one for promises and guarantees, but the plan he and Jan were attempting to see through to its conclusion did require certain absolutes. Timing was important. Theo was walking a thin line between holding back the Sabbat and leading them on. Jan had other responsibilities that were just as vital and was undoubtedly the best judge of how much time he needed.

"You need two weeks, you got two weeks," Theo said.

Seeming reassured, Jan returned to his seat. He took another small sip of whiskey and then placed the glass on the desk. "How about Isaac? Is he proving easy to work with?"

"Easy enough. Him and Gainesmil don't try to interfere with the defenses, really, since we included them in the original planning. And I know about as much about the city as they do now. They got suggestions now and then. I listen and nod and then do whatever the hell I was going to."

"So becoming prince hasn't gone to Isaac's head?" Jan asked.

"Oh, sure it has. But it don't bother me. He likes to walk around and look like the prince. You know, mix with the poor refugees once in a while, give the troops a pep talk. That kinda bullshit."

Theo leaned forward in his seat. "So tell me. Just out of curiosity, what scraps did you toss Gainesmil to get him to lay off? 'Cause I know you had him lined up before you suggested Goldwin."

"I merely impressed upon him the importance of unity of command in these trying times," Jan said with a straight face.

"And..."

"And I assured him that he would have my full support when the time came for a successor to Prince Goldwin."

Theo nodded and sat back in his seat again. Betting against the longevity of Isaac seemed reasonable enough, and it would be easier to follow on the heels of a weak prince than someone like Garlotte. *Sounded* like a good deal, all right. That was the beauty of it. Theo decided he'd have to make a point of being around when Gainesmil realized just how completely he'd been out-maneuvered by Pieterzoon.

"You know," Jan said, raising his glass and dipping it slightly toward Theo as if in a toast, "the title of prince was yours for the taking."

"Hmph. Like I needed that pain in my ass. *And* if I ever did want to be a prince—and I don't—I don't plan on having myself nominated by a Malkavian. Jesus fuckin' Christ." They both laughed quietly at that. "Anything else?" Theo asked.

"Just one thing. I've heard about some grumbling among the rank and file."

Theo stood. He stretched, popped his knuckles. "Let 'em grumble."

"Fair enough."

"Fair enough," Theo echoed, and headed for the door. He stopped just before leaving and turned back to Jan. "Oh yeah. With our perimeter shrinking, there's gonna be more of a chance that some fuckin' Sabbat asshole might get farther into the city and come gunnin' for somebody. I should assign a team to you for more security."

"Don't bother," Jan said. "They're better spent on patrol. Besides, I'm not planning on going anywhere, and Anton and Isaac's men have the inn sealed tight."

Theo frowned. "Whatever you say." He shut the door behind him.

Theo only vaguely noticed the chimes as the elevator passed each floor on the way down. What he kept hearing instead was one of the last things that he'd heard on the seventh floor, one of the last things that Jan had said: *I'm not planning on going anywhere.*

That statement might be completely true. But then again, Theo had known a lot of Ventrue over the years. He'd also worked closely with Jan for several weeks now and seen the childe of Hardestadt in action. Pieterzoon had coopted, for the most part, a jealous and defensive Garlotte, and basically done the same with Gainesmil, a Toreador of some standing. Jan had maneuvered Victoria out of the limelight and then out of the state. And what about Theo himself? He wasn't giving the Ventrue any grief. Instead, he was just playing along.

But that's 'cause what the man's doin' makes sense, Theo thought. He wasn't conflicted about how to do his job, even if, this time at least, it meant giving a Ventrue a free ride. What it came down to was this: Theo was here to blunt the gains of the Sabbat however he could. Jan was basically in Baltimore for the same reason, and the two seemed to be on the same wavelength most of the time. Seeing eye to eye was not the same as selling out.

No, Theo thought. *If I sold out, it was when I stayed on as archon when Pascek became justicar.* But that was something else altogether. What concerned Theo the most at the moment was Jan.

I'm not planning on going anywhere, he'd said.

Then why, Theo wondered, *is Slick fixing up a Lexus for you on the sly?*

Probably there was a perfectly normal and legitimate reason. That's why Theo had brought it up in a roundabout way—to let Jan tell him in the course of normal conversation. Theo wasn't hoping to catch Jan in a lie. He was hoping *not* to. It was still possible that Jan wasn't lying, that the car really was incidental. But if Theo had asked outright and there *was* something underhanded going on, then Theo would never have found out—until it was too late, maybe. Jan would have covered it up, changed his plans, whatever. This way at least Theo could keep his eyes open. Because a working relationship, which is what he currently had with Jan, was not the same as trust. There was too much potential of getting screwed to turn a blind eye.

We're Kindred. We drink blood. We fuck people.

It was that simple. And Theo was accustomed to making sure that he was not the one who got fucked.

The elevator dipped and binged and the "L" above the door lit up. Theo ignored the staff in their colonial garb as he tromped across the lobby. In front of the inn, chatting up a cute little female valet parking attendant, was Lladislas. The former prince of

Buffalo evidently wasn't bringing any of his Kindred charm to bear, because the girl, still a teenager, clearly didn't know what to make of this apparently middle-aged guy who might or might not be hitting on her. She was being polite and noncommittal. Lladislas was standing just close enough to violate her personal space and make her feel uncomfortable without being too obvious about it.

"Yes, indeed," Lladislas told her, with that same enthusiasm that he always seemed to exude, no matter what he was talking about. "The internal combustion engine has changed the world. So many ways. So *many* ways."

"You don't say," said the girl. Her valet partner was keeping his distance. She was on her own as far as he was concerned. The girl's eyes, searching for any excuse to slip away or busy herself, fell on Theo as he exited the hotel, and in that split second when he was about to slip away himself, Lladislas followed her gaze and turned around.

"Theo Bell!"

Theo sighed but didn't stop walking. Lladislas abandoned the valet and fell in beside the Brujah archon.

"Hi, Lladi. You know the hotel staff are off limits? We've had too many go missin' already."

"I was just *talking* to the girl. She seems intelligent enough." Almost instantly, Lladislas's casual manner fell away. He grabbed Theo's arm and the two Brujah came to a halt. "We could've been ruling this city together, Bell. You know that, don't you? All I needed was your support. Pieterzoon wouldn't have bucked you, and Vitel just wants Washington back."

Theo jerked his arm away. "You don't want this city."

Lladislas's face screwed up, as if Theo had just said something incomprehensible. "You seem to have strange ideas about what I do and don't want. First you think that I *want* to abandon my own city. Now you think I want to remain a wandering mendicant for the rest of eternity. Well, let me tell you," Lladislas grabbed Theo's arm again, "I got kind of used to having a city to call my own. Buffalo might not have been Paris or Rome, but it was *mine*—until I listened to you!"

Theo glared down at the smaller man and spoke in an even, obviously restrained tone: "We both know why Buffalo had to go. I'm not gonna go into that again. And I know what you're used to. But let me tell you what I am *not* used to. First of all, I'm not used to a white man grabbin' my arm. Second of all, I'm not used to the same white man grabbin' my arm *twice*."

As Theo continued to glare, Lladislas slowly eased the pressure of his fingers and then just as slowly pulled back his hand. "Sorry. But none of that changes the fact that—"

"Listen," Theo cut him off. "I'm not gonna say this again. I'm not gonna argue, and I'm not gonna answer any questions or listen to you bitch. You don't want this city. Trust me. Stick with me on this. I won't forget about you."

Lladislas's skepticism was plain to see, but, for once, he didn't argue. He took a step back, never taking his eyes from Theo. "Don't sell me out on this, Theo."

The archon didn't say anything to that. He turned and continued on to his bike, which was parked about a block and a half from the Lord Baltimore Inn. "Shit," he muttered as he cranked the engine and pulled away from the curb, wondering if he'd said too much to Lladislas.

The former prince of Buffalo was a straight talker. He'd never been anything but up front with Theo. Theo couldn't say as much in return. Sure, he'd had a good reason to lie to Lladislas in Buffalo. It was part of the plan. Llad never would have given up his city and brought quite a few of his people here to Baltimore, where they could be more effectively used, if he hadn't thought an overwhelming attack was on the way. And, hell, an attack *had* come. A lot sooner than Theo had expected. So it wasn't really a lie at all if it turned out to be true, right?

Hell yes it was, Theo thought. *That's what I get for hangin' out with a Ventrue.*

Still, they'd had a reason for lying, just like Theo had reasons now for warning off Lladislas, even though he probably shouldn't have. One deception necessarily created another, and that one another, and another…. The lies about Buffalo had led to lies about Hartford—and more deaths. But that couldn't be helped. Just like in Buffalo. Part of the plan, a plan in three parts.

Buffalo and Hartford had been part one of the plan.

Part two was up to Jan. That bothered Theo as much as anything. Part two was out of his hands. He had to trust Jan. And he couldn't quite bring himself to do it.

That night in August after Buffalo had fallen, the two of them had talked. They'd worked out many of the details of the plan. First, though, they'd arrived independently at the same conclusion about the debacle in Lladislas's city and what the Sabbat must have known.

"They didn't divert forces from Washington," Jan had said.

"They didn't need to," Theo had pointed out. "Those were babies with fangs they were facing."

"But they shouldn't have known that."

"I know."

They'd both been reluctant to suggest what they each had already decided.

"Could it have been a raid that got lucky?" Jan had asked.

"Too big for a raid. Too small for an all-out assault—unless they knew what to expect." It's what Theo had already decided, when he'd learned of the attack during his trip back to Baltimore, had to be the case. And Jan agreed.

A spy. The Sabbat had to have known exactly what to expect in Buffalo. And so Hartford had been sacrificed, for three reasons: to concentrate more Kindred in Baltimore, to confirm Theo and Jan's suspicion about inside information getting out, and to convince the spy that he or she was still undiscovered.

That led to part two of the plan: While Theo made sure that Baltimore held firm against the Sabbat, Jan, by whatever means he could employ, had to find out who the spy was. If he didn't, then part three was going to be the biggest cluster fuck since the Bay of Pigs.

That same night in August, Theo and Jan had discussed who the spy could be. Victoria? She'd been captured by the Sabbat and then had conveniently escaped. Jan had since arranged for her to be sent elsewhere—back to Sabbat-controlled Atlanta. Garlotte? If he were the spy, that matter had very neatly taken care of itself—unless the explosion was a decoy and he'd faked his own destruction, but it seemed unlikely that Katrina would play along, unless she too were duped…. Malachi, the Gangrel? Ditto as for Garlotte. Gainesmil? Theo thought that the Toreador had been too genuinely disturbed by the initial reports of the Sabbat's early victories for it to be him. Vitel? Isaac? Colchester? Roughneck? Hell, anybody with fangs might have motivation, and too many people had access to news of what was going on. That was the big problem—*one* of the big problems—with rule by committee, and that was the reason that Theo and Jan had undertaken the plan secretly. That narrowed the field considerably, as far as opportunity for a spy to get his or her hands on damaging information.

But it didn't necessarily solve the problem.

Theo pulled his motorcycle to the side of the road and cut the engine. He was still on the waterfront. Without really meaning to, he'd driven to within a few blocks—to within sight of—the scarred portion of dock where Garlotte's ship used to be secured. The explosion, just four short nights ago, was one of several things—probably unrelated things—that were bothering Theo.

He kept playing the events over in his mind: seeing Katrina coming off the ship, talking to her, being blown through the air, letting her go. He still didn't have a good explanation for why he'd spared her. Just a gut reaction. But what bothered him more than that was the basic facts of what he'd seen: Katrina had blown up the prince.

"She blew his ass up," Theo said to himself, trying to convince himself of what he'd seen—but he couldn't. Not quite. He'd practically said as much to Gainesmil the night after. Katrina didn't seem like the demolitions-expert type. Theo had seen what he'd seen, but that didn't mean he'd seen everything. Katrina might have blown Garlotte up, but the more Theo thought about it, the less he believed that she'd managed to pull it off by herself.

So maybe it was a good thing that he hadn't ripped her head off. She might lead him to whomever else was involved—*if* somebody else really was involved; *if* Theo ever found her again. Surely she'd taken his warning seriously and gotten out of the city.

For quite a few minutes, Theo sat on his bike and stared at the blackened portion of the dock where the ship used to be tethered. The debris had all been cleared away, but Theo could almost feel the smoking detritus landing all around him—the small pieces fell in slow motion, gently, as naturally as snow or a gentle rain. He saw Katrina lying on her back in the street, and there was a light rain falling all around her too, falling on her, changing her skin from pale white to dark red. The rain was not water but blood—

blood of a Kindred centuries old, blood spilled in the gutter.

Theo squeezed his eyes closed hard, and when he opened them, there were only the deserted street and the damaged dock. Gone was the image of a young woman manipulated, the panorama of murder and injustice.

"Shit happens," Theo said to himself. He started up the bike again. He didn't have time—or the stomach—for sentimentality, for idealism. His was the world of the street and realpolitik. He pulled away from that place, but the strands of thought that bound him were twining themselves together into a cord he couldn't long ignore.

Wednesday, 20 October 1999, 3:12 AM
The Presidential Hotel
Washington, D.C.

The chambers of Lady Sascha Vykos had ceased to look anything like the luxury suite she had appropriated from Marcus Vitel, the deposed prince of Washington, just four short months before. Or perhaps the months were not so short. Parmenides was not sure. In many ways, he felt as if he had always resided with his Tzimisce mistress. The being he now was, Parmenides/Ravenna, had of course always dwelt with Vykos. She had created him. His nights among the children of Haqim seemed so long ago, though it was the blood of that clan that claimed his allegiance still. Parmenides allowed himself to hide behind Ravenna, behind the face and the body of the ghoul he had killed and then replaced. At times, like now, Parmenides felt very close to the surface. The hands, the face, though their appearance was altered, did his bidding; they responded to his will. Other times, however, he seemed to be submerged beneath an ocean of blackness. The eyes were those of the departed ghoul; the hands were but clumsy, useless things. Not the magnificent tools of an artist. Parmenides held the hands before his face. He moved each finger in turn, trying to trace the impulse for each motion from brain, along nerve, to muscle, trying to tie will to action, soul to body.

"Bring me blood!" Vykos called from the other room.

The iciness of her voice churned the black waters; Parmenides suddenly was not sure if he was above or beneath the surface. But he was moving to obey.

The largest room of the suite, what had been the living room, was more or less converted to storage. Most of the furniture was pushed to one side, where what wasn't reduced to kindling-sized pieces was stacked so as to take up less space. Tables had been erected and were crowded with Vykos's notebooks, various sets of surgical tools, and the occasional spare body part—the fresher ones. Parmenides wove among the tables and made his way to the kitchenette. He opened the refrigerator and removed a pitcher full almost to the rim with blood. At times when he anticipated that Vykos would desire blood, he had been removing the pitcher in advance and allowing it to warm on the counter, but he could not always outguess her, and thus far she had expressed no preference for her blood to be served either chilled or at room temperature.

Parmenides took the pitcher, careful not to slosh onto the floor, and moved quickly past the door to the suite's smaller bedroom—storage area for the not-so-fresh parts. Vykos would dispose of the gallimaufry when the mood struck her, but for several weeks now she'd been completely absorbed by her experiments and unwilling to divide her attention.

He stepped within the master bedroom, noticing instantly the incredibly strong odor of vitae—not the pleasant tang of merely mortal blood, but rather the enticing aroma of fragrant Kindred vitae, Vykos's own blood.

Parmenides's concentration wavered momentarily. He stopped where he stood and locked his knees, so as to keep them from buckling.

Destroy her. That was his mission now. Fatima had ordered him...or had it been that creature that lowered itself down from the ceiling? Parmenides's thoughts grew foggy; the various relationships grew suddenly confusing. *No,* he told himself, *the thing from the ceiling was Nosferatu.* It wouldn't give him orders. It hadn't shown its disgusting face again. Fatima had been the one to tell him...

Destroy her.

Destroy Vykos. Parmenides had to concentrate very intently for the idea to make sense. He was Assamite, hiding behind Ravenna the ghoul. Vykos had made him this. She knew of his charade but thought herself immune from his wrath. But he would wait, would bide his time, and would strike.

Destroy her.

Parmenides felt himself sinking back beneath the blackness, but the fog was receding. He was distant, submerged, but he could see through the eyes of the ghoul.

To his right was a small couch, and on the couch lay a body, bloodied, naked, cut and splayed open from sternum to pelvis. This most recent of the thinbloods, the third so far, was not strong enough to heal herself. She lay uncomprehending, eyes wide, mouth lolled open. Now she was oblivious to her surroundings, though she had been aware enough when Vykos had opened her, had hollowed out the belly that had been so full. The girl smelled of her own blood; she was covered in it, as were her clothes that were cut away, the couch, the carpet. This was not the odor that first struck Parmenides, however.

The bed, too, was a bloody, king-sized monstrosity. Spread, blanket, and sheets were twisted and saturated. Tacky puddles of vitae pooled in every depression. Tangled among the bedclothes was Vykos, and she reeked of the Curse of Caine.

"Blood!" she called again.

Parmenides stepped closer. The feet that were but were not his own moved him to stand over her. Like the thin-blood, Vykos was naked. Her skin, where it was not streaked with blood, was the purest alabaster. Her legs were bent at the knees, spread apart, her feet secured in leather stirrups. Parmenides looked upon her hairless, sexless body. Her small breasts were a remnant of the feminine she had affected—those and the writhing fetus in her own open belly.

"Give it to me!" She strained for the pitcher with both hands.

Parmenides gave it to her and she drank, greedily. Trails of blood ran down both sides of her face and onto her pillow, where they splattered new patterns atop the already encrusted layers.

She finished the entire pitcher and cast it aside. Blood pulsed through exposed arteries into the child within her. She clenched her teeth against pain, twisted the sheets in her fists, pressed outward against the stirrups. Parmenides stood above her, in all her vulnerability.

Destroy her, a voice commanded him. But he was far away; he could not fight his way to the surface.

He could only watch through the eyes of the ghoul that was not him.

A strangled moan escaped Vykos's lips. It was not a cry of pain but of anger. As blood pumped into the tiny semblance of a child, its partially formed limbs jerked spasmodically, splashing some of the liquid pooled about it within Vykos's open bowl of a belly. The unborn child struggled, like a fish out of water, despite—or perhaps because of—the life that Vykos tried to force into the small body.

Then as suddenly as the thrashing had begun, there was stillness. Vykos lay still, though her every muscle was taut. The babe, torn from the womb of its undead mother and fed upon more powerfully cursed vitae, lay still.

Vykos's lingering moan gained strength, grew into a primal roar of undeniable rage. She grasped at her belly. Her fingers, long and sharp, dug into the soft, fleshy cranium, as she ripped the offending child from her body, paying no attention to the arteries and organic cords she ripped asunder. With the crescendo of her scream, she cast the tiny body to the floor and raked her bloody claws across her smooth, white scalp.

It was at that moment that Parmenides heard the distant sound of a bell. The elevator, beginning to ascend. Vykos heard it too.

"No!" she screamed, jerking upright in her naked, bloodied glory.

For the briefest instant, Parmenides stood transfixed by the sight of a single drop of blood sliding slowly across the perfect curve of one of Vykos's exposed ribs—but then Ravenna sprang into action.

He hurried from the master bedroom, pulling the door closed behind him. The arrow above the elevator door tracked the progress of the car from the second floor to the third. The management of the hotel, once loyal to Vitel but easily won over, had long since been ordered to suspend any and all services to the penthouse suite. No employee was to set foot on the sixth floor except to respond to a specific request from Vykos or her retainer, Ravenna.

Yet the elevator was now at the fifth floor and ascending still.

Parmenides stood patiently in the foyer. He quickly checked the various blades hidden on his person. By the time the doors slid open, he was leaning casually on the cane he no longer required to get around. As the retainer of Lady Sascha Vykos, archbishop of Washington, he was prepared to berate whoever was so foolish as to violate her privacy. As an assassin, trained and disguised, he was ready for violence should an attack be forthcoming.

Even so, he was surprised when Francisco Domingo de Polonia, archbishop of New York, flanked on either side by Lasombra lackeys, stepped from the elevator.

"I wish to speak with Her Excellency, Archbishop Vykos," Polonia said forcefully, his words tinged with the Spanish accent of his mortal days. He was tall and held himself with the graceful bearing of a fighter confident of winning. From beneath the black ocean, Parmenides wanted to test him, to challenge him, but this was not the time. Polonia wrinkled his nose only slightly at the stench of decaying flesh to which

Parmenides had grown accustomed over the past weeks. Polonia's companions were less discreet.

"Jesus *Christ*!" said Costello, a lieutenant of the Polonia faction, a middle man from New York. "I've been in Nossie shitholes that smell better than this."

To Polonia's other side stood Joseph Hardin, a Lasombra hatchetman—or knifeman, more accurately—who'd made a name for himself during the early blitzkrieg from Atlanta to Washington. He'd become noted for his casual brutality, against the Camarilla as well as among his own subordinates. "The maid is definitely gonna be pissed," he said.

"Her Excellency," Parmenides said calmly, "is indisposed."

The humor instantly drained out of Hardin and Costello; they grew tense, edgy. Polonia, on the other hand, who had been all business thus far, smiled. It was a cold smile, a crocodile's smile. "I am not asking your permission," he said.

Polonia was not, Parmenides noticed, wearing a sword, reportedly his favorite weapon. The faux ghoul instinctively took in such martial details because there was a palpable tension in the room, despite the fact that Polonia and Vykos were both part of the Sabbat high command; both, in theory, on the same team.

Costello moved to step past Parmenides. Parmenides raised his cane. blocking the way. Costello's eyes bulged; he puffed up with indignation. "What the fuck do you think—"

"Ravenna," came Vykos's cool voice from behind him. "Do fetch a few chairs for our guests." Costello's gaze shifted over Parmenides's shoulder; the

Lasombra's anger evaporated. "I'm afraid the decor simply has not held up well," Vykos added.

She stood before the closed door to the master bedroom. A dark silk robe hid most of her body and made her face, hands, and feet seem to glow white in contrast. No blood was visible. Her skin was freshly scrubbed, and small ridges streaked front to back over her head, as if she had been running her fingers through hair that, tonight, was nonexistent. She held her robe tightly closed at the neck. Parmenides wondered if, beneath, her abdomen was still laid open, an exposed, barren womb. Without comment, he moved to obey her.

"We do not need chairs," said Polonia, no longer smiling. "I do not intend to stay long."

"Such the pity," Vykos intoned.

Parmenides watched her closely for signs of weakness. He knew the physical stress she'd been inflicting upon herself, the amount of blood that she'd both consumed and expended. But as always seemed to be the case, Vykos showed no weakness, physical or otherwise.

"I'm sure," Polonia said, "that you are aware of the latest news from Madrid, Archbishop."

Vykos regarded her rival from behind emotionless, alien eyes. In that instant, she seemed to Parmenides not an aristocrat of the Sabbat, not female, not *human*, but rather a god, a being completely detached from the slaughter and infighting that swirled around her. He felt himself rising to the surface of that black ocean. Impulses of his blood, of violence, filled him, but absent was his own detachment, that fruit of his professional training. Visceral hatred—for his master, for his mistress—filled him. And a love just as powerful.

"There is always *some* news from Madrid," Vykos said, and the illusion of her otherness vanished—or perhaps the illusion of her humanity reasserted itself. Her gaze enveloped Polonia and his underlings, dissected them where they stood.

Parmenides stepped aside, allowing access to the suite, but none of the Lasombra moved. Costello and Hardin could not help but look back and forth between Polonia and Vykos.

"The reports are confirmed," Polonia said. "Cardinal Monçada, your benefactor, is destroyed." The words hung in the air, overpowering even the stench of rotting flesh. Costello and Hardin, who clearly had already heard the news, seemed cowed by what Polonia said nonetheless. They watched Vykos sharply for any reaction—and were rewarded not at all.

Vykos stood perfectly still and silent, not frozen but centered, not shocked but aloof. "And…?" she asked finally.

"And," Polonia responded, "I am now cardinal. I claim the title, and the regent concurs."

Vykos, still expressionless, bowed deeply from the waist. One hand rested easily against the door behind her (Parmenides suspected she needed the support to remain upright, yet there was no indication of weakness). The other hand traced an elegant flourish in the air. She rose and regarded her guest exactly as dispassionately as she had before, paying no attention whatsoever to Costello and Hardin, who were trying, mostly successfully, not to fidget.

Polonia nodded, acknowledging her gesture. "Without Monçada's aid—"

"His interference, you mean," Vykos suggested.

"A firm hand is needed," Polonia continued, ignoring the interruption. "I'm sure you understand." The crocodile smile again, but this time only in his eyes. "Vallejo and his legionnaires have returned to Madrid. The poor soldier was badly shaken, though he put on a good show of sternness. The Little Tailor has departed as well, but he and Commander Bolon have…reconstituted our supply of war ghouls somewhat. The commander has, of course, sworn loyalty to my person."

Slowly, Vykos bowed a second time, this time not holding on to the door, and performing smaller flourishes with both hands. "My felicitations and," she added, rising, "of course, my loyalty. Let us drink to the cardinal of the United States."

Polonia laughed knowingly. "*Eastern* United States. You flatter me, Archbishop."

"Hardly."

They stood there for a long, uncomfortable moment, the four Cainites and the Assamite in their midst. "Any new word from your spy?" Polonia asked at last. "Or have you been too preoccupied?"

"There are so few new words," Vykos said cryptically. The response was obviously inadequate, and another strained silence deepened between cardinal and archbishop. "Nothing of consequence from my contact, Your Eminence."

"Contact me at once with anything you receive," Polonia said. "The attack will fall soon. Very soon."

"As you wish, my Cardinal."

Polonia, grudgingly satisfied, nodded and turned to leave. Costello, relieved enough to sneer, and Hardin followed, but then their cardinal stopped and turned back toward Vykos. "Do look in on your city once in a while, Archbishop," he said. "My people have been distracted from planning the attack on Baltimore by the need to settle disputes—hunting grounds and the like—that should have been your province."

"As you wish, my Cardinal."

Now, slightly more satisfied, Polonia and his underlings turned and left, leaving Parmenides again to look upon those cold, alien eyes that stared after.

The electronic hum of the small, battery-pow-
ered printer, far from seeming incongruous among the
hewn rock of the cavern, was a comfort to Ramona.
Whatever need Hesha was feeling to take and then
print pictures of...of everything they had found,
Ramona was thankful. He didn't seem inclined to
talk, was too busy with his photographs, thank goodness. He'd said something about hard copies and
technology. She hadn't really been listening. Her
mind had been too occupied by the grotesque statue,
the sculpture of stone and flesh and blood.

She was grateful for the rhythmic purr of the
printer. Otherwise, the silence would have been too
much, would have driven her over the edge. Talking
wouldn't have been any better, though. Even if she
could wrap her mind around thoughts and words. The
sound of speech seemed a violation of this place, a
violation of...of the dignity of her dead. Their blood
dried on her hands, on her own monstrous claws.

There was only the electronic hum. Thank God.
Otherwise, she would have heard the ghosts.

Seeing them was bad enough. She had seen the
ghost of this place, of the meadow outside. From the
helicopter. The meadow had been how she knew it
would be—burned, pock-marked, scarred by dried
flows of molten rock. She hadn't even pointed at first,
it was so obvious. Then she'd realized that Hesha
didn't see it, the pilot didn't see it. Even after she'd
pointed out the swath of destruction amidst the pris-
tine forest, they didn't see. They *couldn't* see.

"Just fuckin' land!" she'd yelled over the roar of the helicopter.

They'd put down south of the meadow—the opposite direction from Table Rock, from Zhavon. But from the ground, everything had been wrong—or right. Normal. She saw what Hesha saw. A winter forest, foothills, nothing more, nothing less. Her ghost sight, the vision that Edward Blackfeather in all his strangeness had imparted to her, had deserted her. Or else something more powerful was fucking with her mind, hiding what was there, what she *knew* had to be there. But, still, she couldn't see it.

She wished she hadn't seen what was in the cave. No, that wasn't true. She had a responsibility, a duty. But that didn't change the fact that now she felt bile or blood or whatever the hell was in her stomach churning and churning.

She kept her head down, listened to the printer. She stared away from the heart of the sculpture, in the direction of the bloody scrawl that was separate from yet somehow completed the monument of carnage. She had finished what she had come here to do. She didn't need to look anymore. The memory was bad enough without reinforcing it. It would haunt her the rest of her nights.

She wouldn't have recognized Tanner if not for the ghosts. Like the others, he was part of the statue, but unlike the others, he'd recognized her. None of them, none of the Gangrel, were whole of body. Only Tanner, her sire, was whole of mind. She saw the torture in his tired, desperate eyes. She saw again her own claws slashing his throat, letting the blood drain away, then digging still, tearing away flesh and bone, until the ghost disappeared.

The other ghosts were fainter. The other Gangrel moaned and struggled weakly as Ramona crawled among the spires, but whatever imitation of life remained was just that, an imitation, pale and pathetic. She had done what she could for them, though, and now fresh blood trickled down through the crevices of the grand sculpture. No moans, no feebly waving arms. Silence. Stillness. Only the sound of the printer humming steadily on.

In the helicopter, the ghosts were silent, maybe even at rest. The earth itself pretended that nothing was wrong, that nothing had ever happened. The scar was hidden. Trees, hillside, quiet nighttime forest.

Now Ramona wanted to talk. She didn't like being in the helicopter, so far above the ground, and the whirling rotors were too close. They sounded too much like the thunder of exploding monoliths, of fire and death. The ghosts were silent, but the memories were not.

"You were here before," she said to Hesha, nearly shouting to be heard over the din. She had to think about something other than the night of that slaughter, *anything* else.

Hesha nodded. He'd told her a little about his previous trip to the cave, about possessing the Eye, about losing it again. He'd grudgingly and cryptically mentioned Leopold, the crazed being who had reclaimed the Eye, who had very nearly destroyed Hesha, who *had* destroyed so many of Ramona's clanmates. It had to have been Leopold also, Ramona realized, who created the sculpture, who had bent the stone to his will and tormented those he'd already defeated. How had Hesha *not* seen it?

"You didn't see that...in the cave before?" Ramona asked. *That.* The sculpture.

Hesha shook his head. No, he had not. If he was telling her the truth. But why would he lie? Ramona wondered if a better question might be, why wouldn't he? After spending time with Khalil, she didn't know if any Kindred ever needed something so basic as *a reason* to lie. She herself had lied to Jen and Darnell different times. Liz had been emphatic about not trusting Hesha. *Whatever he told you was a lie,* she'd said.

It was hard. In a way, Ramona wanted to trust Hesha, wanted to believe the things he told her. But Liz had been such a nice, smart woman, and although Khalil had fucked her over royally, she'd seemed more upset, more worried and bitter, about Hesha. He was a Setite; he'd made Liz a Setite, a monster like Ramona, just a different flavor. Ramona had sensed that it was Hesha, more than Khalil, that Liz had needed to escape.

Ramona gave Hesha a long, hard look. He'd taught her a lot in the past weeks—things that would hurt their kind, things that wouldn't. Lord knew that he'd been much more forthcoming than Tanner had been, and there was no point in even beginning to compare him to Khalil. Still, Ramona did feel that Hesha wasn't helping her out of the goodness of his heart. He had his reasons. If he didn't lie to her, it was because he wanted something, wanted to gain her trust—but Ramona wasn't sure if anyone would ever gain her trust again.

So maybe he'd seen the sculpture before and thought to bring his camera this time, or maybe he hadn't seen it and he was just prepared. He hadn't seen the bleeding scar that was the meadow, after all, just like Ramona could no longer see it. Either way, they were helping each other find the Eye, and that was the most important thing. For the time being.

Thursday, 21 October 1999, 11:14 PM
Broadway East
Baltimore, Maryland

The storefront blended in with the other buildings on the block: old brick, narrow, no exposed glass,
just plywood painted black, a red neon sign that read
just plain "bar." Lydia liked the sign. No cute play on
words for the name, and the establishment followed
the same no-nonsense suit. No bouncer, no line of
beautiful people waiting to get in. Sometimes the
random kine wandered in. That was okay. There was
a bar stocked with liquor and beer for the minority of
customers who could still drink that stuff. Everybody
up front, either at the bar or at one of the few tables,
knew to be on their best behavior if a "live one" was
in the room. If nobody was too hungry, the kine might
even wander back out after a few drinks. If somebody
took a shining to him, however, he might be delayed
in the back room for a few hours and wake up the
next morning a few quarts low and with a hell of a
hangover. Either way, none the wiser. So far, no mortals tonight.

Lydia had heard stories about Sabbat hangouts
where kine, still barely alive, were kept hanging
around—literally, on hooks—and the night crowd
just dug in whenever they wanted. The idea repulsed
Lydia. It seemed to her as bad as a gang bang, or taking a shit in front of somebody. Feeding was a private
thing. She wouldn't go as far as to say spiritual, but
she'd never had much appetite for feeding, or even
hunting, in packs. Was it, she wondered, something
about a Sabbat vampire's blood that led it to act like

a fucking animal? That was tricky, because there were some Camarilla folks just as bad, or who would be just as bad if it weren't for the higher-ups threatening to kick their deviant asses. Was it just the social conventions, then, that set apart the Camarilla and the Sabbat? Most of the clans in the Camarilla, after all, had members that had bolted to the other side, *antitribu*, and vice versa for the Sabbat. Couldn't be the blood, at least not absolutely. Maybe bloodline set a general pattern, and some individuals strayed from that pattern.

Too bad Christoph wasn't around instead of doing whatever it was he did by himself. He'd probably have an interesting take on the question. But this was their first time off from patrol in four nights, since they'd gotten the car back from Slick's, which was just a few blocks away. Those four nights for her and her boys hadn't been boring either: five firefights, two confirmed Sabbat kills, three high-speed chases, one after Sabbat, one from Sabbat, one from cops. She'd taken a bullet through the face, damned painful, teeth splintered, took a chunk of her tongue. That had taken some blood to fix. Frankie had had his left hand cut off and still hadn't regrown all of his fingers yet.

Frankie was at the table with Lydia, as was Baldur. So instead of the chance to have a serious philosophical conversation with Christoph, she was sitting with the two members of her gang who were endlessly fascinated by questions like why do you drive on a parkway and park on a driveway?

"Hey, Frankie," said Baldur, "wanna go find a piano bar? You could play Chopsticks."

Frankie was less than amused. "Shut the fuck up, you ignorant fuckin' bastard."

"Was you givin' me the finger? I couldn't tell!" Baldur slapped the table at his own wit.

"Why don't you *both* shut the fuck up?" Lydia suggested. She wanted nothing more than to sip her drink—served in a dark glass, a small enough concession to the occasional mortal patron—and to ignore everyone else in the bar. "I can't even hear myself think."

"You must not be thinkin' loud enough," Baldur said, apparently finding something about his comment funny and laughing hysterically.

Lydia glared. Frankie glared. And Baldur, not as dumb as he seemed, shut the fuck up.

What was I thinkin'? Lydia wondered, deciding it was her own fault. If she'd wanted privacy, she should have gone someplace private. Any place with Frankie and Baldur was not private. And even with the two of them piped down, there were other people in the bar to aggravate her. People in general didn't aggravate Lydia; she wasn't one of the great loners, like Theo. But of the four Kindred in the bar other than herself, Frankie and Baldur, and the bartender, one of them was Jasmine. And that was a real pisser.

Jasmine herself was harmless enough. She was some hippie throwback chick: long, straight hair parted in the middle; bell bottoms; cowboy boots; tight shirt and boobs perkier than they had a right to be. She was a powder puff as far as getting her own hands dirty, but she talked a mean game—mean, loud, and constant—and that's what she was doing now at the table in the corner.

"*We* shouldn't be doing *their* dirty work," Jasmine said to her small crowd of admirers. She jabbed her finger at the air at least two times every sentence to emphasize her points. Maybe she was trying to hypnotize her audience. It seemed to be working. The three Kindred listening to her were all guys—Lydia knew the type. They looked like jerks. In life, they would've been the kind to follow their dicks around, and now that those particular appendages didn't carry the same drive, the owners were pretty much without direction and susceptible to forceful speech, and it didn't hurt that it was attached to a pretty face and erect nipples.

"If those *bigshots* over at the Lord Baltimore Inn are so worried about the Sabbat," Jasmine was saying, "*they* should be the ones riding up and down the highways keeping watch."

Lydia took another sip from the opaque highball glass half-filled with blood that she held in her hands. She'd heard Jasmine's rants before, directly and second-hand from Baldur and Frankie, but this time it bothered Lydia more. This time she had to restrain the urge to pull her .38 out of her jacket pocket and plug Jasmine one right in the forehead.

"*They* aren't taking any risks. *They* aren't putting their privileged asses on the line."

Let it go, Lydia told herself. *Everybody knows she's all talk.*

"*They* just sit up there and just sit up there and *talk*, talk, talk. *We* are the ones who do the *dirty work*."

Let it go. Nobody's listening. But they were listening. The three rebels without a clue were listening. Frankie and Baldur had listened, although they were oblivious to what was being said at the moment.

Frankie was too busy brooding, and Baldur was occupied with making a tower out of salt and pepper shakers.

"What time is it, Frankie?" Lydia asked. Maybe there was a late movie they could go catch or something. Anything but staying and listening to flower child shoot her mouth off.

"About 11:30."

Baldur started laughing, tried to keep it in, unsuccessfully.

"*What?*" Lydia, against her better judgment, asked him.

Baldur forced a straight face. "You can ask him what time it is…but don't ask him to tie his shoe!" He couldn't control himself any longer and burst out laughing. He also ducked the angry swipe that Frankie sent his way.

Lydia's vision clouded over red. "Okay. That's it." She reached into her jacket pocket.

"It's not worth it to them," Jasmine said, "to risk *their* sorry hides. No, *we* are the ones they call—"

The wall right above Jasmine's head exploded in brick and mortar dust. The crack of the gunshot rocked the small room like a sudden clap of thunder. Jasmine flattened her face and arms across the table. Her admirers were on the floor. The bartender was out of sight. Frankie and Baldur just stared in dumbfounded disbelief as Lydia swaggered toward the other table, her smoking .38 held casually at her side.

"You talk *a lot*," she said.

Jasmine, her cheek still pressed against the table, slowly peeked over her own forearm. Lydia stood by the table with her gun in hand but not raised, so Jasmine cautiously sat upright in her chair. "There's a lot to be said," she responded, not, Lydia noticed, jabbing her finger at the air any more. One by one, each member of Jasmine's audience began raising his head above the table and glancing around furtively.

Lydia ignored them. "There's a lot of people busting their asses to make sure the Sabbat don't just run right over this place," she said.

"You're right," Jasmine agreed, some of her fire returning, "and those fat cats at the Lord Baltimore Inn ought to be *with* us."

"What do you think Theo Bell does every night?"

"He's a Ventrue lap dog," Jasmine said, jabbing toward Lydia.

Lydia pulled back the hammer on her .38. "Say that again." The three heads that had been rising above the table slowly sank out of view again.

Jasmine opened her mouth, paused, placed her palms flat against the table top. "He risks his ass," she agreed reluctantly, "but he's still just taking orders."

"You don't know what you're talkin' about."

"And you do?"

"More than you." Lydia eased the hammer back into place. As if on cue, the three heads slowly peered up over the table again. "What do you want us to do?" she asked. "Just give Baltimore to the Sabbat?"

Jasmine shook her head, said, "Of course not. All I'm saying is there's no equality. Pieterzoon and that crowd decide what's best for *them*. They don't give a rat's ass about us, but *we* are the ones who get cut to shreds every night when the Sabbat come creeping this way."

"How many of us have *you* seen get shredded?" Lydia asked. Jasmine didn't answer, didn't meet her eyes. "That's what I thought. Too damn busy bitchin' to get your hands dirty."

"That's not true!" Jasmine objected. "I go out. I patrol. I don't think it's as bad as they say."

Lydia crossed her arms, tucking the revolver under her armpit. "Why don't you make up your mind? Are we gettin' cut to shreds, or is it not as bad as they say? You can't have it both ways."

Encouraged by the lack of further gunfire, Jasmine's admirers eased back into their seats. The first and boldest of the three, a punk with a nosering, dusted off his shirt and smiled at Lydia. "I ain't seen that many Sabbat," he said.

"Then you been in the wrong damn place," Lydia said, gesticulating and inadvertently waving her gun about.

The punk shrank back. "Why don't you put that thing away, babe. You can't finish all of us with it."

Before anybody could move, Lydia had the .38 pressed up against the punk's nose. "No, but it sure would hurt a fuckin' lot, don't you think? Wanna give it a try? You want one more big fuckin' nosering?" She cocked the hammer again.

The punk's hands were in his lap. He didn't move a muscle. Lydia backed away slowly, let down the hammer, and then casually slipped the gun back into her pocket. She opened her mouth to call Frankie and Baldur over, then realized that they were right behind her already, both ready to back her up if there was trouble.

"Frankie," she said, "show this dumb-ass, peacenik bitch how safe it is out there."

Without a word, Frankie raised his left hand and started unwrapping the loose bandage that covered it. When he was done, they could all see the skinny, still-growing hand, muscles and tissue not yet fully formed, fingers only about a third as long as they should have been.

"Don't you tell me it's not that bad out there," Lydia said quietly, threateningly. "Don't you tell him that. You just like to hear yourself talk and then blame other people for—"

A shrill chirping sound interrupted her. Lydia reached into her other jacket pocket—Jasmine and her admirers involuntarily tensed just the slightest—and pulled out a cell phone. She clicked it on. "Yeah."

"I need you to come over here," Theo's voice, still deep and strong if faint, said over the line into her ear. He gave her the address. "Don't bring your boys. Got that?"

"Yeah. No problem."

"Good." The line went dead.

Lydia almost took the phone away from her ear but then had a better idea. "Oh, yeah, Theo," she said to the phone, "You got a second? I got somebody here that has something to tell you." Lydia held out the phone to Jasmine. "Here you go. Your chance to tell it straight to the top...."

Jasmine stared coldly at the phone but did not reach out to take it.

"No?" Lydia shrugged. She put the phone back to her face. "Guess I was wrong. I'll be right there."

Lydia clicked off the phone and stuffed it back into her pocket.

"I gotta go. You fellas mind keeping Jasmine and her boys company?" Lydia asked Frankie and Baldur.

"Sure."

"No problem."

"Good," Lydia said. "Tell her some war stories. Maybe tomorrow night we'll take her on patrol with us."

Friday, 22 October 1999, 12:20 AM
Front Street
Baltimore, Maryland

Theo was waiting in the parking lot of a convenience store when Lydia drove up. "Took you long enough," he said. "I catch you in the middle of something?"

"Nah," she shrugged off his question. "You keep me south of the city most of the time. I don't know my way around downtown as much. Got here as fast as I could."

Theo nodded. "Anyway, I got something for you to do. It's gonna be boring as shit, but it's not something I'd ask just anybody." Lydia didn't protest, and he could tell she was hooked. He wasn't just blowing smoke up her ass. He did trust her—as much as he trusted any Kindred. "I'll have Slick send your boys another car. You can't tell them—or anybody—about this. Okay?" Lydia nodded.

"You see that beige Lexus over there?" Theo pointed toward a parking lot just down the block on the other side of the street. The lot was next to a local playhouse. There was no show tonight and just a few cars in the lot.

"Third from the end?" Lydia asked.

"Yeah."

"You sure that's beige? Looks gray to me."

Theo shrugged. "Maybe it's dirty. But you see the car."

"Yeah, I see it."

"I need you to keep an eye on it—all night, every night, until somebody comes and gets it. I got somebody else watchin' during the day. But if somebody comes to take it, you call me, and you stay on 'em until I catch up. Got that?"

"Yeah. No problem. Gonna be anybody that would recognize me?"

Theo thought about that for a second. "Probably not, but maybe. So don't be too obvious."

"Gotcha."

They stood there for a minute, both staring at the car like it might move without anybody there to drive it. "What you packin'?" Theo asked.

Lydia pulled her .38 Special partially out of her pocket.

Theo frowned. "Let me see that."

Lydia glanced around to make sure they weren't attracting any attention, then slid Theo the gun. He held it flat on his open palm, evidently unconcerned that anybody else would see it, and tested the weight.

"Smith 'n' Wesson. What's it made of, paper?"

"Don't be talkin' about my piece," Lydia flared.

Theo handed it to her. "It's very cute. Put that back in your little pocket. Here…" He reached under his jacket behind his back, pulled out a massive handgun—three times as heavy and the barrel twice as long—and handed it to her.

Lydia's hand dipped several inches. "Jesus. All I gotta do is hit somebody over the head with this."

"Desert Eagle," Theo said. ".44 Magnum, seven-round clip. Little more range, lot more stopping power."

"Shit. I'll walk lopsided if I carry this damn thing."

"Happy birthday," Theo said without a smile. "I hate to think of a friend of mine walking around with that little pea-shooter." He gestured toward her pocket. "Here's an extra clip."

"Shit. Thanks, man. But I hate to think of you all defenseless."

Pause. "I'll manage." He turned and started to leave, then stopped. "Oh, yeah. Where are your boys? So I can send somebody to get 'em."

"You know the little rat-ass bar a few blocks from Slick's?"

"Yeah. I know it." He turned and started to leave again.

"Hey, Theo."

He stopped, turned back to her.

"I gotta ask you about something," Lydia said, not sheepishly exactly, but Theo could tell she didn't want to waste his time. He liked that.

"Shoot."

"You know Jasmine?" Lydia asked.

Theo frowned, nodded, folded his arms.

"Yeah, yeah. I know she's full of shit," Lydia continued rapidly, "but she was at the bar, and she was sayin' that she's not seein' heavy action."

"What's it got to do with you?" Theo asked, stone-faced.

"Well, I...you know..." Lydia shifted her weight uneasily back and forth from one foot to the other. "Shit. I feel like an asshole, a fuckin' tattle-tale, but I'm not...I mean, I figure, she's not seein' action, she must not be goin' out, and somebody's not patrollin', we got a hole to look out for. I mean, we're seein' shit *every night.*"

Theo didn't like the sound of that. Somebody not pulling his or her weight was a problem, even if Jasmine was no more than another body, a speed bump in the road when the shit came down and bodies were what Theo needed. Just went to prove that nice tits didn't count for much.

"I'll check it out," Theo said simply. "You just watch that damn car."

The call from Lydia came on the fourth night after Theo had set her watching the Lexus. "He picked up the car," she said over the crackling line of the cell phone.

"Who?"

"Van Pel."

"You sure?"

"Yeah."

"Where are you now?"

"Just leaving the lot."

"Stay with him." Theo was several minutes south of the city and turned north immediately. "Keep me posted."

Damn bastard, he thought of Jan. They'd talked just last night, made the risky decision to pull back the second defensive line, except for the salient of the airport itself, and Jan had not said a damned thing to ease Theo's mind. In fact, the Ventrue had only made Theo more suspicious.

"Still seein' some packs gettin' into the city," Theo had said. "Might be another hit squad. Sure you don't want more security?"

"I'm fine here," Jan had assured him, then added, "and I'm not planning on leaving the inn until this is all resolved."

Lyin' bastard, Theo had thought then, as he did now. He leaned on the gas and shot northward, closer to the city. He wasn't looking for reassurance about the change in the defenses; that was, if dangerous, still all part of the plan. What concerned Theo was another part of the plan they had decided on back in August and not talked much about since: the spy, the high-level mole they both had decided had to be operating. That was Jan's job, to uncover the turncoat. God knew Theo had enough on his plate already. But as far as the Brujah archon knew, the spy was still operating. And they were getting very close to the point in the plan when a breach of secrecy would mean the failure of the whole undertaking. *And now Jan was lying to Theo.* Maybe it was all unrelated…but Theo couldn't help instinctively connecting the dots, even if the shape of things they suggested was the last thing he wanted to see.

Theo's thoughts were interrupted by the chirping of the phone in his pocket. "Yeah."

"Van Pel just picked up somebody at the Lord Baltimore Inn, out back, real quiet like."

Lyin', fuckin' bastard. "Who?"

"Couldn't tell. Just one, though."

"You still on 'em?"

"Yeah. Headin' back toward downtown."

Theo could see the city proper ahead. He was inside the city limits now. He sped up even more. "Call back in three minutes."

"Gotcha." The line went dead.

Pieterzoon, you lyin', fuckin' bastard. Don't make me kick your ass. For a Ventrue—hell, *any* Kindred—to lie was not a big deal in and of itself. Theo had lied himself when he'd suggested that another hit squad might make it deep into Baltimore. No Sabbat was getting anywhere near the Inner Harbor. But Theo and Jan had established a fairly effective working relationship, and Theo was pretty sure that the Ventrue had been straight with him since that night in August when they'd found out about Buffalo. Now Jan was lying, and Theo couldn't help but suspect the worst. Could going rogue be Jan's best shot at upward mobility? After all, the old boys like Hardestadt weren't going anywhere, fast or otherwise, and that meant that nobody under them was going anywhere either. Theo hoped that he was wrong, but if he wasn't, the Camarilla here in the U.S. was sunk. And that would reflect poorly on him, as the archon of Clan Brujah present on the scene. And *that* made him mad.

Three minutes. The phone rang again.

"Turned away from downtown," Lydia said. "Headin' north on Charles. Just passed…Saratoga."

Theo was near Charles Street, but farther south. He stuffed the phone back into a pocket and pressed on northward as quickly as he could without waving a red flag for the cops. There wasn't too much traffic. The lights were the problem. He caught one red, took a quick right, left at the next two green lights, then right back onto Charles.

The phone again. "Turnin' left onto Franklin."

"I see you," Theo said. He put away the phone, shot forward to the intersection with Franklin Street and left through a yellow. He saw Lydia in the Pontiac ahead and made sure he had a bead on the Lexus before he waved her off. She'd done her part. He would handle it from here. She made eye contact, hesitated, gave him that questioning look: *Are you sure?* He waved her off again, and she turned down a side street.

Theo turned his full attention to the Lexus. It was about a block and a half ahead of him. He dropped back a little farther—a motorcycle was not the most inconspicuous way to follow someone—but kept a close eye on the traffic signals. He didn't want to lose sight of the beige car. A forced detour around the block to avoid a red light was no longer a good option.

As Theo followed along behind, he felt a fire rising in his gut, a cold fire, one that he knew if he didn't hold down would grow red hot, and then would open the way for hunger, the uncontrollable hunger. He felt the fire more keenly than the rumble of his bike or the wind against his face. His anger, which was never far away, was stoked by frustration, resentment. Kindred like Lydia, he knew, were trying to do their part, to do what was right, to keep the Sabbat from taking everything. Because as depraved and deceitful as the Camarilla was, the Sabbat was ten times worse, a hundred times. But so many of the Kindred were in it only for themselves, for their own personal agendas. Damn the Camarilla, and the city, and everyone else in the world for that matter.

Theo had his own long laundry list of damnables, and it was growing more extensive every night: Damn all the dead weight that Theo was compelled to move around. Jasmine and others like her might be good for a debate society or a campus protest, but on the street, once bullets started flying, they weren't worth shit. Damn Pieterzoon for lying and for his ambition, for whatever angle it was that he was playing. Damn Hardestadt and all the other old-timers. If they weren't so hell-bent on keeping all the younger Kindred in their places, then Jan and his type might not be driven to scheme and *seize* power, giving the elders that much more reason to be paranoid. Damn all of Clan Ventrue for always being such lying, conniving pricks, for forcing Theo to be suspicious of them. There was no way that he could come right out and ask Jan about the spy, or about why he was lying about the car. The Ventrue would lie and lie again, and Theo would never find out the truth. The only way was to confront Pieterzoon once there was no turning back.

Basic decency was too much to ask for; it was too lofty a goal. Mutual self-interest, if you were lucky, was the closest you were going to get. That was the way of the world, Kindred or kine. The best you could do was stake out your own moral ground, draw that line in the sand, and then fucking bust the head of anybody that stepped over.

Those were Theo's sentiments as the Lexus turned off Franklin Street and he followed. They were soon cruising through a portion of Baltimore reserved for the old-money families. Majestic homes on walled estates spoke of wealth and luxury—and of isolation from the real world. The Lexus was easing along at thirty-five, and there were few other cars on the road here. Theo dropped farther behind. He killed his headlight. He toyed with the idea of ditching his bike altogether—he could easily keep up with the Lexus on foot at this speed—but there was always the chance that van Pel was only cutting through the ritzy neighborhood and would get back on a highway, so Theo watched from as far away as the gentle curves allowed. All the while, the fire in his belly was growing more intense, gaining strength and heat.

It was the red fire, the hunger, that over a hundred years ago had taken hold of him the night he had rid the world of Master Bell, plantation owner, slave holder, violator of Theo's family. It was the red fire, the hunger, that had not let Theo stop at that. He'd come to his senses amidst flames and carnage, the plantation house an inferno, and at the slaves' quarters, the ground littered with bodies. Bodies he recognized, too many of them actually members of his mortal family. It was not the last atrocity Theo would commit over the years, but like all the other times, he had been driven to it. Circumstances, injustice, cruelty, and then the anger, always the anger and the fire.

He was holding it down tonight. Mostly. Still, he wasn't completely in control. Tonight he wasn't the same calm and collected man who regularly tracked down Sabbat interlopers and splattered them all over the pavement. He was aware of that. He was also aware that tonight's dealings were a bit touchier than the usual search-and-destroy outings. He was aware—but he wasn't feeling inclined toward finesse.

And so, when he saw the Lexus start to pull into a gated drive, Theo felt almost as if he were merely a spectator. His rational mind watched as he gunned the engine and his motorcycle shot forward, as he flicked the headlight back on and barreled toward the passenger's side of the Lexus. He closed the distance to the car before the large, electronic gates had swung halfway open. As the motorcycle slid and screeched to a halt just at the front bumper of the

Lexus, two armed guards, ghouls both, were rushing forward. Theo had his shotgun unhooked from within his jacket, in hand, and cocked before the guards could get off a shot. He didn't level the SPAS at them, and they somehow sensed his restraint and held their own fire, avoiding for the moment a certain blood-bath. For a long, tense moment, they all faced one another. The Lexus idled quietly, Theo's bike less so, and the gate, with a slight rattle, swung open.

Then the rear passenger's window on the Lexus rolled down with a calm hum. The tinted glass gave way to the shadows of the interior, and a thin, un-naturally pale face. The paleness was not a result of fright or agitation. The face was fairly expression-less, in fact. A streetlight reflected off Jan Pieterzoon's glasses. He straightened his tie ever so slightly.

"It's all right, guards," Pieterzoon said. "He's with us."

The guards hesitated, but holstered their weap-ons. Theo hooked the SPAS back in his jacket and backed up his bike a few feet. The tinted window hummed closed again, and the Lexus moved forward slowly up the sloped drive. Theo followed.

As they drove up the hill, Theo was glad at least that Jan had faced him. Maybe the Brujah's suspi-cions were totally baseless—at least about the spy business. Or maybe that's what Pieterzoon wanted him to think. Could Jan have faced him that calmly if there was something going on here that the Brujah couldn't find out about? Maybe. Pieterzoon had balls. Theo had to give him that. He'd watched the Ventrue, alone, outgunned, and seriously injured, outmaneuver a Sabbat hit squad. That as much as anything had convinced Theo that Jan was worth helping and had allowed them to put into effect a plan that might just salvage Camarilla prestige, if not all of the cities that were already gone. Still, though, Theo only trusted a Ventrue about as far as he could throw him. Hell, not even that far.

"Good evening, Theo," Jan said as he and van Pel were getting out of the Lexus.

Van Pel handed the keys to one of two waiting ghouls playing valet. Theo didn't offer his bike keys, and the second ghoul didn't ask. Hans van Pel, Jan's executive assistant, or some bullshit like that, was tougher looking than his boss: taller, burlier, chin and jaw more squared, he looked older too. He looked, Theo thought, like a Nazi, but maybe that was just Theo's Brujah showing. Van Pel opened the door for the two Kindred and managed to look at the same time both respectful of Jan and discreetly disdainful of Theo. Theo let it slide. He'd found over the years that he could get a lot of mileage out of other clans' snobbery. He welcomed being underestimated. It was made easier to take by the knowledge that he could, any time he wanted, reach out and break van Pel's goddamned neck, and Jan wouldn't so much as blink. Nobody was going to jeopardize their relationship with an archon over a ghoul. Apparently van Pel hadn't thought that matter all the way through to its logical conclusion. He couldn't know how close he'd come to catching Theo on the wrong night for that kind of shit.

Because the fire wasn't gone. The confrontation at the gate had only tempered it slightly. Theo was completely in control again. He was glad that Jan had faced him. If the Ventrue had tried to cut and run, Theo knew what could have happened. The two ghouls would have been no problem—the three ghouls, make that, because van Pel would have found himself stuffed through the windshield and with his dick for a hood ornament. The trouble would have come after the fact, after Theo had broken Jan in half. Probably the Brujah wouldn't have killed Jan permanently, because Theo still had questions about the spy, and the plan hadn't yet run its course. He would have gotten an earful later from Pascek, though. But, hell, it wouldn't have been the first time. And probably not the last.

But Jan had rolled down the window instead of making a break for it, and now they were playing nice. For the moment. So Theo held the fire down.

As they made their way across the main entry hall, Jan, not looking at Theo, said, "Your company is an unexpected pleasure." It was the kind of smart-ass Ventrue bullshit that Theo had no use for.

"Yeah," Theo said. "Imagine my surprise, meetin' you out here when you weren't leavin' the inn until all this was resolved."

They began to ascend a large curving staircase. This mansion, despite being architecturally different, reminded Theo of the Bell plantation house. It reminded him also of so many of the halls of power he had gained access to as a representative of Clan Brujah—as an archon he'd gained that access, but not a taste for the surroundings. They were always so similar. No matter what city or continent; whether the estate was in the wide spaces of the countryside or tucked in among others of its kind in town; no matter last century or this; classical, neo-classical, art deco, southwestern; it just didn't matter. The elders, just like Master Bell, were part of the privileged class, the haves who wanted both to flaunt their status and to hide away in safety from the have-nots who made up most of the world.

And this, the insular world of privilege, was the world that Jan Pieterzoon belonged to, that he felt comfortable in. Theo knew that instinctively, and tonight only served to prove him right. Whatever gains he and Jan achieved, whatever level of success they reached against the Sabbat, it was still just a marriage of convenience. Theo wanted to stop the Sabbat because the world would be fucked if he didn't. Jan wanted to stop the Sabbat because his sire told him to.

Climbing the steps, Theo still wasn't sure what exactly he'd busted in on. Jan wasn't about to say. He enjoyed too much knowing more than anybody else; he liked to lord it over people, kind of like the Nosferatu, except they weren't generally so arrogant about it. Maybe because a lot of their so-called secrets were worthless bullshit. Small return for spending eternity going through people's garbage. At least when the Ventrue held out on you, it was usually important—which wasn't necessarily a good thing.

So Theo tromped along with Jan and his flunkie. The Dutchman seemed to know where he was going. At least there wasn't a fucking butler, although van Pel had enough of a stick up his ass to make up for the fact. Theo was ready for anything—

Anything except what he saw when van Pel opened a set of double doors for the Kindred, and they walked into some kind of sitting room. There was the small fire in the fireplace—always the damned fire, never mind the idiocy of it; it was a status thing—and the giant mirror and the grandfather clock and the fucking satin upholstery, but what shocked Theo, *surprised the shit out of him*, was not what but *who*.

Occupying two of three ornate, straight-back chairs were two other Kindred. Two whom Theo recognized. Two who by all rights should not have been there.

The first was a very young woman—*appeared* to be a very young woman—delicate, almost frail, but Theo knew better than to trust that impression of her. He knew that a better, more accurate gauge of her capabilities was to be found in her eyes. For the brief instant that he met her gaze, her eyes shone with an intensity that had borne her through more centuries than Theo had seen. For a moment, the intensity bordered on hostility, irritation—she hadn't expected him—but then it was as if a shield descended over her face. Emotion and human sentiment vanished, but not activity; she took in and assessed every detail, formed conclusions and convictions in mere seconds, asserted her superiority over the circumstances before the first word was spoken.

"Archon Bell," said Justicar Lucinde of Clan Ventrue, "what an unexpected pleasure."

An unexpected pleasure. Exactly what Jan had said. Nothing, Theo noticed, was ever *a surprise*, even when it was. Never, *What the fuck are you doing here?* which was what Theo thought but didn't say. *An unexpected pleasure*. That must be what it said in the Ventrue Handbook under: "What to say when some asshole barges in where you don't want him."

The other Kindred did not speak. His presence was, if less astounding—he was known to operate in Baltimore, after all—potentially more troublesome in its implications. Hesha Ruhadze's right hand rested easily atop the sterling-silver handle of his cane. His skin, his handsomely bald head, was slightly lighter, a richer brown, than Theo's skin. If Theo had not recognized Hesha, the Setite would not have seemed out of place. He was completely at ease amidst the trappings of wealth, sitting straight in his pressed suit. The firelight sparkled against his cane and against the monocle partially tucked within his crisp shirt's breast pocket.

"Jan," Lucinde's voice was pleasant, but formal and curt, "have your man bring another chair."

As van Pel hastened to obey, a series of competing thoughts were running through Theo's mind: Lucinde was in town. How long had she been here? Why keep her presence secret when that knowledge could easily prop up the morale of the city's Camarilla defenders? What the hell was she doing meeting with Ruhadze? Sure, the Setite might be able to help the cause, but those arrangements could be handled at lower levels. Pieterzoon was enough of a luminary in the clan that Hesha would be shown appropriate respect meeting with him instead of a justicar. There had to be something else going on, something bigger than this city, bigger than the plan—the plan as Theo knew it.

Jan waited to claim the third chair until van Pel returned with a fourth.

"Do join us, Archon, Mr. Pieterzoon," Lucinde said.

Theo sat. She wasn't going to kick him out. Theoretically she could; she out-ranked him, even though Pascek was his boss and Theo didn't owe the Ventrue justicar any personal allegiance. But it would be messy if she tried and Theo wanted to kick up a fuss. He was the highest-ranking official on the ground, had been from the start. If Lucinde didn't want to rankle him too badly, which seemed to be the case so far, either it was simply more useful for her purposes to keep Theo on board, *or* there was some agreement between her and Pascek behind the scenes. Not that Pascek, the fanatical, paranoid bastard, would bother to tell his own archon. So Theo was left to puzzle it out.

"Archon," said Lucinde, her eyes maintaining the hard shield of formality, "I believe you might be familiar with Mr. Ruhadze?"

Theo nodded, almost imperceptibly.

"We have met," said Hesha.

The Setite's presence complicated matters for Theo. Even with a justicar, he would have tended toward the blunt confrontation; he had already committed himself to that path, barging in uninvited and unannounced. Lucinde and Jan would have told him something, and he would have set about confirming or disproving their story. With Hesha there, however, Theo was reluctant to air any dirty laundry. Suspicion among members of the Camarilla, especially among key players, was not something to vent in front of a Setite, especially this Setite. Not that anybody denied the distrust, but it just wasn't smart to give a snake an opening to slither into.

"And, Jan Pieterzoon," Lucinde continued, "I believe you know Mr. Ruhadze."

"Only by reputation," said Jan, self-consciously ambiguous, disarmingly making light of the tension between the clans. Hesha nodded appreciatively.

"I believe, Mr. Pieterzoon," Lucinde said, "that we should attend to the archon's business first, so as not to waste his valuable time." "I agree. Archon Bell," Jan said, adopting Lucinde's formal parlance, "As we have discussed before, Mr. Ruhadze had various and long-standing interests in Baltimore, and naturally the recent passing of Prince Garlotte is of great concern to him."

Theo's mind shifted back to that whole matter. He hadn't really considered Hesha as a possibility. Did the Setite have his fangs in Katrina somehow? Did he see an opening to slide in and take the city that might slip through the cracks between Camarilla and Sabbat?

"As a gesture of goodwill and mutual concern," Jan continued, "Mr. Ruhadze has brought to our attention certain information that might be relevant."

Goodwill, my ass, Theo thought.

Jan removed his wire-rimmed glasses and cleaned them with a silk handkerchief as he spoke. "Apparently, the prince's childe, Katrina, did not in fact go down with the ship, so to speak."

Theo leaned back slowly, pressed his back against the back of his chair, and folded his arms. "And…?"

"The fact that she survives is perhaps less significant than the fact that she has been in hiding since the explosion." Jan replaced his glasses.

"You think she had something to do with it?" Theo asked.

"Perhaps," said Jan.

Theo scratched the rough stubble of his chin. He stared for nearly a full thirty seconds at the small flames dancing above the gas logs, as if he were considering the possibility that Katrina had blown up her sire. What the Brujah actually wondered was why, if they knew Katrina was still around and they thought she'd done it, hadn't they just taken her down? It wouldn't be that hard. Maybe they planned to, and with him showing up unexpectedly, this was the easiest bone to toss him. It was possible, the Brujah knew, that they had already found the girl, that they knew he had let her go that night. Or, he knew, it was possible that Hesha, or *all of them* for that matter, had been the impetus behind Katrina's revenge. If they wanted him to finish her, that would be a nice, tidy little end to the affair.

"You think somebody put her up to it?" Theo asked. He looked from Jan to Lucinde to Hesha. He wasn't accusing them, not explicitly, but he wanted to expand the area of questioning. He didn't want to give them too easy an out.

"It is…possible," Jan said.

Theo sat silently again. He didn't bother to look more at the other three. They were too practiced at deceit for him to learn anything from their expressions or body language. He was the same way, he knew. On the street sometimes lying was required. The farther from the street, the higher up the ladder, the more it was required. Except these three would call it "dissembling." They couldn't even be honest about lying.

"Archon," said Lucinde, her confidence belying her youthful appearance, "could you look into this matter? Prince Goldwin has yet to name a new sheriff, and I fear there would be a certain conflict of interests, regardless."

Yeah, he might conflict with your interests, Theo thought, then said flatly, "I can do it."

"Good." Lucinde's smile seemed amazingly devoid of ruthlessness. "Good."

"Hans," said Jan, lifting a hand toward the ghoul but not looking. Van Pel produced a small pad of paper, which he handed to his master. Jan uncapped a fountain pen and made a brief notation. He tore loose the sheet of paper and handed it to Theo. "Here is the address where she is staying."

Theo looked at the address; he knew the area. He stuffed the paper into his pocket. The other three Kindred were watching him, waiting, but Theo didn't have anything else to say. He couldn't very well address his real concerns, not with Hesha there, but there would be time later. Theo would make sure of that.

For now, he stood, grimly, nodded to each of the personages, "Lucinde, Jan, Hesha," and left.

"Can you arrange the meeting?" Lucinde asked, perhaps an hour after Theo Bell had left.

"Certainly," said Jan. "I don't foresee any difficulties."

"Other than the usual Malkavian proclivities," Lucinde suggested.

Hesha smiled, politely, not genuinely amused. He, appropriately, did not wish to convey the impression that he was allying himself with the Camarilla, with the Ventrue, so he let slip occasional glimpses of his disdain for them. Lucinde took no offense. The Setite's scorn was no more sincere than the thin veil of civility through which it glimmered. They were not all so very different, Jan mused.

"Of course," Jan said. He too smiled politely at the handsome African. The younger Ventrue's graciousness was slightly more forced than was his justicar's, however, and intentionally so. He harbored considerably more reservations than did Lucinde concerning this agreement into which she had just entered. Undoubtedly because she merely made the agreement; it was Jan's responsibility to carry it through. Better, then, he decided, not to appear too willing to cooperate; better to keep Hesha at an obvious arm's length, to make sure the Setite fulfilled every letter of the agreement. There was no call for camaraderie with clans that didn't claim their rightful place—and fulfill their obligations—among the Camarilla, but instead attempted to use the sect when it suited their purposes.

Why, Jan wondered, should he treat Ruhadze any better than they would someone like Bell, who had proved his worth, many times over, to the Camarilla? Jan considered the task, the test, that they had set before Theo. The Ventrue was troubled by the possibility that Theo's services might be lost to the Camarilla. But, as Lucinde had pointed out, they had to be sure. Besides, one only went so far in arguing a point with a justicar, especially on someone else's behalf. Add to that the fact that Pascek apparently agreed. One did not argue with two justicars. Period.

So Jan was left to deal with the Setite. And to hope that Theo passed the test.

part two:
bait and switch

Theo didn't like it at all. Not one bit.

Lucinde was in Baltimore. He didn't know how long she'd been in the city. He still wouldn't have known she was there at all if he hadn't decided something was fishy about the car that Pieterzoon was having fixed up on the sly.

Even knowing, Theo still wasn't happy. Far from it. But he felt a little better now that he was tearing through the night on his motorcycle. The roar of the engine was very like the Brujah's style, much more than the quiet machinations of the Ventrue, the deceivers. Deceive your enemies—that Theo understood. Work with your friends. Work for a common goal. That's how it should be.

Fuck them, Theo thought. He knew it didn't work that way. But it should. The problem was, there were no friends, only allies. Allies of convenience; allies while you were within earshot, if that.

It wasn't even that Jan and Lucinde had done anything really horrible. Hell, Theo knew that. He would even count the two of them among the "decent" Kindred, which wasn't saying too much. They were barely in Pascek's league as far as conniving, fuck-you, bend-over-and-take-it-up-the-ass politics went. Still, they pissed Theo off.

Lucinde, of course, could go wherever the hell she wanted to go. Theo could have quibbled protocol, the fact that she didn't bother to let him know she was around—how was he supposed to defend the damned city when he didn't know the true extent of his resources?—but he would be on shaky ground. Besides—protocol. When the hell had Theo ever argued points of protocol?

It wasn't some silly Toreador thing either, like he had his feelings hurt, or thought that he'd been snubbed. Those were sensibilities that Theo hadn't known during life—a slave doesn't have feelings, not like that; he's too busy surviving—and he hadn't developed them during unlife. The truth of the matter was that, by pulling this stunt, Lucinde was undercutting what confidence Theo had in Jan, confidence that they could work together, that they could carry out the plan—or that Jan could or would carry out his part of it. If Jan had kept this from Theo, what other important details were hidden? Lucinde was making Theo's job harder, and that was making it less likely that the Camarilla would hold out on the East Coast, and *that*, promoting the interests of the Camarilla, was supposed to be her number-one fucking job.

But maybe her sneaking around had more to do with Hesha. Theo didn't buy for a second that shit about a gesture of goodwill. The Setite might actually have had information about Katrina, but no way in hell was that the only thing he was there to talk about with Lucinde. The more Theo thought about it, the less it made sense for Hesha to have orchestrated Garlotte's destruction. The former prince and Ruhadze had more or less coexisted for many years—unless some major disagreement had come up in the recent past that Theo didn't know about. Possible. Besides that, though, it was not the most auspicious

time to take over a city, with the Sabbat closing in—
unless the Setite had a deal with the Sabbat. Again,
possible.

Shit, Theo thought. Too many possibilities, and
none of them as urgent as what he was doing at the
moment. Unlike the ritzy part of town where Lucinde
was hanging out, the Cherry Hill neighborhood was
not asleep and quiet. Here, at night, the dregs rose to
the surface. Pimps and prostitutes. Open-air drug
markets. Young men, mostly black, who'd be lucky
to live beyond twenty or twenty-five. Overdose. Violence. AIDS. They either thought they were
indestructible, immortal, or else they just didn't care.
Fatalism led to fatalities. Theo didn't seem out of
place. Nobody bothered him. Maybe it was the touch
of death that rode with him. Somewhere in their gut,
those people on the street recognized him, knew him
for what he was, kept their distance.

The address that Jan had given Theo, the address where Katrina was supposedly hiding out, was
not far from the house that had been her haven before she blew her sire to bits. Not very smart, staying
so close to home, and apparently some flunky of
Ruhadze's had spotted her and followed her. Then
again, this particular childe of Garlotte's was not exactly noted for her subtlety and misdirection. Blowing
up the prince and his entire ship in the middle of his
city was a lot of things, but subtle was not one of
them.

Theo parked down the block and made his way
along the cracked sidewalk. The house was a bro-
ken-down shack, flimsy, maybe forty years old,
without much hope of making it to be much older.

The front door had even less hope. Theo kicked it in, sending splintered wood from door and door frame cascading into the living room.

Before the black girl Katrina was sitting beside could open her mouth to scream, Katrina was off the couch and away in a blur. Theo was ready for that. The mortal was opening her mouth but still had not screamed when Theo cut Katrina off at the kitchen door. He gave her an elbow to the jaw, and she sprawled into the kitchen table. The lone chair clattered across the room.

Finally, the scream.

Theo looked back at the black girl, maybe eighteen years old. He pointed toward the front door—what *had* been the front door. "Get the fuck out. Now."

The girl's scream died away instantly, but her mouth stayed open. She almost fell over herself scrambling out the door. Theo turned back to Katrina. She was about to jump up and bolt again.

"Don't," Theo said, "or it'll be the last fuckin' thing you do."

Katrina froze. Then, slowly, she picked herself up from the floor. She rubbed her jaw. It didn't seem to be broken, although Theo's blow could have broken a mortal's neck.

"Your friend gonna bring help?" Theo asked.

"Like who? Who the fuck's gonna help me?"

"I feel real sorry for you," Theo said. "I thought I told you to get outta town."

Katrina crossed her arms, set her hip defiantly. "Where am I supposed to go?"

"I look like a travel agent?"

They stood staring each other down for several seconds. "So you here to finish me?" Katrina asked finally.

"If I wanted you dead, you'd be dead by now."

"That's what I figured. What do you want then, or are you just slummin' tonight?"

"Sit down and shut the fuck up."

Katrina glared but righted the chair and sat. She brushed off her jeans and the tight, sleeveless T-shirt she was wearing. "Havin' second thoughts about lettin' me go?"

"More every minute." Theo eased back against the chipped, dirty counter. "Listen good. Two things. First, I've got a question for you."

"Then you're gonna finish me."

"I *might* if you don't shut the fuck up. Where'd you get the explosives? I don't figure you for the type to have a chemistry set in the basement."

"Some guy. He offered. I took him up on it."

"This guy have a name?"

Katrina shrugged. "Probably. He didn't say. I didn't ask."

"So let me get this straight. This guy you don't know, don't know his name, comes up to you for no reason at all and offers to sell you a case of dynamite."

"Plastic explosives. Showed me how to use 'em too. And he gave 'em to me, didn't sell 'em."

"Kindred?"

"Yeah, I think."

"Who'd he work for?" Theo held up his hands. "No, let me guess. He didn't say. You didn't ask."

"You're pretty damn smart for a Brujah."

"You're gonna be pretty damn flat for a Ventrue, you don't watch it." The threat was not made in jest, and Katrina, still defiant but not quite as confrontational, sank back into her chair. "How did you meet him?"

"He found me. Said he had something I might want. Just went on from there."

"It happen around here, this neighborhood?"

"Yeah. I'm not hard to find."

"Yeah, and that better change if you wanna keep on wakin' up." Theo ignored Katrina's sneer. "He give you the stuff right then, or come back?"

"He told me to get in touch with him if I was interested. I was supposed to go to this bar up at Park Heights called Dewey's Sweatshop."

"Sounds classy."

"Tell me about it. I ain't picky, but this was a real lowball joint. But I went, like he said. I asked the bartender if Johnny was around—"

"That the guy's name?" Theo interrupted. "Johnny?"

"I don't know. I think it was more like a password, you know? Anyhow, I ask if Johnny's around. Bartender says no, but I give him a piece of paper with a time written on it. Then I meet the guy the next night at that time."

"What about the bartender?"

"Fat guy with a beard. Not one of us. Too sweaty. Must be Dewey."

"And you didn't even try to find out who this Johnny guy was workin' for?"

"Why the fuck should I care?" Katrina asked.

"So, you'd know who was settin' you up to kill Garlotte and then let you take the fall."

"Look, man…" Katrina stood up and knocked the chair back against the counter. She started pacing, agitated, not nervous, back and forth in the tiny space of the kitchen, like a rat in a cage. "Maybe it's different for you, being such a big badass and all, but anything I do, *somebody's* gonna be yankin' my chain. I got what I wanted out of this, and that's all that mattered. Garlotte's history. *He's* not yankin' my chain anymore. If somebody else got what they wanted too, fine. If I get fucked before it's all over, well that's just too fuckin' bad for me. You can send me a sympathy card, you Brujah archon asshole. But I tell you one thing, it won't be Garlotte tellin' me what to do. Not anymore."

Theo just watched her, watched her get herself all worked up, watched herself blow off steam, this little white girl who wasn't going to play by anybody's rules. Her type was a dime a dozen. Maybe cheaper than that. She just happened to have had access to a prince, to a careless prince, and she'd made the most of her opportunities. But there was something else. Otherwise, Theo would have crushed her that night on the dock. She sounded more like a Brujah than a Ventrue; there was enough anger. But that was true of any number of Anarchs or, of the occasional Ventrue who jumped to the Sabbat, *antitribu*. As Theo watched her, he finally, after two weeks of wondering about it on and off, realized what it was that had prompted him to spare her: She just didn't care.

It wasn't that she didn't care about what she was doing. In fact, she cared so much about whatever she had set her mind on—revenge against Garlotte, standing up to Theo—that she didn't care about the consequences. That night on the dock, she hadn't run. Sure, after the explosion she'd been knocked senseless, but she hadn't run before, when Theo wouldn't have known to chase her. And tonight she wasn't cowed by facing an archon who could, quite justifiably, put her down. Confidence? Fatalism? Stupidity? Balls? Whatever exactly it was, it could take her a long way…or it could get her killed. Really soon.

"Is there anything else you can tell me about the guy?" Theo asked when Katrina realized that he was watching her, studying her.

She glowered at him for a long moment, then sighed. "Yeah. He's ugly. Not Nossie ugly, but ugly. When I saw him, he needed a shave and a shower. Receding hairline. And he couldn't keep his fuckin' hands to himself."

"What?"

Katrina seemed to grow angry at the thought. "He kept, like…not feelin' me up or anything, but touchin' my arm when he was talkin' to me. Gave me the creeps. I went home and took a shower." Theo waited, but Katrina just smiled sarcastically and shrugged. "That's it, cowboy. You know what I know. Now what? Lights out?"

Theo laughed, and enjoyed the fact that that seemed to make her angry all over again. "You must be the luckiest damn person in the world for nobody to have killed you already."

"We're all—"

"Yeah, yeah," Theo cut her off. "We're all dead already. Save it, sister. Look. I told you once to get the hell out of Baltimore, and I guess it turned out okay that you didn't. But you're damn lucky that whoever set you up for this didn't decide to clean up afterward. Why, I don't know. Unless he figured you were stupid enough to get yourself killed without his help—which ain't too far from the truth."

"Well, you can—"

Theo pointed a beefy finger at Katrina, and she stopped mid-protest.

"I can do whatever the fuck I want, that's what I can do," Theo said. "And this is what I want to do." He stood there for a few seconds, finger stretched toward Katrina like a dagger. The slightest signs of hesitance crept into her face, her posture. Then Theo took an old newspaper, a half-finished crossword, from the counter, and a pen that was lying nearby. He tore a small strip from the paper and jotted down a name. He held the strip of paper toward Katrina. Very cautiously, she took it from him.

"This is what you do," Theo said. "You get that girl that was here…what's her name?"

"Angela."

"You get Angela. You steal a car if you have to, and you drive. West. You drive at night. She drives during the day. You ride in the damn trunk. You change your name, and you stay the hell away from here, away from the East Coast. Go to San Francisco. Ask around till you find that guy," Theo pointed at the slip of paper he'd handed her. "You should be able to find him around the docks."

Katrina looked at the name on the paper. "Friend of yours?"

"No. Matter of fact, don't mention my name or he'll kick your fuckin' ass and dump you in the Bay. You don't know me. Leave me out of it, he'll probably help you get set up out there. Got it?"

"Uh…yeah."

"And I mean *tonight*. I mean you're gone in the next hour, the next half fuckin' hour. You don't listen to me this time…"

"Right. All right."

Theo waited, glared at her long enough to make sure that she was taking him seriously, then he turned and walked past the splintered pieces of door and door frame that littered the living-room floor.

Outside, the drug dealers scattered at the sight of him. Fatalistic or not, they could see death walking, and, this time, they were smart enough to get away.

Tuesday, 26 October 1999, 10:15 PM
Presidential Suite, Lord Baltimore Inn
Baltimore, Maryland

"Tell Pieterzoon I'm here."

Anton Baas, head of Jan's security detail, regarded Theo for a moment with that aloof, European detachment that annoyed Theo so much. Then Baas nodded to one of the two men beside him—all three were ghouls—who slipped within the double doors to Jan's suite and reappeared a few seconds later to nod back at Baas. Baas opened the door wide and stepped aside for Theo to pass.

Inside, Pieterzoon and van Pel were seated at a table that held a sizeable stack of leather-bound ledgers. Jan removed his glasses, folded them, and slipped them into his breast pocket. He closed the portfolio before him and placed it atop the stack of its mates.

"Theo, I was expecting you," Jan said. "I imagine we have much to discuss."

At least, Theo thought, the Ventrue wasn't pretending that nothing had happened last night. "I imagine that too," Theo said.

"That will be all for now, Hans," Jan said. He and Theo watched each other closely, neither speaking or moving, as van Pel gathered together the ledgers and showed himself out.

"How long has she been here?" Theo asked as soon as the doors closed.

"Not long. Two weeks."

"When were you gonna tell me?"

"There was no need."

The answer seemed truthful enough to Theo, and that in itself was something. It would have been easy enough for Jan to dangle some assuaging lie about how they were going to let Theo in on the secret in just another night or two.

"Theo, I did not know more than a few nights in advance that she would be arriving, and I was given explicit instructions to say nothing. To anyone."

Theo took the seat that van Pel had vacated. Jan's explanation seemed likely enough—not that that meant it was true. The truth could just as easily be that this was a line to insulate Jan from the subterfuge, to keep Theo on board and happy.

"Two weeks," Theo said. "So she got here just before Garlotte's big bang. Her idea? Yours?"

Jan's eyes narrowed, almost quizzically. He was not the least insulted by the suggestion. "Because he would never agree to the plan? No. Though that was actually one of the reasons for her coming. I did not have great hopes for your embassy to Garlotte that night. I also thought, as did the justicar, that I had perhaps expended as much of the prince's favor as was wise and that a new, more highly and more officially placed voice was called for. No, we did not destroy Garlotte. We were quite surprised by that turn of events, in fact, and not greatly pleased. The justicar could have persuaded him to accept the plan."

Shit. Theo kicked himself for not seeing that one. But it was so easy to assume the worst, most devious motivations after discovering deception—easy, and often correct. Not this time. Maybe. Theo had even suspected Jan of being the spy, and though he hadn't disproven it, the Brujah had to believe that Lucinde wouldn't be working closely with the bastard if there was any question of his passing on information to the Sabbat.

"I couldn't tell you any of this last night," Jan said. "Not with Hesha there. Not with Lucinde there too, really. She would prefer to play the hand closer to our vest."

"Then why are you tellin' me?" Theo challenged him.

"Why did you support me when it would have been easier to take Garlotte's side, or that of Lladislas, your clansman?"

Theo didn't answer at first. He sat back in his chair, crossed his arms, then said, "We needed somebody from outside, somebody with broader connections, somebody less provincial."

"My thoughts exactly. In short, you chose what you thought would be most effective for our cause, despite whatever you thought about me. I don't have illusions that we'll leave this city, this situation, and exchange postcards. I'm not speaking with you tonight out of any sense of friendship or altruism, and I know you'd never expect that. But no matter what our respective justicars may think, I think that you will be the most service to the Camarilla if you know the broader picture."

Theo's first impulse was anger. Who the fuck was this Ventrue to tell *him*, an archon, about the broader picture? But, Theo realized quickly, Lucinde seemed to have taken Jan into her confidence, and that might provide information from a circle that would otherwise be kept from even an archon. No point getting pissed off and being insulted.

"Okay then," Theo said. "You said talkin' to Garlotte was one reason she came. What were the others?"

"That was the primary reason she wanted to be physically present, but she's also been quite helpful in my negotiations with the Giovanni. Isabel and her folk proved resistant to my Boston gambit. I'm afraid that Jacques Gauthier was less than adequate as an envoy. At any rate, with Lucinde's backing, I was able to exact the concessions we require from the Giovanni—"

"How?" Theo was skeptical.

Jan, on the other hand, seemed to relish divulging the details of this particular scheme. He was proud of his accomplishment—that, Theo noted, might be something he could use against the Ventrue some night, if the need arose. "A few like-minded financiers can indeed produce miracles—provided they are the right financiers and are amenable to guidance." Jan rubbed his hands together. "Several strategic sell-offs were sufficient to spark a rapid devaluation of the Italian lira and, not coincidentally, to convince certain individuals within Clan Giovanni that it was in their best interests to agree to a few limited and reasonable requests. It wasn't even a risk to the Masquerade, really. The only thing that collapses in Italy more often than the exchange rate is the government."

"What about Hesha?" Theo pressed, less than interested in exchange rates. "A Setite doesn't offer a token of goodwill unless he's gonna get something out of it."

"Just like a Ventrue?" Jan asked with a wry grin.

"Same ballpark."

"Hesha actually approached us. He did bring the information regarding Garlotte's childe, but that was less significant than what he was able to offer about the Eye of Hazimel."

"The Eye of what?"

"Not what, whom. Or perhaps what applies as well. Hazimel. According to legend, an ancient Ravnos, a stone mason by some accounts, who ruled much of India. Pre-history. He extended his domain by bestowing his Eye upon a succession of rulers in exchange for their loyalty."

"And the Eye…"

"Quite powerful," Jan assured him.

"Like what Xaviar was talkin' about."

"Quite possibly."

"Shit. So that was his Antediluvian…and the Leopold guy that Victoria went lookin' for…"

"Exactly. Hesha evidently knows a great deal about this Eye and…Lucinde has offered our cooperation in this matter."

"She what?" Theo asked in measured tones. Jan studiously removed his glasses from his pocket and began to clean them. "What the hell is she thinkin', workin' with a Setite? I don't like it."

"Nor do I." But resignation was obvious in Jan's voice.

"She can offer *your* cooperation…."

"I don't foresee that the matter will involve you at all."

"Good," Theo said, then shook his head and muttered, "Workin' with a Setite…"

"There is something else about last night that we must discuss," Jan said, putting his glasses back on.

Theo nodded. "Katrina. I found her. She told me—"

"—who gave her the explosives," Jan finished the Brujah's sentence. "A Kindred who may or may not be named Johnny. She told you how to contact him, and then you sent her to San Francisco. She followed your advice, by the way...this time."

This time. That meant that Jan knew about the last time, on the dock, and about everything that Theo and Katrina had said last night. *This is a set-up,* Theo thought instantly. *Blackmail, maybe.* But then why, he wondered, would the Ventrue have gone to all the trouble of briefing Theo about Lucinde, or why would Jan have bothered fabricating such elaborate lies? Was it possible that Jan wasn't after blackmail? It would be risky after all. Theo could simply bull his way through, argue jurisdiction and bullshit like that—but if Lucinde, a justicar, threw her support behind Jan's accusations...

"Nossie followin' me?" Theo asked.

"Not you, actually. Her."

"Katrina? Since when?"

"Since she met with a local Sabbat operative."

"Johnny."

"He generally goes by Jack."

Theo tried to absorb all that. The Nosferatu had been trailing the Sabbat who'd given Katrina the explosives. That meant that they would've been following her the night she blew up Garlotte. "They saw it all, didn't they, the sewer rat fuckers."

Jan nodded.

"Why the hell didn't you say anything before?" But as soon as Theo asked the question, he knew the answer—and it set the fire burning deep in his belly once again. "You thought I put her up to it."

"The possibility existed," Jan said evenly. "Why else would you let her walk away?"

Good fucking question, Theo thought. It was one that he'd just begun to come to grips with, and he didn't think it would make much sense to someone in Jan's position, an establishment man. Even if Theo felt inclined to explain, which he did not.

"Not my job to clean up city matters," Theo said.

Jan frowned. "Is anything really just a 'city matter' in the middle of a war?"

"Hey, if Garlotte can't keep his young'ns in line, fuck him. If Goldwin can't straighten it out, then fuck him too." The fire was growing. Theo didn't show it externally, but he was wishing more and more that this was a problem he could beat into submission, that he could just rip Jan's head off and be done with it. But it wasn't that simple. It never was. Theo had thought Jan was the spy; Jan had thought Theo was the spy. How the fuck were they supposed to prevail over the Sabbat when nobody on their *own* side was ever above suspicion? What was it about the blood, about the curse of Caine, that made them all such arrogant, shifty, devious, deceitful bastards? Or was *that* the real curse, and the blood-drinking was just symptomatic?

Jan ran a hand through his spiky blond hair. He took his glasses off, tucked them back into his pocket again, and started massaging the bridge of his nose.

"I didn't doubt you, Theo. It was so unlikely...and after the success we've had..."

Theo held the fire in check, fought it back down, but not without effort. "So the whole thing with Katrina last night," Theo said, "it was a...set-up. A test."

"A test," Jan acknowledged. "Yes."

"If I did her in, then I was covering up. Turn her over to you and I'm okay. So tell me," Theo leaned forward in his chair until only about two feet separated his face and Jan's, "where do I stand after hustlin' her off to the other side of the country?"

"You have our trust," Jan said in measured tones. He seemed to sense that, if last night had been Theo's test, tonight was his own. "Why else would I tell you what I've told you?"

"*If* what you've told me is true," Theo said. Slowly, he eased back in his chair. It made sense. It would have been much easier for Jan to say nothing than to conceive such elaborate lies. Theo took a cigarette from his jacket, lit up, swallowed the smoke, didn't let it back out.

For several minutes, the two Kindred sat in silence, Jan alternately cleaning his glasses and massaging the bridge of his nose, Theo staring at the floor, thinking, fuming. Jan wasn't the enemy, not the real enemy, Theo kept reminding himself. It was all just part of this fucked-up world he inhabited where blood was food and sunlight was death. He and all his kind were monsters living on human blood—but there were worse monsters, those that had forgotten, *forsaken*, their distant humanity. The worst of them were among the Sabbat. They were the enemy. They were the ones who would treat mortals like they were slaves, like they were animals. Jan was not the real enemy.

Jan seemed to sense Theo's gradual calming and spoke again. "After the explosion, Colchester came to Lucinde and me. He told us about your being there and letting the girl go free. I found it...odd. But not treacherous. Lucinde wasn't so sure."

"Because there's a spy out there," Theo said. "She thought I was the spy?"

"No. We'd already determined the identity of the spy."

Theo just nodded his head, more sickened than surprised—another secret, more information kept from him that could have been useful.

"Lucinde wanted to make sure that you weren't in league with the spy," Jan explained. "Just to cover every angle, she spoke with Pascek. He said to test you however we could, to make sure that you were completely loyal."

Pascek. Paranoid motherfucker. Theo didn't tense a single muscle; he didn't scream or curse aloud. He just filed it all away, pushed it all down to be fuel for the fire when he needed it next.

"If you had wanted Katrina silenced," Jan said, "you would have destroyed her. I held to that the night of the explosion. I hold to that now."

"Okay," said Theo. He laid his palms flat against the table. "So you stood up for me, and Lucinde and my boss, like most justicars, are paranoid bastards. So fuckin' what? Where does that leave us now, if all the bullshit games are over?"

Friday, 29 October 1999, 1:23 AM
Hemperhill Road
Baltimore, Maryland

Theo stood by the mantelpiece staring into the huge, gold-framed mirror that dominated the study. The room was furnished with antiques, every piece. He couldn't name the style of the chairs or the exact period of the porcelain vases or even of the overall motif. The decor was old, older easily than Theo. Old and expensive. But Theo had seen older. He'd spent years travelling with Don Cerro in Europe, meeting many of the old and powerful Kindred to whom these antiques would be little better than patio furniture.

Those years of study—study of casual excess, of how stagnant Kindred society could become over time—had been good for him. They had shown him that injustice and cruelty existed everywhere, even beyond the slave plantations of the American South, even for whites. Oppression was not the exception, it was the norm. Those years had sparked the realization that the fire was not always enough, not even the fire fueled by hunger.

In the halls of power, creatures existed to whom years were playthings and the real world was a distant, dangerous thing. Yet the real world had a way, on occasion, of making its presence known, of asserting itself. Theo had not been around for the Anarch Revolt or for the first wars against the Sabbat, but reality had intruded upon the elders with a vengeance. Change, so long held at bay, had come crashing down upon them, an avalanche sweeping all before it. Perhaps another time like that was at hand. The Final Nights, Xaviar had said. And even though the Gangrel had been wrong about his supposed Antediluvian, events in these modern nights were moving at an accelerated, alarming pace. The world could not be kept at bay. Not forever.

Behind Theo, among the antiques, sat Marcus Vitel, deposed prince of Washington, D.C. He wore an expensively cut suit, more old-fashioned than the type Pieterzoon tended to wear, with a small golden eagle pinned to his lapel. Vitel had enough gray streaking his dark hair to make him look distinguished among a group of mortals—if he chose to consort with mortals any longer. He still appeared strong of body and mind, but the loss of his city and perhaps of his childer had left him visibly bitter. His dark blue eyes had a hard glint. As he had for much of his stay in Baltimore, he remained aloof from other Kindred, royalty tossed among the commoners. He often, but not always, attended the council meetings, which themselves had grown less frequent. Otherwise, however, Vitel kept to himself, creating an expanding circle of ghouls to meet his needs and wants.

"Do you feel it is wise," Vitel asked, "to fall back so close to the city?"

Theo scratched the stubble on his chin as he answered, and continued to watch Vitel in the expanse of the mirror. "The shorter the lines we have to watch, the stronger our defenses can be. We stay spread wide, they slip through. We pull tight, nothin' gets through."

"But if they do get through," Vitel protested, "they are in the city proper. We must press our lines forward, not withdraw them so the enemy can strike swiftly at our heart."

Theo shook his head, patiently but firmly. "We can't match them for manpower. We're taking some losses every night. Others of our folks are kinda melting away. Not a lot, but it's starting. They can see the writing on the wall. We've gotta concentrate our force, just like pulling folks in from Buffalo and Hartford."

"But surely we must have contingencies, the airport—"

"We'll keep a screen around the airport," Theo said. "When the big push comes—and it's looking sooner every night, judging by what they're throwin' at us—those who can afford it and have it set up ahead of time, yourself, Pieterzoon, Gainesmil, maybe a few others, you guys'll jet out. Everybody else," Theo shrugged, "this has gotta be it. We'll never get this many Kindred together and more or less organized again. We've let slip talk about some escape routes to the north—ground runs to Pittsburgh and Phillie— but that's just to sooth some nerves. Those orders will never happen. We make our stand here. In Baltimore. But we wanted to keep you informed, 'case you wanted to line up a plane or anything."

Vitel sat quietly, his hands and interlocked fingers resting in his lap. "If Baltimore falls, there is little chance of getting Washington back."

Theo turned from the mirror, leaned back against the mantel, and crossed his arms. "I agree," he said. "It would be a longshot, even with the Tremere chantry holdin' out in D.C. But I think we can hold on here. We have to. We shorten the lines, make sure we're not broken. Pieterzoon's sources say the Sabbat high command is gettin' antsy now that Monçada's out of the picture. We figure time is on our side. We hold out long enough, those bastards'll start slittin' each other's throats and forget all about us."

Vitel pondered that, nodded thoughfully. "The Sabbat is not known for its solidarity," he agreed.

Jan was not surprised to see Hans van Pel escorting Hesha along the concrete corridor precisely on
time. The Setite had proven himself prompt, respectful, and professional—which was not to say that Jan
trusted him the least little bit. But Lucinde had pro-
nounced that they would deal with Ruhadze. Jan
could see how, from her perspective, it might seem
that keeping the Setite happy was the best way to
forestall his interference in the plans that were now
unfolding. From Jan's view, however, accommodat-
ing Hesha was at best a distraction from far weightier
matters; matters that, should they sour, the blame
would undoubtedly fall squarely upon Jan. Not to
mention the fact that he doubted Lucinde's underly-
ing assumption that *anything* they did would prevent
the Setite from tampering. Could the Eye really mean
that much to Ruhadze, that he would forego his natural proclivity, namely treachery?

The Eye of Hazimel. It had proved extremely
potent, if Xaviar's account of the Gangrel massacre
was given credence. Why then, Jan wondered, hand
the device—an actual eye; how macabre—to a Setite?
Perhaps Lucinde merely wished to aid Hesha by has-
tening his journey to his own doom. Reasonable
enough.

Whatever her reasons, though, Jan was left to
play his part. He'd arranged the meeting that Ruhadze
had requested. The Ventrue felt much more comfortable in this facility than he had three months ago in

a sub-basement of the Wesleyan Building, where he had met with the Nosferatu underlings of Marston Colchester, who had arranged the employ of a certain Lasombra *antitribu*. That basement had been a maze of puddles, exposed pipes, and, Jan had gleaned, Nosferatu deathtraps. This non-public level of the Convention Center, on the other hand, was, if austere, at least dry, clean, and well lit. Colchester was here personally this time, in his guess of mild-mannered, well-dressed, African-American businessman.

Ruhadze, as usual, was tastefully and expensively dressed, black turtleneck and slacks, camel's-hair jacket. The monocle, a thin chain trailing to his jacket pocket, was propped before his left eye. The syncopated tap of his silver-handled cane fell precisely between the clicks of his shoes, each of the three distinct sounds echoing slightly from the bare cement corridor. Van Pel's footfalls, though louder, lacked the musical quality of the Setite's. Hesha carried a leather attaché case in his left hand.

"Good evening, Mr. Ruhadze," Jan said.

"Mr. Pieterzoon." Hesha nodded to Jan and to Colchester, but no further introductions were extended.

"You won't mind if we observe from the adjacent room?" asked Jan.

"By all means."

Van Pel opened the door by which they were standing and gestured for Hesha to enter.

Hesha stepped inside the room and the door closed behind him. The only furnishings were a large metal table and three folding metal chairs, two of which were occupied. A wide mirror took up most of one wall. Behind it, in the next room, Jan Pieterzoon, Marston Colchester, and Pieterzoon's ghoul, van Pel, would be watching, listening, recording.

The two men seated at the table were the ones Hesha had asked to meet. He could have contacted them directly, of course, but the political circumstances were somewhat unsettled at present, and Calebros had suggested that Hesha go through what he called "proper channels." The advice had seemed reasonable enough—aside from which Hesha wanted to keep in the good graces of his Nosferatu allies—so the Setite consented. Little had he known that he would end up dealing with a justicar. Hesha was neither intimidated nor impressed by Lucinde's station—though impressed upon him were the implications of her very presence and the secrecy of it. Something unusual was definitely afoot, and Hesha would as always keep a sharp eye. For from war always arose opportunity for the prepared.

"Gentlemen," Hesha said to the two Kindred, "I thank you for agreeing to see me this evening."

Roughneck and Quaker looked on silently, suspiciously, perhaps from general distrust of Hesha's clan. He had checked with his brethren in the area— the two Malkavians had neither grudges nor indebtedness toward any Setites in the area. Had the latter been the case, then Hesha *would* have contacted the two directly, no matter what Calebros had recommended.

As Hesha moved closer and took his seat across from them, he became aware of a faint but distinct odor—that of dumpster refuse. It was not so pungent

as the fecal odor that many Nosferatu, through preference or artifice, cultivated, and it suggested unlife
spent not in the sewers but on the streets. Each man
looked the part of the vagrant. Both wore over-sized,
threadbare clothing, worn and dirty. Both were unshaven and unkempt. Roughneck's beard was long
enough that he tucked the very bottom tip of it into
his belt. The role of mendicant was one that Hesha
had affected upon occasion when necessary, but these
two Malkavians seemed to come by it honestly.

Hesha removed from his attaché case a folder
and placed it before him on the table. "I have some
pictures I would like to show you. I am willing to
compensate you—in addition to what you'll receive
for coming tonight, of course—for anything you
might be able to tell me about them."

The Setite opened the folder. The pictures were
from the cave in New York that he and Ramona had
each visited twice. The girl was still in New York, in
the city. She had been less than excited by the pros-
pect of flying, and there would have been little reason
for her to accompany Hesha at any rate. Of course,
he had not suggested that to her. If he'd told her to
stay where she was, she probably would have fought
to come to Baltimore. The girl was not ignorant, but
she was rash and headstrong—one might even say
obstinate to a remarkable degree; Hesha had said that
and much more to himself. Ramona possessed all the
follies of her youth, her clan, and her temperament.
She was a quick study, but Hesha wondered if she
would survive long enough to learn what she needed
to know.

He had not brought the pictures of the statue with which she had tampered. That work of perfection and genius had nothing to do with the Malkavians. There was madness amidst the sculpted rock, the fused bodies, but it was an insanity far darker and more pervasive even than that exhibited by the descendants of Malkav. The sculpture was an emanation of the mad Toreador Leopold, his tortured artist's soul physically rendered. There were implications for the Eye there, if Hesha could puzzle them out. Hesha would not risk revealing those photographs to these Kindred or, more importantly, to those beyond the mirror.

The pictures that he had brought, that were before him on the table, were rather the legacy of the Prophet of Gehenna. Much of the cave had been covered by the writing, the unintelligible scrawl, penned in Anatole's own blood. Hesha had taken a sample of the vitae, and he had taken the pictures of the bloodsigns, but he could no more translate the marks than unravel the mysteries of the Prophet's blood. A linguist—among many other skills—by trade, and fluent in or familiar with literally dozens of languages and dialects, Hesha could not read the scrawl. He could *sense* meaning, but he could not penetrate the seemingly random array of pictograms, runes, sigils, and—for the lack of any discernible paradigm—scribbles. Though he could not be certain, Hesha's instinct told him that Anatole had created the sanguinary panorama, had used his own arm as stylus and his own blood as ink. Who else could have so mutilated Anatole, if not himself? Leopold, with the Eye? Possible. But Hesha could not overcome the impression that the statue and the writing were fashioned by different hands, that the statue was the welling up of some great...malignancy, and that Anatole had found it, had imparted his own revelation—for those who could unravel it.

Let those see who have eyes, the Biblical prophets often said—the words more often than not spoken to the unfortunate masses, the predestined, the damned, who were doomed *not* to see.

Hesha slid the photographs across the table to those who shared, if not the prophet's power, at least Anatole's affliction. The Setite intended to watch carefully for any minute signs of recognition, for the slightest indication that either of the two Malkavians knew what it was they were viewing; he was ready to read the most subtle nuances of their reactions.

He was not prepared for the chaos that suddenly engulfed him.

"Hm. Two-way mirror. Nice," Colchester said, as he, Jan, and van Pel filed into the observation room. "I used to have one of these." The Nosferatu added, his demeanor, if not his visual disguise, reverting to its more usual, grotesque state. "My second wife liked to watch me bring other women home."

Jan sighed audibly. Colchester heard and also seemed to realize that he was rubbing his hands together in reminiscent glee. The Nosferatu cleared his throat, resumed his serious manner.

"Gentlemen, I thank you for agreeing to see me this evening," Hesha's voice came to them over a speaker by the mirror. Roughneck and Quaker regarded him warily.

They're smarter than I thought, Jan mused.

"I have some pictures I would like to show you," Hesha said. "I am willing to compensate you...."

"Have you seen the pictures?" Colchester asked.

"No," Jan said. That was not part of the agreement that Lucinde had arranged. She apparently had no interest in the photographs and therefore had decided that there was no reason for Jan to see them. Or perhaps she had merely assumed that Jan would install a recessed camera over the table, which he had. There was no need to try to read over Hesha's shoulder. Everything would be reviewed in good time.

At that moment, however, everything went haywire.

"*My God, what's happening?*" van Pel yelled in response to the sudden eruption of chairs, table, photographs and bodies on the other side of the mirror. The ghoul began at once for the door, but was stayed by Jan's hand on his shoulder.

"We are here for observation only, Hans," said Jan with rapt fascination, not once shifting his gaze from the room beyond the glass.

There were one hundred forty-seven photographs. Quaker glanced at the first for maybe two seconds, then flung himself back from the table with the force of a hurricane. His chair crumpled beneath him; his legs whipped upward, striking the underside of the table.

Hesha leapt back out of the way as the table upended and a geyser of photographs erupted into the air. Quaker's gyrations knocked his friend to the floor as Quaker himself landed hard on his back and head.

He convulsed, sharp violent spasms, and began to spit bloody, frothy drool.

"What'd you do?" Roughneck, climbing to his knees, yelled at Hesha. *"What'd you do to him?"*

Hesha prepared for violence. The bearded Malkavian started crawling toward him. Quaker was still writhing, his contortions growing more violent. He began vomiting vitae, his body heaving. He spewed a watery mix of blood and bile. It covered him, covered the floor and many of the pictures.

Roughneck, crawling toward Hesha, slipped on the mess. *"What'd you do?"* The Malkavian took one of the blood-splattered photographs, started to rip it apart in his hands, but stopped suddenly. He held it for a moment, staring, then slammed it down on the floor. He tried to smooth the folds and creases, to piece the ragged edges together; he pressed it compulsively against the floor, as if the blood there might hold the damaged paper together.

Hesha was trying to take it all in. After the first instant when Roughneck had started toward him, there seemed to be no immediate physical threat. But he could feel an energy in the air, an almost electrical charge. For an instant, the blood on the cold floor seemed to be boiling. Bubbling and spitting. But that had to be just Quaker's gurgling and coughing, spraying more droplets on what was already there. Had to be…didn't it?

Roughneck, Hesha saw, was smearing the blood on the floor…no, using his fingers to draw in it…to *write*. As the Malkavian's eyes rolled up in his head, his fingers traced paths and left figures that Hesha recognized—that Hesha recognized but could not translate. Roughneck was reproducing exactly, one after another, the symbols from the cave walls, from the pictures—from the pictures that Roughneck had not yet seen!

Hesha glanced at the mirror. Pieterzoon and the others didn't seem inclined to intervene, and with a similar detachment, the Setite watched Roughneck and Quaker. Quaker's eyes remained rolled upward, only the bloodshot whites visible as he blinked uncontrollably. His tongue flicked from side to side like a live snake, and his teeth clamped down as if trying to capture—or kill—the creature. His own blood mingled on the floor with that of his companion. Roughneck continued writing, recreating Anatole's symbols, at the same time sliding over what he'd already written and smearing it beyond recognition.

While Roughneck scribbled in the blood, Quaker suddenly ceased convulsing. His body grew rigid, back arched. He hacked, expelling a clot of blood and phlegm from his throat, and then in a cracking, tortured voice he spoke:

"The light…the last of the light…it fades, fades…high above, far far away. Night…the Final Night. Walls too slick…can't climb…surrounded by bulging eyes, blank, bloated faces…too slick…can't climb."

Quaker began writhing again, scrabbling at the floor in terror. His fingers clawed at the bloody cement, nails digging into the floor, snapping, splintering.

Roughneck was now scooping into his arms all the photographs he could reach. They were torn and bloodstained, spread across the floor. He gathered together those he could, began tearing at them, stuffing the pieces into his mouth, swallowing, gagging, stuffing more into his mouth.

"*The children!*" Quaker shouted. "*Down the well...they point the way...beneath the children...they are not yet quick...they point the way.*"

Hesha did not try to prevent Roughneck's destruction of the photographs. The Setite had copies. Neither did he attempt to unravel Quaker's ravings. Rather, Hesha depended on the tape recorder in his jacket, and the recordings that Pieterzoon was making.

Suddenly Quaker ceased thrashing; he grew perfectly still. "*The children fear their shadow, but the shadow fades with the last of the light,*" he intoned. As unheralded as it had come about, his respite from terror ended, and Quaker again clawed frantically at the cement floor. "*They show us the way!*" he cried frantically, the last of his strength seemingly spent. "*They show us...light fading...Final Night....the children.*"

And then Quaker was silent, still; Roughneck with him. And as Hesha looked on, the two Malkavians crumbled to dust, their bodies sifting away amidst the pooled blood and photographs from the cave.

Jan stood perfectly still and stared at the aftermath. Van Pel and Colchester did the same. Several drops of blood had splattered against the mirror and now seemed suspended in time between the two rooms—the present on this side of the glass: quiet, orderly, following predictably from what had preceded; the future on that side: blood-soaked chaos, incomprehensible warnings of doom.

The children down the well.

What in the bloody hell…? Jan could not comprehend what he had seen, what he had heard. The room beyond the glass grew unfocused, the mangled photographs, the remains of the two Malkavians. Jan's gaze latched onto the suspended droplets of blood—the blood that would connect the present and the future.

In the end, it was Hesha who came to them. He opened the door to the observation room where they stood speechless.

"I would appreciate a copy of the tape," the Setite said.

Jan slowly turned his head, shifted his gaze from the suspended blood to look at him. Ruhadze appeared completely unfazed. Jan nodded. Satisfied, Hesha left them.

Sunday, 31 October 1999, 10:52 PM
Presidential Suite, Lord Baltimore Inn
Baltimore, Maryland

"Do you think he believed you?" Jan asked.

Theo settled back into the plush couch. "How many times are you gonna ask me that?" he grumbled.

Jan didn't answer. He didn't need to. Theo hadn't given anything away, not that they were aware of, but neither had Vitel. There was every indication that Vitel had believed Theo—he *had* to have. If Vitel had seen through Theo's ruse, then they were doomed, and the Camarilla presence on the East Coast was a thing of the past. But if Vitel *was* convinced that Baltimore really was the last stand, then there might still be hope....

Jan found the digital video cassette he was looking for, slipped it into the player, and turned on the television. The picture that sprang to the screen was not of the best quality, but the image was clearly the exterior balcony of a hotel at night. The row of doors, aside from the sequential numbers, were identical. All of the curtains were drawn; some of the rooms behind the curtains were lighted, others not. The small white date in the corner of the screen indicated it had been filmed last night.

"This is one of Vitel's havens in the city," Jan said. "He alternates days among them. No apparent pattern. Colchester took these shots himself. We're lucky there was no woman who forgot to pull her curtain in a room nearby, or he would have fogged up the lens." Theo laughed under his nonexistent breath. "Vitel has a block of eight rooms reserved permanently," Jan went on. "Ghouls stay in the others, but he..." Jan paused until a dark figure came into view, a tall man in a dark overcoat, his equally dark hair streaked with gray. "He stays in this one." The picture zoomed in as Vitel entered room 337. The door closed, and a light came on behind the curtain.

"Now," said Jan, picking up a remote control and fast forwarding through a couple of uneventful hours, then returning the tape to normal speed. As Theo and Jan watched, another figure moved into the picture, a disheveled man with dirty, receding hair.

"Look familiar?" Jan asked.

"I haven't seen him before," Theo said, "but he could be the guy Katrina described."

From a shelf by the television Jan took a dossier and dropped it on the table in front of Theo. "He's our man," the Ventrue said. "Tzimisce. Active in the Sabbat around Baltimore and Washington for years. Leads a pack at times, but a bit of a loose cannon."

Theo thumbed through the thick file, looked at the pictures, skimmed the text. "Helluva body count he's racked up."

"And those are the ones we know about. He's the one that approached Katrina. He'd been flying under our radar until one of Colchester's people recognized him coming out of a meet with Vitel. A meeting very much..." Jan aimed the remote control again, rewound the scene slightly to show Jack skulking up the last few stairs, and then played it forward at normal speed. Jack knocked on the door of room 337. The door opened. Jack stepped inside, and the door closed.

Theo was not impressed. "Shit. You can't even see if it was Vitel that let him in. That the best Colchester could do?"

"He's the one," Jan insisted. "I can show you the footage from later last night when Jack drops off his message to Sascha Vykos in Washington, and other messages too, from the past few weeks."

Theo continued to flip through the dossier and scowled at the large TV screen. The seconds and minutes in the corner passed by. Jan stood silently and watched. After about twenty minutes, the door to 337 opened again, and Jack slipped out of the room and down the steps. He was carrying a large, folded envelope.

"How did Colchester's guy just happen to catch Jack, or Johnny, or who the hell ever he is, meeting with Vitel?" Theo asked. "Not this time, the first time."

Jan clicked off the television and moved with deliberate steps to a chair opposite Theo. "After Hartford," Jan said, "we began a series of observations."

"'We,'" Theo repeated. "You and Colchester."

"Yes. Vitel was one of the subjects. We couldn't be sure whom to watch, so we cast a wide net."

"How wide?" Theo wanted to know. "Who else?"

Jan paused for a moment, but the hesitation removed any surprise from what Theo was about to hear. "All the principals," Jan said. "Vitel, Garlotte, Goldwin, Gainesmil, Lladislas, Quaker and Roughneck, Malachi...yourself...."

It didn't bother Theo to find out that he'd been spied upon like that. Why should it, after finding out about the test he'd been subjected to the other night, after finding out that his own boss, Pascek, had urged the Ventrue justicar to test him rather than standing up for him? Theo took it in stride. It all had the stink of Kindred politics, but he was the one who'd let himself wade so deep into the shit. It was one thing serving as archon for his sire while his sire was justicar. Theo hadn't had to stay on when Jaroslav succeeded Cerro. The archon could have walked away, but he hadn't. And all the maneuvering, which had never been pretty or nice under Cerro, had just gotten uglier and meaner with Pascek at the helm.

"Vitel is the one," Jan said quietly at last, trying to keep the meeting focused. "I have records of the meets with Jack, dates, times, locations, pictures, transcripts of some. You can see whatever you want."

Theo tossed the dossier back onto the table. "I want to see it," Theo said. "All of it. Every fuckin' thing you got."

"Has Ruhadze shown you the pictures of the sculpture?" Emmett asked.

"No," Calebros said, shaking his head. A single candle struggled to illuminate the chamber of hewn rock. "The writing, Anatole's legacy, is more important, I think. I respect Hesha enough—"

"Hmph," Emmett snorted. "Respect a Setite. Augustin would puke in his grave."

"Don't speak of our sire in that tone. Or Hesha for that matter. In Bombay—"

"Bombay, shmombay. Give it a rest already." Emmett rolled his eyes.

"Do you want to look at the pictures we _do_ have?"

"Of the writing? The ones that turned the Malkavians into Shake 'n' Bake? No thanks."

"I looked at them," Calebros gently taunted him. "Hesha looked at them. Even the Gangrel whelp did."

"Oh yeah? Well…good for you."

"Stunning retort."

"Up yours."

1 November 1999
re: legacy of Anatole

As usual, nothing straightforward about
Prophet of Gehenna; as many
perspectives as individuals involved.

Ramona claims hillside at cave scarred,
ruined—would seem to fit with Xaviar's
account. But neither Hesha nor <u>Jeremiah</u>
able to confirm. In fact, contradictory
accounts.

Two Malkavians in Baltimore destroyed
after looking at pictures (barely!),
yet others of us unscathed. <u>Clan-
specific response?</u>

↳ Sturbridge might have insight?

Jeremiah still somewhat
troubled after his time with
Anatole.

"Hey, big sugah, I give you the *ride* of your life."
That's what had started it, the prostitute's comment
while Theo was pulled up to a stop sign.

He'd been riding through Katrina's neighborhood—what *had been* her neighborhood. He wasn't
sure why exactly he was doing it. After leaving
Pieterzoon, Theo had checked up on several patrols,
which were going as well as could be expected with
the Sabbat pressing northward a little more forcefully every week. One dumb-ass Kindred refugee from
Charleston had tried to be a hero, tried to stop a drive-
by single-handed and ended up half road kill, half
hood ornament. Otherwise, things were relatively
quiet. Theo had found Lydia and told her what he
needed. Then he'd wandered for a little bit—and
found himself here, in Katrina's old 'hood.

The prostitute wasn't really different from any
of the others. Younger than some, not haggard and
used up, not yet. Older than some of the others, the
ones that didn't look old enough to be thinking about
boys, much less pulling down their pants for them.
She was heavier than a lot of them. Maybe she wasn't
a junkie, not yet.

"Hey, big sugah…"

Her voice cut through the rumble of the bike's
engine while Theo was idling at the stop sign. Without thinking, he reached over, grabbed her wrist,
pulled her toward him.

"You wanna play rough, sugah?" she teased him.

He checked her arm. No tracks. Checked the other arm.

"I'm clean as a baby's bottom," she said.

"Babies shit all over the place. Get on," Theo growled. He couldn't stand to look at her there on the corner. She wore a tight, low-cut spandex top that slid down when she moved, giving a free preview of a large, dark nipple. Her skirt was short and hugged tightly against her bulging ass and thighs. Her spiked heels were tall enough to stake a Kindred. She stopped to hike up her stockings before sliding one leg expertly over the seat and climbing on the bike behind Theo.

"I'll make you happy, sugah," she purred in his ear.

"Shut the fuck up." Theo found himself wanting to turn around and shake her, throttle her. *Is this the best you can do for yourself, sister?* he thought. *Is this why good people risked their lives and died? So you could sell yourself on the street corner, instead of somebody else selling you on the auction block?*

"You wanna know my name, sugah?"

"No."

"Suit yourself."

He didn't want to know her name. He didn't want to acknowledge that she existed. For a brief moment, as he pulled away from the curb, he wanted to fool himself, to pretend that that corner would remain free of anyone like her for more than just an hour or so. This was the real world, but it was the worst of the real world. At least when Master Bell had crept down to the slave quarters in the dark of night, Theo's mother and sisters had had no choice. They had been dependent on that man for their lives and the safety of their family. He had taken from them; they had not given.

But then, as Theo felt the prostitute's arms latching onto his broad chest, he saw again everything else that was around. Clusters of hopeless people, desperate people, selling drugs because there was nothing else to do, no opportunity, no jobs, not here.

Then get the hell out of here, Theo thought. *Or get on the damn bus and go find a job.* But he knew it was never that simple. Some of them *were* just evil, predators. Theo had known enough people, Kindred and kine, to know that. Eat food, drink blood, didn't really matter. Some individuals existed for no other reason than to prey on others. But some were just lost, overwhelmed by a world they didn't understand. In the city, these people couldn't just go out and work in the field; and without an education getting a job anywhere, bus or no bus, was next to a miracle. The only greater miracle was surviving long enough to get that education, surviving intellectually and morally in a culture that didn't encourage or reward that kind of achievement, in a world where decisions made so early in life so often led to jail time, pregnancy, death. Meanwhile Pieterzoon, and his mortal counterparts, flaunted their wealth, their connections, their power, like that was their birthright.

Theo kept driving. Knowing what he did still did not ease his resentment of the woman sitting behind him. *He* had been born in the lowest part of this sick world, but he had risen above it. He had refused to accept the status quo. He'd had injustice after injustice heaped upon him: his family split up when he was barely five years old, his mother, some of his brothers and sisters sold away from his father and other siblings; Theo's mother and sisters raped while he, chased from the slave quarters, shivered in the darkness outside. Theo could recollect every night that it had happened. Every single night. He remembered. He remembered being whipped as well. Some of the scars still marked his back. He could recall how many lashes he'd taken on each occasion and which overseer had administered the punishment. Theo had found them all, one at a time, years later, and evened that score. The memories had driven Theo; the offenses against his dignity had led him to led him to assert his right to determine, as much as possible, his own destiny.

But that was not the case with the broken individuals whom he saw around him on the streets of these modern nights. What the fuck was wrong with these people? How could the world acknowledge their humanity if they didn't acknowledge it themselves? Black men shooting black men. Impoverished families, shattered by drugs, living in filth. Self-respect, Theo had long ago decided, stemmed from empowerment, but empowerment thrived only with self-respect. That was the problem. To break out of the self-destructive cycle of hopelessness and victimization and into the self-sustaining cycle of empowerment and self-sufficiency. In his own mortal life, Theo had taken the initiative to break from one cycle to the other, and from that first step everything else had followed. He had escaped slavery, had returned time and again to the South to help others escape, and when Don Cerro had imparted the gift—what Theo had then considered a gift—of unimaginable power, Theo had broadened his activities from mere redemption of those in need to revenge against those in charge. He'd taken the whip to Master Bell, and worse. But seeking revenge, Theo found, was adding fuel to the fire that had always burned within him, the fire that mingled with his newfound hunger until they were one and the same. Old Master Bell was not the only one to pay for his crimes. Many of the Bell slaves did as well. Many members of Theo's family.

"Where you wanna go, sugah?"

Theo flinched at the sound of the voice so close to him. It took him a second to orient himself, to remember that he was riding the rough streets of Baltimore, not the hidden back roads of Mississippi. He turned down a dark, deserted side street, turned between two buildings and stopped the bike. The woman got off, smoothed her clothes.

Theo got off the motorcycle. "You got kids?"

She smiled, ran a finger down the sleeve of Theo's leather jacket. "You don't wanna talk 'bout kids." There was a small smudge of bright red lipstick on one of her front teeth.

Before he realized he was doing it, Theo grabbed her hand and squeezed, not breaking her fingers, but the woman cried out in pain. "*Do you have kids?*" he demanded.

"Yeah…yes!" Her fear caught up with her pain as she looked into his eyes. Tears started streaming down her cheeks.

"*How many?*"

"Two," she cried. She began trembling all over. Her teeth chattered together. Her lipstick was smeared somehow. The cool, damp air seemed suddenly to bite all the way to her bones, to sap her strength, but she was sweating. She tried to pull away but couldn't.

The fire rose up within Theo. He hated this woman who was both symptom and cause of evil. Still holding her, he turned her face roughly with his other hand, and then tore into the taut flesh at the base of her neck. Blood filled his mouth, her blood, her basic humanity, same as anyone else's. Her frantic scream died away to a pathetic whimper, but still her heart pumped spurt after spurt of fresh blood into Theo. He drew strength from she who lacked strength. He drank greedily to quench the fire, to extinguish the hate and pity he felt for her.

In the end, though he was full, he felt completely spent. He licked the wound closed and let go of her. She stumbled a few steps before her knees buckled and she landed hard on the ground. She sat, dazed, tears wet on her cheeks.

Theo stood over her. He still hated her for what she was, for her weakness. He hated himself for the compassion he couldn't find in his heart. These were his people, yet he was one of the predators. He knew he'd need the blood in the nights ahead, but he didn't like to feed like this. But she had spoken to him. She had asked him to make her a victim. He could not change her. He could not save her from herself. She would be back on the street, tomorrow night or the night after. If she pulled herself out somehow, there would be others.

Theo reached into his pocket, pulled out a wad of twenty-dollar bills. He peeled off five, six, tossed them at her. They landed by her knee. Her stocking was torn. Angry but tired, Theo climbed back onto his bike and left her there.

Lydia stepped into the joint for the second time
in two nights. Cigarette smoke hung thick, and the
jukebox was cranked up loud playing ZZ Top. The
bartender, busy enough with the six or so guys at the
bar, didn't appear to notice her. He was fat and greasy.
It wasn't hot in the room, but his shirt was stained
with sweat on the chest, back, and armpits. Two of
the patrons at the bar were familiar to Lydia: Frankie
and Baldur. They were each nursing a beer, taking a
sip every now and then and generally keeping busy
not noticing Lydia, although they were sitting near
the front door.

A couple of hard-up-looking types were sitting
by themselves at two tables, but the other tables were
empty. Lydia picked one and took a seat with her
back to the wall. Almost before she'd touched ass to
seat, one of the guys from the bar was sidling over to
her table. He was the kind who seemed more cocky
than successful with women. He wore a threadbare
army jacket and had thinning red hair.

"Buy you a drink, beautiful?" He gave her a wink
that he must have thought was suave.

Lydia sighed. "What do I look like, president of
the Hair Club for Assholes?" He laughed. Lydia did
not.

"That's good. That's good. Come on, gorgeous,
let me buy you a drink. I'm just trying to be friendly."
He pulled out the chair opposite Lydia and made himself at home.

"I don't need no more friends," Lydia said. She glanced at his couple of drinking buddies at the bar, who did piss-poor jobs of pretending that they weren't watching. "Besides," Lydia added, "I don't go for guys." She tried not to laugh as his smile drained away. The lesbian ploy was always good for some mileage, and her statement, as far as it went, was mostly true these nights. Sex just wasn't what it used to be.

Her visitor, after his initial surprise, managed a forced smile. "Don't go for guys? You just haven't met the right one." He winked again.

Lydia rolled her eyes. She took a second to look around the room at the other patrons. Aside from Frankie and Baldur, they all seemed to be mortal: coloring was right, they were drinking too much to be faking it. She turned back to her guest. "And you would be the right one?"

"You bet your little lacy panties."

Lydia sighed again. She looked at her watch and decided she didn't have time for this. "Okay, sport. Let's arm wrestle for it."

He was taken aback by the suggestion. "Huh?"

"Arm wrestle. You know…." She propped her right arm up on the table. "You win, you and your buddies can stretch me out on the bar and take turns fucking my brains out. I win, you piss off."

He laughed, but his grin now was more suspicious than confident. He hesitated, gave a good hard look at the small, pale woman across from him, then laughed again. "Okay, baby. You're on, and you're in for the time of your life."

"Yeah, whatever."

He put his elbow on the table and made a big production of caressing her fingers when he took her hand.

"Whenever you're ready," Lydia said, "just say the word."

He took a deep breath and started pushing just before he said, "Go."

Lydia let him have about three inches, just to get his hopes up, then slammed his knuckles onto the table top.

"Ow! Shit!"

"Were you ready?" Lydia asked, full of concern. "I couldn't feel you pushing."

"How the hell did you—?"

"Tell you what, sport. Just to be fair, why don't we go left handed, double or nothing. You win, you and your boys can fuck me, then turn me over and fuck me in the ass. Sound good?"

He glared at her from across the table, spoke menacingly in a low growl, "You're gonna regret this, you fucking bitch."

Lydia shrugged. "Maybe. Put your money where your mouth would like to be." She propped her left arm up on the table.

His pause was longer this time. His friends at the bar no longer made any pretense of being disinterested. Some kind of trick, he had to figure. She'd tricked him somehow. But not twice. He pulled up his sleeve, put his left arm on the table, grasped her hand with a firm grip, no suggestive foreplay.

"Whenever you're ready, sport."

He didn't say go this time, just started pressing with all this strength. Lydia held him at straight vertical for five seconds…ten…fifteen. A vein was bulging at his temple. He gasped and sucked in air. Lydia grimaced, then all the strain left her face. "Tsk, tsk, tsk. Maybe you should try two hands," she said.

Surprised and totally crestfallen, he only had another second before she slammed his knuckles against the table. He was leaning in so hard that a joint or ligament or something made a loud popping noise. He roared in pain and frustration and grabbed his elbow.

"That didn't sound good, sport."

He glared threateningly at Lydia and started to stand.

"Think twice, sport," she said very quietly, and he stopped partway up. "That was just your elbow. You touch me again, I'll rip off your dick and stuff it up your fuckin' ass."

He paused for a few seconds, hovering between up and down, holding his elbow.

"That's better," Lydia said. "Now, why don't you go home to your wife or your girlfriend or your thirteen-year-old neighbor, whoever it is you fuck, and smack her around? You'll feel like a big man again. Everything'll be okay."

Without looking at his friends, he eased up out of his chair and hurried awkwardly out of the bar. His drinking buddies, with raised eyebrows, turned back to their drinks. Frankie and Baldur, less surprised, turned back to their drinks as well.

Lydia glanced at her watch again. 11:56. She'd come here last night, after she'd talked to Theo, and asked the fat bartender if Johnny was around. When he wasn't, she'd handed the bartender a note that said simply, "11:45 pm." *So where the fuck is he?* she wondered. Frankie and Baldur had been here early to get a good spot. They would have let her know if he'd already shown up and left, or if something weird had happened. But there they were, sipping on their beers, arguing very quietly and reasonably about whether or not Cher could kick Madonna's ass.

Lydia didn't have to wait much longer. When the door opened a few minutes later, he came inside the bar—the guy whose picture Theo had showed her. He was dirty and unshaven with seriously receding hair. He shuffled more than walked and was kind of hunched over a little, not like some Nossie freak, just a normal, lowlife scumbag. He looked around and seemed puzzled, then ambled over to the bar, where he exchanged a few words with the bartender. The bartender pointed toward Lydia, and "Johnny" looked her way. Lydia met his gaze evenly, didn't smile, didn't blow him a kiss, didn't flick him off.

He shuffled over to the table with a sneer, much as Lydia's earlier suitor had. He stopped and stood over her, raised his palms on either side, said, "Here's Johnny."

Lydia turned her head and spit on the floor. "I heard your friends call you Jack."

"If I had friends," he said without missing a beat, "and if I did, you wouldn't be one of them, whoever the fuck you are."

"Oh, you're breakin' my heart." She crossed her arms and leaned back in her chair.

He turned to make some smart-ass quip to the bartender, and in that instant of distraction, Lydia moved. More quickly than her target could react, she reached for the Desert Eagle that was tucked under her belt in the small of her back. Right as Jack looked back at her and his eyes grew wide, she fired. Three shots. They slammed into his chest, blew him backwards through the air into the bar.

The bar patrons dove for cover, all except Frankie and Baldur who were up, 9mms in hand, and blocking the door. Frankie plugged the bartender who was going for a gun. The fat man crashed into the counter behind the bar and sent bottles of liquor cascading to the floor. One bullet passed through him and shattered the mirror behind the counter.

Lydia looked at the Desert Eagle in her hand. She blew on the tip of the barrel. "Damn. Theo was right about this thing."

That was when Jack hit her. Despite the three gaping holes in his chest, his arms had transformed into long, muscled tentacles. One whipped across Lydia's face, knocking her off her seat, backwards into the wall. She was on her feet in mere seconds, but Frankie and Baldur were down beneath the blows of the second tentacle, and Jack was breaking for the back door. Lydia was off balance and her head was still ringing, but she squeezed off two quick shots. Her fire tore apart the door frame over Jack's head. His arms contracted to normal length as he ran. They looked like strings of sausages being sucked down a garbage disposal. He rushed headlong out the back door—and square into the arc of the fire axe.

Theo took the Tzimisce's head off with one clean blow—if a decapitation spewing blood and black ichor could be called clean. Jack's body ran a few more steps before tumbling to the ground. It was just momentum, but it looked like it took him a few seconds to figure out that his head was fucking gone.

By the time Lydia, Baldur, and Frankie reached the back door, Jack's blood was dry and crystallized. Slowly, before their eyes, his body too began to harden, dry, and crumble.

"That's what we've got to look forward to," Frankie said solemnly. "Some night."

Theo wiped the handle of the axe and tossed it aside in the alley. The four Brujah ignored the few terrorized customers who scrambled frantically out the front door now that the way was clear.

Theo turned to Lydia. "Don't give up on a fight before it's over," he said. She nodded somewhat bashfully. "Let's get out of here," he added, and turned to do just that, but then stopped and turned back to Lydia again. "Arm wrestling?" She smiled sheepishly. "Showboating'll get you killed, kid."

Nobody argued, and they all left.

Tuesday, 2 November 1999, 1:59 AM
Hemperhill Road
Baltimore, Maryland

The Lexus screeched to a halt at the curb. Almost before the car had stopped moving, Theo was out the front passenger's door and moving briskly toward the townhouse. He touched two of the eight steps and pounded uncharacteristically loudly on the front door. Waiting only a few seconds, he pounded again.

When a startled ghoul opened the door, Theo simply said, "Get Vitel now. *Hurry*." Then he stepped inside.

The ghoul rushed to obey; this was the closest he'd ever seen the Brujah archon to a state of agitation. While Theo waited, he unclipped his SPAS 12 from inside his jacket and checked the ammo, then unfolded and secured the stock. Within a few moments of the ghoul's hasty exit, Vitel was coming down the stairs. He paused at sight of the shotgun in Theo's hands, the Ventrue's eyes narrowing suspiciously.

"We gotta go," Theo said at once. "They've broken through."

"The Sabbat?"

"They hit us heavy from the west, I-70 and National Pike. We got 'em bottled up 'round Leakin Park, but I don't know how long." Vitel hesitated, so Theo pressed his point, speaking rapidly. "They'll be hittin' from the south too. Or if they get past Leakin and down Mulberry, we'll be cut off from the airport.

Pieterzoon's got a plane waiting, or if you've arranged one I can get you there, but we gotta go now."

Vitel hesitated a moment longer, then turned to his ghoul, who was rushing back down the steps. "Frederick, get the briefcase from the safe. *Now*." Vitel turned to Theo. "You have a car waiting."

"Yeah. We'll change it on the way, just in case a pack has snuck in town and this one's marked."

"Very well."

Vitel followed Theo out the door and down the steps to the Lexus. Theo, out of habit, tucked his shotgun mostly under his jacket. He opened the back door for Vitel, then got in the front. He turned to Lydia, behind the wheel. "One more on the way." Theo scanned up and down the street. "All clear out here?"

"Yeah," said Lydia. The Desert Eagle was lying in her lap. Both her hands were on the wheel.

What seemed like forever passed before Frederick came out with the leather briefcase. He stopped only long enough to lock the door, then ran around the car and got in behind Lydia. He handed the briefcase to Vitel. Lydia pulled away from the curb with a jerk.

Within just a few minutes, three different police cars had rushed past heading westward, lights flashing, sirens blaring. Also to the west, Theo could see thick smoke rising from the horizon. The black billows were readily visible against the ambient pink of the night-time city sky.

"You have a plane standin' by?" Theo asked Vitel, who the Brujah noticed was also watching the distant smoke with some consternation.

"No," Vitel said. "Mr. Pieterzoon's graciousness is appreciated. I wasn't expecting anything like this. Nothing so soon."

"Me neither," Theo said. "They screened their movements pretty damn well. Everything came at once, whole fuckin' convoy. They get in, we'll never root 'em all out."

"Yes, the Sabbat is like that," Vitel agreed.

"You want me to call and have another car or two go by for your other ghouls?" Theo asked.

"There is no need."

Suddenly all the passengers lurched to the right as Lydia took a left turn hard enough to squeal the tires and leave skid marks through the intersection.

"Damn, girl!" Theo braced himself against the door. "The cops are all headed the other way. You tryin' to convince 'em to come back after us?"

"Sorry."

Lydia sped on down the street. Her next turn, not noticeably more gentle than the preceding one, was through the open bay door of an old brick warehouse. The wide metal door rolled down quickly behind the car, blocking out the external light, and as Lydia screeched to a halt, the large, empty, cement-floored space of the warehouse fell into darkness.

"Where is the other car?" Vitel asked.

With those words barely spoken, Theo turned and fired a shotgun burst into Vitel's face, dragonsbreath rounds. The white phosphorous charges tore through the head and torso of the former prince of Washington, burning through the seat and the rear windshield.

At the same instant that Theo fired, Lydia whirled with the Desert Eagle and blasted a .44 magnum slug between Frederick's eyes. The top half of his head exploded. He bounced off the back seat and slumped forward against Lydia's headrest.

Theo sprang from the smoke-filled car just as the warehouse lights flashed on. He threw open Vitel's door and leveled the SPAS at the Ventrue's body. What remained of the head leaned back, slack-jawed, against the smoldering seat. Large portions of Vitel's tailored suit, not to mention his flesh and the melted globule of gold that had been a pin shaped like an imperial eagle, steamed and sputtered.

Frankie and Baldur rushed forward from their assigned positions at the breaker box and the door. Christoph approached more cautiously.

"Holy shit!" Frankie marveled. "You blew his head clean off!"

"Nah, it's still attached, just fucked up," Baldur pointed out.

Lydia was out of the car now also. She wiped splattered blood from her face and licked her hands. The four Brujah all turned as one as the bay door clanked suddenly upward and open. In marched Jan Pieterzoon with Anton Baas and a dozen other heavily armed ghouls.

"Shut the fuckin' door!" Theo yelled at them. Several ghouls rushed to comply.

"Uh…Theo…?"

Theo turned back to Lydia, who was suddenly looking very perplexed. He followed her gaze, past the blood-soaked corpse of Frederick—to the empty, smoldering seat where, a moment before, Vitel's body had been.

"Shit." Theo took a step back from the car. "He's gone. Heads up, everybody."

That was when Frankie went down. One second he was standing there next to them, the next he let out a startled yell and was yanked under the Lexus.

"Shit! Under the car!"

"Frankie!"

Everyone was yelling at once. Theo scrounged a few more dragonsbreath rounds from his pocket and slammed them into the magazine. He started to squeeze off a burst under the car, but stopped. Frankie was down there.

"Shit!" Theo said again. He should've known better. A Ventrue can take a pretty good shot and survive to heal himself if he's got enough blood. But Vitel had to be way fucking old to hold together after what Theo had given him. And how the hell did he get past them out of the car? Frankie was going to have to take his chances, Theo decided. They couldn't afford to let Vitel drain him.

"Watch out!" Theo squatted and fired a burst under the car.

Yells from all around, and then Vitel shot out from beneath the Lexus. He was a blur, knocking Lydia and Baldur aside. Then the prince was gone again. The warehouse was suddenly quiet, except for Baldur scrambling to pull Frankie from beneath the car and cursing as he burned himself on the steaming phosphorous.

"Baas, your men by that door and that one," Theo shouted. "Nobody gets out. Lydia, Jan, you others, by the big door. *Keep it closed!*"

"He broke his neck," Baldur was saying in disbelief. "He broke Frankie's neck like a...like a..."

Theo shut out the sounds of Kindred and ghouls rushing to obey his orders. He scanned the interior of the warehouse. Vitel was there somewhere, and he was proving as tricky as any Nosferatu.... There. The slightest bit of movement, away from the ghouls and the other Kindred. *Can't give him time to heal*, Theo thought. He fired another burst, emptying the magazine toward where he'd seen the motion. He saw Vitel, heard him cry out from the blast, but then everything went dark.

What the...?

Blackness. Living shadow. A cloud of it enveloped Theo, blocked out his vision, muffled sound. He heard gunfire, but it sounded far away. The inky blackness coated Theo like a second skin. Chills shot through his body, his muscles starting to spasm. The sensation was repulsive, unnatural, evil. Theo had seen this before, had fought his way free before—but what the hell was a Ventrue prince doing firing off this kind of shit?

Theo was disoriented by the shadow, but he dove hard to the side—what he hoped was away from the car. He felt the drag of the darkness clinging to him like a greedy lover, but the force of his lunge tore him free. He landed on the cement, rolled, and jumped to his feet. The gunfire was much closer now. Pieterzoon's ghouls had opened on Vitel with their submachine guns. The cloud of darkness that had assaulted Theo was rapidly dissipating as Vitel took more and more hits from the ghouls.

Vitel was ragged. Much of his face was burned away, and his chest and clothes were in tatters. But the cursed blood that animated him was potent enough to hold him together, to pull him back from the brink of the abyss. And he was proving far from helpless, even after expending what must have been much blood.

As Theo's head cleared, Vitel, with a simple gesture, sent tendrils of darkness hurtling toward the impertinent ghouls who were dogging him. The ghouls, in self-defense, shifted their fire. The bullets shredded one of the snaking black tentacles, but several others found their marks, knocking ghouls aside, crushing some against the solid brick walls.

So much for a quiet hit, Theo thought. The warehouse was full of smoke and gunfire, snake-like tentacles crushing the life out of ghouls, and if any of the phosphorous had splattered too close to the Lexus's gas tank, the car might go up in a fireball any second. And Theo still couldn't quite believe that a face full of dragonsbreath hadn't toasted Vitel. That should have done in most any Kindred. The Brujah had never fought a creature quite this old before. *And this ain't no Ventrue neither.* Not throwing around shadow magic like that.

In the short space of time it took one of the tentacles to pound a ghoul into pulp, Theo reloaded the shotgun and fired another burst. Vitel staggered back, and a couple of the shadowy tentacles frayed and faded out of existence. The dragonsbreath might not be finishing him off, but it was taking a toll.

Theo charged in behind the blast. He fired again, but Vitel jumped out of the way. No—not jumping, hovering. Vitel was just floating in the air, hanging there as if he were suspended by a cable. But just as this was sinking in for Theo, Vitel was coming down, claws flashing, right at him. That moment of unexpected floating was enough to throw Theo's timing off. He tried to dodge, but Vitel's claws raked across his face and chest. Vitel closed again. Theo clubbed at him ineffectually with the emptied shotgun, but it was a sword slicing through the air, just over Theo's head, that drove Vitel back. Given a second's reprieve, Theo glanced back to see Christoph, broadsword in hand, wading into the fray.

But then Christoph hesitated, and Theo saw why.

Vitel's hands were no longer claws. What confronted the two Brujah was worse. Balanced on Vitel's right palm was a ball of flame, fire conjured from thin air—or perhaps from hell itself. Theo and Christoph each dove as Vitel hurled the fire. It passed right over them, shot across the warehouse, and landed amidst the second group of ghouls. The fireball erupted into a true inferno. Theo rolled to his feet to the sound of shrieking, burning ghouls. The smoke in the warehouse was growing thicker every second, threatening to block out the dim light from the ceiling units.

As Theo rummaged through his pockets for more dragonsbreath shells, others were pressing the attack. Lydia and Baldur were advancing on Vitel, with Pieterzoon and Baas each flanked out to opposite sides, all four assailants' guns blazing. The bullets were striking Vitel, driving him back half a step every few seconds, but the entry holes were closing over as quickly as they appeared—and Vitel merely smiled.

Theo slipped his last handful of dragonsbreath

rounds into the SPAS and looked up to see another ball of flame in Vitel's hand. The archon was instantly ready to dive clear, but Vitel launched the fiery sphere in another direction. Lydia flung herself to the side, but Baldur wasn't so quick. The flame struck him and burst into a great conflagration. He whipped around and flailed madly, but the fire raged, burning away clothes, hair, undead flesh.

Lydia launched herself again, this time at her friend, knocking him to the ground. But the fire was more than she could take. As soon as she landed, she jumped away from Baldur as if she herself were now burning. She screamed, a panicked, terror-filled sound, as if he had been thrown at her instead of the other way around. She slapped at her legs, her chest, her face, trying to put out flames that were not there.

That was all Theo saw of her. He was charging Vitel for a better shot. But Jan and Baas were moving in also, blasting away with their MP5s, and Christoph was edging closer with his sword. Theo didn't have a clear shot and held his fire as he moved forward.

Vitel, practically ignoring the hail of submachine-gun fire from the two Dutchmen, watched the several Kindred and ghoul approaching. The former prince had remained incredibly calm throughout the fight, despite the seemingly long odds he'd faced. Now that most of the ghouls and several Kindred were dispatched, he took on an almost demonically gleeful aspect. His eyes shone with delight in the destruction, in the bodies broken and burning. Far from thinking of escape, Vitel was preparing to finish the job. He was reveling in the slaughter.

And as Theo and the others moved closer, Vitel changed. Not merely his attitude, or his bearing. His form itself changed, grew taller, darker—as if the smoke and shadows now filling the warehouse were drawn to him, drawn *into* him. The warehouse was growing darker but, Theo realized, the darkness was spreading *from* Vitel, not the other way around. He was growing shadowy, pools of darkness seeping out from his many wounds, as if his body could no longer contain his black soul. Some of the bullets passed through him now; others seemed to disappear into the darkness without effect. At some point, his arms became, no longer arms, but spiraling black tentacles, four rather than two, obsidian cobras poised to strike. All this was shifting among the smoke and deepening shadows. Nothing remained clear except his eyes, glowing red and fierce.

Suddenly, as one, the tentacles shot out, the cobras striking. A whip of solid darkness struck Theo across the face, ripped open further the ragged claw wound. Baas went down, his knee shattered. A tentacle whipped around Christoph's sword arm and jerked him off his feet, shaking him like a rag doll until his screams and the sound of snapping bones filled the air. His broadsword clattered to the cement below. Pieterzoon was caught by a giant black constrictor, arms pinned to his side. His MP5 fired harmlessly into the floor until the ammunition was spent and the weapon fell silent.

Theo climbed to his feet, blood seeping from the rent in his face, the gash in his chest. As he gazed upon the beast of shadow before him, the archon's studied battle calm suddenly drained away. He saw standing ahead, thrashing his compatriots, not Marcus Vitel, Ventrue pretender of obviously Lasombra blood, but a creature purely of the Beast. The fiery red eyes, the pure darkness spilling over through a man-shaped portal from hell. This was the Sabbat. This was a demon that would subjugate them all.

And the Beast within Theo answered. The fire that was hatred and anger, violence and hunger, rose up within him, took hold of his limbs and gave them strength. Theo fought the Beast before him with the Beast within his own breast, the demon that would one night consume each and every one of them.

His allies down or immobilized, Theo charged. The first blast from his shotgun ripped apart the appendage that had struck him. The second blast, the last of his dragonsbreath, he poured into the heart of the creature that Vitel had become. The shadow demon staggered. Theo threw himself at it. He swung his gun again like a club. Vitel stumbled back farther. They were at the brick wall now, the rear of the warehouse that was transformed into one of the nine fire- and smoke-filled levels of hell.

Then the remaining tentacles converged on Theo. They sprang back from their far-flung targets to strike him, hitting him from behind on the head, back, legs. His knees buckled, but he didn't fall. A black cord lashed him across the face. Another tentacle whipped at him—Theo caught it, stopped it in midair. He held it in both hands and, fueled by his blood and the fire of his belly, ripped it apart. The shadow demon Vitel roared in anguish. The tentacle that Theo had severed with his bare hands dissolved into nothingness.

Before Vitel's cry had completely left his gaping black maw, Theo scooped Christoph's broadsword from the floor. The archon swung, seeking blood but settling for viscous shadow. He cut away another tentacle, and then the last. Vitel, eyes burning with bright hatred, cursed in pain and fury. Darkness flooded out of his body and swept over Theo in a tidal wave of oblivion, but the Brujah would not be denied. He swung again. The sword clove through the shadow, through the trunk of the Vitel beast, the tip of the weapon scraping the brick wall behind and showering a spray of sparks into the darkness. Whether the terrible sound was the force of steel against brick and mortar or the bellow of Vitel, Theo couldn't tell. But as he raised the blade to strike again, the shadow began to break up. The darkness contracted, seemed to wither and crack, and a moment later, where the demon Vitel had stood, fine black powder floated to the ground, oily dust upon the cement.

"Damnedest Ventrue I ever met," Theo said laconically.

Jan attempted a smile, but the pained result was not particularly effective. "Yes...quite."

The smoke still hung heavy in the warehouse. Opening the doors would only have attracted attention to the building—something they didn't want—and there was no one inside in danger of succumbing to smoke inhalation. Jan's few remaining ghouls were keeping watch outside. The warehouse walls were solid, but there had been a lot of gunfire, and nobody wanted the cops stumbling in.

"Don't you guys have a secret handshake or something?" Theo asked. "Us, we don't have to worry about that kinda thing. Nobody ever pretends to be a Brujah, especially a prince. Hell, there's probably ten or twenty Brujah princes pretendin' to be something else."

Jan fidgeted a bit and tried to concentrate on the lock on Vitel's briefcase. It had been a long time, Theo decided, since he'd enjoyed someone else's discomfort this much, and it didn't hurt that the enjoyment was at a Ventrue's expense.

"How 'bout Lucinde?" Theo asked, leaning very close so no one else would overhear. "She know about this? About him?" He knew the answer to that, but he couldn't resist asking. *God, I'd love to be there when Jan tells her about this*, Theo thought. He waited for some response, but Jan was pointedly not paying attention. He was thumbing combinations on the briefcase's lock and listening for any sign of progress.

"The cop decoy worked fine," Theo said. "The cop cars, the fire on the west side."

"Hm?" Jan looked up for a moment. "Oh, good." He returned his attention to the lock.

"You think it's trapped?" Theo asked, tapping the briefcase.

"I doubt it."

"Okay." Theo took the briefcase from Jan, propped it against his own chest, and pressed with his fingers into the crease by the handle. They dug through the leather and into the metal beneath. Theo kept pressing, working his fingertips into the widening gap, and the briefcase popped open. "There you go." He handed it back to Jan and left the Ventrue to sort through the contents.

Nearby, Lydia and Christoph sat dejectedly by Frankie, who was propped up against the side of the Lexus. The angle of his neck looked distinctly uncomfortable.

"Guess he fucked me up pretty good," said Frankie, seeing Theo.

"Guess so," Theo said.

"But we fucked him too, didn't we? I'll be fine. Just give me a little time, a little blood."

"Yeah. Sure thing," said Theo, but he wasn't convinced. Sure, blood could heal broken bones, but they didn't always heal straight, and spinal injuries could be a real bitch. Hard to figure what might happen with a broken neck. So he turned to Lydia and Christoph, who were considerably less upbeat than Frankie. Then again, Christoph was never upbeat. What was it Lydia had said about him once? *Moody as a damn girl.* Christoph was sharpening his sword.

"Hope I didn't hurt it," Theo said. "I didn't exactly mean to slice through a brick wall."

"It's a strong blade," Christoph said. "I'm glad it finished the job, even if I wasn't wielding it."

Theo nodded. Christoph said stuff like that sometimes when he did decide to talk, but he was good enough in a fight.

"Man, I'm sorry," Lydia said from where she sat next to Christoph.

"Don't need to be," Theo said. He started to walk away—he didn't feel much like a confessional just now; his face and his chest hurt—but Lydia wasn't done yet.

"It's my fault," she said. She gestured toward the pile of ash that had been Baldur, but she didn't look at it. "I should've helped him. And Frankie too."

"Wasn't nothing you could do," Frankie assured her.

"Didn't nobody ask you nothin'," she snapped at him. "He was on fire. I coulda put it out, coulda…" Her voice faltered as she remembered the uncontrollable terror that had overcome her. Her eyes welled up with blood as she relived those moments.

"Hey," Theo said, "one of your people went down for good. It happens. It'll happen again." She shot him a challenging, bloody glare. "Get fuckin' used to it." Then he did walk away.

part three:
the shell game

My dearest Lucius,

How anxiously I await your every missive, you whose name has so long been carved upon my heart; you whose thoughts I know better than the reflection of my own face in the mirror. My greatest fear—which, judging by your angry words and deeds of late, seems justified—is that you might mistake my intentions. You must know, though it seems you do not, that I value your messages purely as agents of verisimilitude, that through your words I might believe myself closer to your thoughts and, by extension, to your flesh. You must know, though you hurl your accusations at me, that it is the wolves at the door, not I, baying for more. They, even among your own esteemed lineage, are the ingrates, the feckless purveyors of incaution. You must know that I, above all others, wish to see you come to no harm at the hands of others.

Rest assured that I bear you no ill will despite the injuries inflicted upon me and mine. Doubtless they arose from misunderstanding, for does not jealousy flourish when kindred hearts are separated? Know that I forgive your every transgression, that I hold you still in as high esteem as any cherished friend or dear pet.

I find your city in good order and commend you for having left it so. There is no step I tread, no sight I behold, that does not usher thought of you to my mind. Fear not that you will lack reward for your sojourn among the infidels. No good deed goes unpunished, or so the wits are wont to say. For now, however, I languish in your absence, wishing only that I might lay hands upon you.

I remain your humble and gracious servant,
—Vykos

Friday, 5 November 1999, 11:24 PM
Presidential Suite, Lord Baltimore Inn
Baltimore, Maryland

"Hmph." Theo handed the letter back to Jan. It was one of several in Vitel's briefcase that seemed to confirm that the deposed prince of Washington was not what he had appeared to be—as if Theo had any doubts after the struggle in the warehouse earlier that week, and after the extensive proof that Jan and Colchester had assembled before that.

"Doesn't look like he and Vykos get along very well—*got* along very well," Theo said. All the letters were in that same mocking tone of love-letter parody. Only a fool would mistake them for true affection, for anything less than pure spite.

"Not surprising," Jan said. "From all I know about Vykos, it doesn't exactly inspire intimacy."

"Neither did Vitel."

"True. Apparently with good reason." This was as close as Jan had come to verbally acknowledging that he and his entire clan had been duped, that a pretender had ruled the American capital for thirty years in the name of Clan Ventrue. Of course, none of the Camarilla powers-that-be had sniffed out the truth—in fact, it had been a veritable cotillion of archons and a justicar that had handed power to Vitel in the late '60s. Such was the insular nature of princes and the "organization" of the Camarilla that in a city the sect "controlled" no one had suspected Vitel of treachery beyond the norm.

"How'd Lucinde take it?" Theo asked, unable to resist one more jibe.

"How are the defenses?" Jan quickly changed the subject.

Theo chuckled but didn't torment the Ventrue further. Then the archon grew serious once again. "Lines are pulled back as tight as we can make 'em. I think we're ready…ready as we can be. Sabbat's hot on our heels. They're shifting west and north. Looks like the push, when it comes—I'd guess in the next few nights—will be from the west, just like I told Vitel was happening. Except this time it'll be for real."

Jan was looking over some of Theo's notes, a list of patrols. Several of the names were very recently crossed off. "What happened to these three?" Jan asked.

"Caught during the day. Ghouls."

"Oh."

Jan was studying the list more closely, obviously tallying the numerous crossed-off names, and counting the few defenders that remained. Many of those marked out, Theo knew, had already fallen to the Sabbat. Some had likely seen an opportunity to save their own skins and stolen off into the night. Had a Kindred who didn't come back from patrol hightailed it out of the war zone, or been tagged by the Sabbat? It was impossible to know for sure. Take Clyde and Maurice, for instance. Last seen near Green Haven. They didn't seem like the deserting type. But who knew if, in a few years, Theo might bump into them walking down the street somewhere. For their sakes, Theo hoped that the Sabbat *had* gotten them.

"It's going to be tight, isn't it," Jan said, still looking at the list.

"Yeah, well, we knew from the start that it would be." Theo reached for a cigarette. "Not a whole lot of room for error."

"You'd been planning on having Vitel available to help, hadn't you?" Jan asked.

Theo lit up, took in a deep, unfiltered breath, then shrugged. "Plans change," he said. "No Vitel, no Garlotte, no Victoria…" Victoria. They'd had not word from or about her since she'd left for Atlanta, and that had been months ago. There'd been vague rumors about something unfortunate happening to a Sabbat Bishop Sebastian down there, but even if true, the reports might or might not have anything at all to do with Victoria.

"We'll do what we can," Theo said. "It's all about timing. How 'bout things on your end?"

Jan nodded. "Everything is prepared."

Theo nodded solemnly. "Good." Because if things *weren't* ready…well, there wasn't any point thinking about that.

Jasmine pressed her back against the side of the car. Her legs were cramping from squatting, but she wasn't about to get up. Not while she could remain out of sight—and maybe relatively safe—among the clunkers on this used-car lot.

Had Borris made it this far? She wasn't sure. The others she was sure about. She'd seen them go down, seen them ripped to shreds by… No. She wasn't going to think about that. She couldn't right now, not if she hoped to somehow get away.

What was that?

She almost jumped up and fled. She wanted to, even though it wouldn't be the smartest thing to do. But now that she'd stopped, she didn't know if she could make her legs do what she wanted anymore. She just wasn't sure. She wasn't sure about anything anymore. Had she heard something, something nearby? Nothing sounded right. There wasn't too much noise, she realized. There wasn't *enough*. The normal sounds were all out there: a car zipping by on the main road, the buzzing of the cheap street lamps that didn't really light the car lot that well. What was missing were the sounds that she should have made, that she would have made if she were still a normal human being: She wasn't breathing hard after running all that way; her heart wasn't pounding from exertion and fear. Not that she wasn't afraid— she *was*. Terrified. But none of her body's normal responses confirmed that anything unusual was happening to her.

She felt dead. And if the Sabbat had anything to do with it… No. She pushed that thought back where it came from, closed her mind to it.

A *normal patrol*. That's what Theo had said. *Bullshit!* Jasmine bit down on her lip to keep from cursing aloud at the arrogant, all-powerful archon. She was convinced that he'd done this all on purpose, intentionally put her in harm's way. A *normal patrol*. He'd said it in that deep, expressionless way he said everything, but she knew—she could feel the snide vibrations; she could tell he was sneering when she wasn't looking. He'd found out that she hadn't been going out every night; she hadn't given in to the oppression of the system—*like he had*. And he resented her. He hated her for it. She had the courage that he didn't, and he couldn't stand that.

It *hadn't* been a normal patrol. She and her three partners had run into at least five other patrols—that was way more than would usually be in one area. That was at least fifteen or twenty Kindred on the western edge of the city, and she had seen what had happened to many of them when the Sabbat struck….

Jasmine looked down at the gun that she clutched in her hand like salvation. They'd just thrust it upon her at the beginning of the night. A something centimeter or millimeter or something. She hadn't fired a shot. Not yet. As she looked down, she noticed for the first time that her bell bottoms were torn. Her mouth grew dry as she saw the blood along the tear— her blood. She became aware of the throbbing, of the gash along her left calf. A weak, mournful cry escaped her lips.

"*Jasmine?*"

She flinched, banged her head against the car door, cursed silently at herself for the noise.

"*Jasmine?*"

Was it Borris's voice? Could it be? Jasmine fought the idea of running again. She wasn't sure how serious her injury was, how long her leg would hold up. She wasn't sure what exactly was out there—

That wasn't true. Not completely. She'd seen enough to guess. The Sabbat had swarmed into the city. They'd come speeding in what seemed like dozens of cars, jumping out when they saw anyone, Kindred or kine, doing awful things.... The patrols that hadn't been swept away by the first wave had responded, and then the police had showed up. From then on, it had been a hundred different small running fights—for Jasmine, mostly running. She wasn't sure exactly where she was now—just hiding among the cars.

"*Jasmine?*" Closer now. He sounded desperate, maybe hurt.

"*Borris, is that you?*" she whispered.

She heard movement, very close now, just on the other side of the car, at the rear of the car. And then he peeked around and over the trunk. Jasmine could tell from the pained expression on his face and the awkward way he held himself that Borris had to be injured.

"Borris..." she said quietly, relieved just the slightest bit for the first time this long, long night. Her relief was short-lived.

As he stepped around the car, Borris was not alone. He was not holding himself awkwardly, he was being held. And the sight of the creature holding him turned Jasmine's blood to ice.

A bony ridge—once a nose?—ran down the center of its face from forehead to upper lip. On either side, the brow and cheeks fell away at a smooth, sharp angle. The jaw was recessed, not seeming to fit the rest of the sleek face, and instead of hair there were sickly white follicles of skin braided and draped over the creature's shoulder.

Tzimisce. Fiend. The name fit only too well.

"Jasmine…" Boris said, his eyes almost rolling up into his head from pain. Edging around the car, he and the fiend turned just enough that Jasmine could see the Tzimisce was not, in fact, holding Boris up by the collar as she'd thought. The thing's hand and forearm were plunged through Boris's skin, into his back. It looked as if its fingers were gripping his very spine, manipulating him like some demonic puppet.

Jasmine couldn't stand the sight of it. For a moment, her fear fled her. With a defiant cry, she stood, raised her pistol at the fiend, pulled the trigger—and nothing happened. Jasmine was not aware of what a safety did. No one had thought to tell her. And so her moment of fearlessness passed in futility. Boris and the fiend were not alone. The other Sabbat creatures swarmed over her, knocked her to the ground, tore the gun from her grasp….

Wednesday, 10 November 1999, 4:07 AM
Friendship Park
Anne Arundel County, Maryland

The hell with this, Lydia decided. She stood from behind the trashcan, scanned the darkness for movement, saw it, and fired her last two shots. "Motherfuckers." She knelt back down, ejected the empty clip from her Desert Eagle, and began refilling it and her two spares from the loose cartridges in her jacket pocket. The trashcan in its wooden container made good enough cover. The motherfuckers most likely wouldn't have found her for several minutes more had she not given away her position by firing, but now they'd zero in on the muzzle flashes and head this way. But that was okay. Lydia was tired of playing hide and seek.

She glanced where she'd last seen Frankie and Christoph, but they were out of sight now. She and Frankie were pretty much in the same boat, except he wasn't as fast as she was. For all the shit she'd given Christoph about his oversized switchblade, he seemed to be having the most luck. Hard to argue with good old-fashioned dismemberment.

So much for the *Friendship* in Friendship Park.

The park had seemed like the last chance to hold the line. The running battle in the car had gotten out of hand really fast. Just too damn many Sabbat swarming all over the fucking place. This was no raid. This was the shit, and Lydia and her boys were caught between it and the fan.

Things might get a little hot, Theo had said.

A little hot. "Kiss my ass, you black bastard," Lydia muttered. *A little hot—yeah, and the sun might make me a little uncomfortable too.*

She slipped in a refilled clip and listened for the footsteps she knew she'd hear. The motherfuckers might be big and damn near invulnerable, but stealthy they were not. *There.* She heard the plodding footsteps. Maybe they were quick for being that big, but they weren't going to keep up with her. She gauged the distance of the footsteps, then jumped up.

The thing was maybe twenty yards away, lumbering toward her. Tzimisce war ghoul. Big, ugly, spiked, partially covered with chitinous bone armor. Lydia had heard lots of stories, but she'd never faced one of these things before tonight.

She unloaded on it. Seven .44 magnum slugs square in its chest from fifteen yards. Nothing. Maybe she cracked the armor a little. Maybe. She popped out the empty clip, slammed in a full one. She wasn't sure if the war ghoul actually could smile—the face seemed to be immutable armor too—but it looked to Lydia like it was smiling as it came closer.

"Oh yeah? Well, fuck you, buddy."

She opened up on it again. Seven shots right in the face. This time it staggered, stumbled a step, hesitated, but kept coming. Lydia could see cracks in its hard face, patches where the armor had crumbled away, even if the thing didn't have more than a headache. What bothered Lydia the most was that it still looked like it was smiling.

"You like that, motherfucker? You want some more?"

She held her ground, ejected that clip, and slammed in her last one. Seven more shots into the face from closer than ten yards. The head exploded. Bone and ragged flesh sprayed into the air and landed all around like grotesque rain on the heels of the Desert Eagle's thunder. The war ghoul continued on for three more laborious steps, stopped as if thinking the matter over, then toppled forward like a fallen tree.

Lydia savored her success for a full three seconds before seeing the similarly mammoth shapes emerging from the darkness, from the same direction her smiling, headless war ghoul had just come.

"Motherfuckers."

"Watch your mouth, kid."

Lydia whirled and leveled her gun—at Theo. He wasn't smiling—he almost never smiled—but just like with the war ghoul, there was something about him, his manner, that suggested a smile.

Theo tapped the Desert Eagle, still aimed at him. "I wouldn't bother pointin' that since you just fired all your shots." He nodded toward the war ghoul's disintegrating carcass, then added, "If you're tryin' to lure 'em all to you, you're doin' a good job."

Lydia didn't say anything to him; she didn't know what to say. Not because she was in awe of him, though she was still to some extent, but because she was angry. Angry about how brusque he'd been about Baldur's death. Theo had told her to get over it, and then hadn't said anything else about it, just gone on like nothing had happened, like Baldur hadn't been doing his job and standing up for all of them. *Well, then fuck Theo*, she'd decided.

And now here he was again, in his black leather jacket and Yankees cap, pretending nothing much was going on. It pissed off Lydia all over again, like they were all in the warehouse again and what used to be Baldur was lying just over there. But this wasn't the place to bring it up. There wasn't time, with the other war ghouls closing in, so Lydia said the first thing that came to her mind:

"Yankees suck shit, man."

Theo cocked his head. "You lose money on the Braves or something?"

"Hey," said Frankie who was jogging up with Christoph right then, "is it true that Greg Maddux is one of us?"

"How the hell would he pitch day games, you moron?" Lydia snapped.

"Sunblock?"

"Uh…" Christoph was perplexed by their conversation. "Does anyone else see what I see coming this way?"

Lydia looked back over her shoulder. The approaching war ghouls were indeed much closer now, their hulking silhouettes clearly visible despite the darkness. She started filling her clips again; she only had enough cartridges left to fill one and a half.

"They're all *over* the place," Frankie said, "like stink on—"

"Yeah, we get the idea," Theo said. "Look. You guys are the last patrol out. I came to bring you in myself. We don't have much time."

"Last patrol?" Lydia thought she'd heard him wrong. "What the fuck you talkin' about?"

He glared at her—maybe there was a little impatience there, a little urgency, but it was hard to say. "I say we take out these three, then we're outta here. You guys take the one off to the right. Got it?"

Lydia and Christoph nodded. Frankie couldn't exactly nod anymore, just like he couldn't quite stand up straight. Something to do with how his neck had healed, but Lydia guessed that having a permanent crick in his neck was better than being permanently dead.

"Their right or our right?" Frankie asked.

"Our right."

"What about the other two?" Frankie wanted to know, but Theo was already gone, swinging around wide to the left. His left.

"Come on." Lydia broke toward the war ghoul that was separated from the other two. Christoph kept pace with her, Frankie lagged behind. When they got within a few yards, Lydia circled to the side while Christoph continued to close. The creature had no neck. Its jaw was embedded in its torso several inches below the top of its massive shoulders. Its arms weren't elongated like those of many of the war ghouls...but it had six, which made up somewhat for the shorter reach. The arms were well-armored too. The ghoul skillfully blocked Christoph's slashes, one after another, and seemed about to grab the Brujah's sword arm after every thrust, but Christoph managed to strike and then evade the grasping hands.

Lydia took up an angle to the side, clear of Christoph, and took potshots at the ghoul's head. She was conservative with her fire, not wanting to hit Christoph or use up all her ammo. Frankie caught up with her and joined in the target practice with his H&K 9mm.

Their shots didn't do a lot of damage to the war ghoul, but they did irritate it. More and more it used one of its hands to try to shield its face from their bullets, and that hurt its coordination against Christoph. He struck more telling blows, chipping away armor, and even drawing blood once or twice.

Finally the beast had enough of the harassment from afar—not that far really. It broke away from Christoph and charged Lydia and Frankie. They weren't expecting the move, but it didn't matter. Christoph, seeing what happened, swooped in behind the war ghoul and struck tender flesh behind each knee. The ghoul, hamstrung, screeched a surprisingly high-pitched wail, and dropped to its knees. It twisted from the waist, trying to fight off both Christoph and the bullets.

Christoph had the definite edge now. He worked quickly and relentlessly, taking advantage of every opening. His blade found chinks in the armor, ripped entire bone plates from the creature's flesh. He began to pare down the number of limbs he had to contend against: One arm hung useless at the ghoul's side; two hands were sliced completely or mostly off, and then a third.

At last, Lydia and Frankie closed in. Christoph stepped back as those two poured enough concentrated firepower into the beast's face that its exo-cranium cracked and shattered like an egg. The three Brujah stood in silent triumph around the monstrous carcass.

"Okay," said Theo from very close behind them. "If you guys are finished, let's get the hell outta here."

The other three Brujah looked at him. There he was again, standing like nothing had happened, like the park, the *city*, wasn't crawling with Sabbat war ghouls. Lydia thought for a moment. She couldn't remember hearing his shotgun go off, but she'd been absorbed in her own fight…. Then she looked more closely and saw the blood on his hands. Not blood dripping. His own blood, around his knuckles, and white patches of his own bone showing through. In the darkness beyond him, she could just barely make out the two mounds that, a few minutes before, must have been war ghouls.

Wednesday, 10 November 1999, 4:32 AM
Lexington Street Metro stop
Baltimore, Maryland

Cardinal Francisco Domingo de Polonia stood beneath the city that was the newest addition to his diocese. The Metro trains were still idle for the night. Their idleness would continue into the day and likely beyond. Some destructive band of vandals had demolished several portions of track, damage that would take the Metro authority quite some time to repair.

Surrounding Polonia was a small group of his hand-picked staff, each completely loyal—each to his own personal agenda of cruelty and ambition. They followed Polonia because he was strong. God had obviously smiled upon the newly anointed cardinal, unlike so many of the other Sabbat notables: Monçada, attempting to spread his reach across the broad Atlantic was destroyed; Borges, having prevailed in Miami after years of struggle, was slain; his protégé Sebastian was fallen in a bizarre combat. The conquest of the U.S. East Coast truly had become the glorious accomplishment of Polonia. He would install his own archbishops and bishops, removing the compromise candidates Borges or Vykos had earlier insisted upon. Vykos was another whose meteoric rise was checked; the Tzimisce's star was certainly descending, though the freakish archbishop seemed hardly to notice. Originally Monçada's legate in this matter, Vykos had been more intent on seizing power than on exercising it. Now, without Monçada's backing, the creature had grown distant and aloof, grossly ignoring the necessities of administration and politics entailed in ruling a city the magnitude of Washington, D.C. For reasons unexplained, Vykos had neither consolidated its power base, conducted the siege of the Tremere chantry with any energy, nor appointed bishops to oversee the affairs of the city in which the archbishop seemed so disinterested. The Tzimisce mind was a mystery to Polonia. If he could not fathom Vykos's motivations, he could—and would—at least soon deal with the shortcomings and be rid of the archbishop. Once Baltimore was completely in his grasp and the Camarilla defenders rounded up and staked for the sun, there would be no more need for Vykos's spy—the only factor that had stayed Polonia's hand thus far from moving against the Tzimisce.

And the city would be his very soon, was practically his already, if the reports streaming in were accurate—not always a safe assumption. But even if half the updates of strategic point after strategic point secured were true, the Sabbat had won a victory more sweeping and complete than even the sacking of Atlanta at the outset of the campaign. There had been minimal resistance on the western edge of the city, and heavier fighting to the south, south of the Baltimore-Washington International Airport. But the Sabbat column—in the loosest sense of the term— that had swept in from the west had quickly cut off the airport from the city itself. What difference did it make if the few Camarilla around the airport held out, if other Kindred from the city could not flee there to escape? According to Vykos's spy, some of the Camarilla dregs might try to flee northward on the ground, and so a significant force had circled to the north to prevent any mass escape in that direction. This would not be merely the capture of a city; it was to be the final scouring of the East Coast, the total annihilation of Camarilla resistance, and the establishment of Polonia's unquestioned dominance.

Waiting for more news, the cardinal surveyed the members of his surrounding staff: Costello, long-time lieutenant who had followed in Polonia's wake to the height of power; Hardin, nomad warchief who had swung securely into Polonia's camp once it was clear which way power was flowing in the Sabbat high command; Bolon, Tzimisce commander of war ghouls, as resolute as he was massive, most physically impressive of the bunch but the least dangerous to Polonia. Significant also were those who were absent. Vykos had not participated directly in the attack but would be along shortly, Polonia was sure, to bask in the glow of victory. Vallejo, too, was gone. The legionnaire had returned to Madrid after the news of Monçada's demise, and as far as Polonia was concerned it was good riddance. If Vykos was unpredictable, Vallejo was too disciplined, too unwavering in his loyalty to Monçada. It was a quality with which Polonia was uncomfortable, even in his own supporters. Armando Mendes, Polonia's ablest lieutenant, had remained in New York where, Polonia was quite aware, he had been maneuvering to usurp the rule of that fine city. That had been before Polonia had been elevated to the post of cardinal. Polonia planned to reward Armando by giving him the city—and then holding him to impossibly high standards of pacification, while at the same time shackling the new archbishop with debilitating tithe demands in both manpower and financial resources.

Yes, Polonia's underlings kept him on his toes, like a man walking upon a line of razors. It was his lieutenants, however, if they crossed him, who would find the blade at their own throats.

"Commander Bolon," Polonia said. "Your latest reports."

"Yes, Your Eminence." The Tzimisce knelt but even on one knee was almost as tall as Polonia. Large spikes of bone protruded from much of the commander: his shoulders, elbows, knuckles, knees, and along the crest of the bone helmet that, evidently, was actually part of his head. "The airport is secured. We've disabled the radar, so even if Cammies get in, they're not going anywhere. The losses we took earlier—"

"How heavy?" Polonia demanded.

"Significant, but not beyond the acceptable range."

Polonia was pleased by this. Those casualties south of the city were the only relatively heavy losses his forces had suffered all night. "Good. Continue."

"Those losses," Bolon stated, "were largely attributed to Theo Bell."

Bell. Damnable Brujah archons. First Julius in Atlanta cutting a swath through the battalion of war ghouls, now Bell blazing a path of destruction near Baltimore. *Shouldn't they be in North Africa trying to excavate Carthage or something?* Polonia wondered. But it didn't matter. The area was secure now.

"And Bell's destruction has been confirmed?"

Bolon paused. "No, Your Eminence. I have no such report."

Polonia was not surprised; neither was he pleased. He turned to Hardin, the fellow Lasombra who had commanded the column from the west. The cardinal had accompanied Hardin's column on tonight's assault, so as to reach the center of the city more quickly and establish a strong presence and command center there. Polonia had forced himself merely to observe initially. How else to gauge Hardin's mettle? And Hardin had performed well, though resistance was light. The Sabbat forces had skillfully enveloped and destroyed the defenders on the western edge of the city, and then had struck decisively for the heart of Baltimore—where there was no resistance to speak of. Polonia, growing less patient with the disappointing enemy body count, ordered Hardin's force to disperse, to scour the city for pockets of resistance. There had been fear in those first hours of a breakout, but then encouraging word had filtered in from other quadrants: The airport was cut off from the city; Gregorio's flanking expedition was in place to the north, and was squeezing southward. There would be no breakout. Now all that was left for Polonia to do was receive word as the enemy was tracked down and destroyed. If he was fortunate, one or more of the Camarilla worthies might fall into his grasp: Bell, Pieterzoon, Vitel. At the very least, however, the city would be Polonia's.

"And your latest?" the cardinal asked Hardin.

"Southern half of the city's in good shape, little or no resistance. Inner Harbor's quiet, except for the Lord Baltimore Inn, which is burning to the ground as we speak. My people are spreadin' north. Most of the Camarilla must have taken off that way. They should run smack into Gregorio."

"Not so!" said a new voice, another opportunistic nomad warchief who'd risen from pack leader to prominence over the course of the war. Gregorio, newly arrived, wore a white smock that blended almost seamlessly with the albino's alabaster skin. His shiny pate was as smooth and pale as a porcelain doll. "My men have worked their way south to the city limits and not seen the first retreating defender. They are not fleeing that direction."

"Impossible," Polonia said.

Gregorio seemed genuinely saddened. Furrows of disappointment creased the Tzimisce's brow: "Yes, I was afraid Hardin would fill the harbor with heads before I'd seen the first Camarilla hair—but all seems quiet here as well."

That fact was far from lost upon Cardinal Polonia. No significant resistance within the city. Secure perimeters established. The airport sealed. No armada of ships escaping the harbor.

Decisive action, that was what these men, these treacherous lieutenants hovering like vultures, respected, and that was what Polonia would give them. This was what he most hated about high command, the fog of war. He was forced to rely upon information provided by his subordinates. They were his ears and eyes, he their mind. He much preferred to be leading the charge, observing everything firsthand, as he had for most of his existence; but leadership carried a price as well as reward. His commanders from all fronts needed to be able to find him; he had to learn what they knew, interpret the situation from the details they provided, even if they themselves did not fully understand the implications of what they said.

"They've gone to ground," Polonia said. "They're hiding, waiting for us to grow overconfident, then they'll counterattack." That had to be the explanation. It had to be. "See that your men find shelter," he said to his commanders as a whole. "It's late. First thing tonight, we'll root them out. We'll find them if we have to burn the whole city."

And Polonia was prepared to do exactly that.

Wednesday, 10 November 1999, 4:45 AM
Eurofreight jet cargo hold
Baltimore-Washington International Airport

Theo was, relatively speaking, in a good mood,
perhaps even approaching what, for him, passed as
the zenith of his mood spectrum: guardedly optimis-
tic. He was ignoring for the moment the fact that his
boss had confided in a Ventrue rather than him. He
didn't really care that Lydia was pissed at him. He
wasn't even too bothered that the Sabbat was march-
ing practically uncontested into Baltimore. That, at
least, was part of the plan. He and Jan had lured the
Sabbat for weeks, drawn them closer and closer to
Baltimore, fed doctored information through Vitel
about a non-existent last stand, and then hustled most
of the Camarilla defenders out of the city. The Sabbat
leaders would have thought that they'd cut off the
airport from the rest of the city and denied that avenue of escape. In fact, two out of three Kindred in
the city had been gathered there and many were already in the air *before* the attack fell.

Theo's sense of satisfaction was tempered by the
reality of heavy—read: *total*—losses among the patrols on the western edge of the city. That fact that
the casualties had been anticipated, like Buffalo, like
Hartford, did little to ease the archon's mind. Neither did the knowledge that he'd chosen Kindred
specifically for the suicide mission. He hadn't been
willing to jeopardize secrecy by calling for volunteers,
by willing other Kindred to determine their own fate.
Instead, he'd purposefully winnowed the chaff, as-
signing to that part of the city most of those who

hadn't been pulling their weight, those he wouldn't have been able to depend on in the nights ahead—because even the ambitious maneuver of extracting Camarilla personnel from Baltimore was merely part of the plan. More lay ahead, and it wasn't going to get easier.

So Theo's guarded optimism leaned heavily to the guarded, but the only immediate hurdle he faced was making sure the cargo plane got in the air. He'd already herded the last defenders south of the city, Lydia, Christoph, and Frankie, away from their increasingly hopeless stand at Friendship Park and to this last aircraft of Pieterzoon's that was waiting on the runway. They were on board and situated comfortably—again, relatively speaking—in the cargo hold. The engines were humming gently. After months of constant toil and strain, Theo was almost ready to relax, even if just for a few hours.

That was when the pilot buzzed the hold. "Radar's out at control," came the static-riddled voice over the intercom. "We're denied clearance from the tower. We can't take off."

Theo's fleeting optimism quickly reverted to his general rule number one—anything that can fuck up, and most things that "can't," will. He jabbed the intercom button. "Take off. Now."

"Sir?"

"*Take...off...now.*"

"We don't have *clearance.*"

"I heard you. That means nobody else will be landin', right?"

"Sir, there are other planes in holding patterns...circling, waiting to land."

"If you don't take off now, there will be people here, probably in less than two minutes, who will blow this whole plane—and you and me with it—to Kingdom Come." There was a pause. "Don't make me come up there," Theo added.

But to add insult to potential injury, the pilot wasn't listening to Theo. The Brujah in the hold heard the distracted pilot over the intercom, however: "What in the world? Who are those folks on the—? Hey!"

Theo heard the gunshots in stereo—over the intercom and outside the plane. So did the others.

"What the hell?" Lydia was shouting, ducking from reflex.

"Get this plane movin'!" Theo had to force himself not to punch the intercom button too hard and break it. There were no windows. He couldn't see what was going on out there.

"*Mary, mother of God!*" the pilot was shrieking.

"Go! Go!" Theo yelled. If the Sabbat blocked the runway, he and the others were trapped. "Go!"

The plane lurched forward suddenly. Theo stumbled, slapped at the wall for support. Bullets punched through the fuselage just a few feet away. Were the Sabbat in cars? Were they blocking the runway? He couldn't hear over the plane's engines. He couldn't see anything.

The pilot was gasping and sobbing over the intercom: "*Jesus-Jesus-Jesus…!*"

"Holy fuckin' shit!" Lydia, Frankie, and Christoph dove for cover.

"*Get us up!*" Theo roared at the intercom as he regained his balance. "Go!"

For a few sickening seconds, the gunshots seemed to get louder. Theo kept expecting the plane to screech to a halt, or to hear the pilot get his head blown off. That would ground them just as effectively. Theo prayed the plane didn't explode. He almost welcomed the thought of being boarded. At least then he could do something! He wouldn't be completely dependent on the pilot getting them off the ground, on the plane holding together. He was jittering like crazy in this forced inaction.

But finally the gunfire began to grow more distant, and shortly it was drowned out completely by the engines. The plane's speed pressed Theo back. He felt the instant when the wheels lost contact with the tarmac.

They were in the air.

"Secure cargo bay for take-off," the pilot's voice quavered belatedly over the intercom. He was obviously shaken, whimpering quietly to himself, seeking relief in checklists, protocol, routine.

The cargo plane didn't hit any of the holding planes. The pilot kept to low altitude, probably breaking several hundred FAA regulations, until they were beyond the immediate periphery of the airport. Theo swallowed. His ears kept popping. He and the others settled in the best they could.

Christoph, now that the excitement was over, was trying not to let on that being in an airplane scared him shitless. As soon as the shooting had stopped, he'd strapped himself down, and every few minutes he unobtrusively added another knot to the nylon straps that held him down. He had enough slack left for two or three more knots. Theo wondered what Christoph would do after that. The archon had seen this kind of thing before; it wasn't that uncommon with Kindred who predated air travel. Christoph, one of those who preferred a sword to modern firearms, would seem to be a prime example.

Frankie was doing well enough—considering that he'd had his head nearly ripped off a week and a half ago. He'd recovered physically, more or less, but there had been some nerve or structural damage or something like that. Not too surprising since Theo and all the others, by all rights, shouldn't be walking around anyway. Undead physiology was not always predictable. For Frankie, though, the physical trauma of having his neck broken, or maybe the emotional blow of losing his friend Baldur, had left him scarred. In the past, he'd always been fairly even-tempered for a Brujah. He'd been predictable and reliable, if not the sharpest nail in the coffin. Now, however, in the cargo hold, he had squeezed himself between two stacks of crates and gone practically catatonic. He wasn't curled into fetal position or anything like that, but he was far from aware of anything that was going on around him. Theo figured he could shoot Frankie in the foot and the other Malkavian probably wouldn't notice for a few hours. It came and went, this detachment from reality. At times, Frankie was his old self, but at others…

Another body, Theo thought. That was all he could count on Frankie to be. Another of the walking dead. But then again, that was all of them. Maybe Frankie had just slipped one step closer to what was in store for all of them eventually. Less a person, more the walking dead.

And if that wasn't enough to make a cheerful bunch, there was Lydia. As the plane bumped through light turbulence, she was glaring daggers at Theo. She wasn't rattled by the shooting anymore, now that they were in the air. Just pissed. No big deal. Let her stare all she wanted. Didn't bother him. She'd either get over it, in which case she'd probably get along okay, or she wouldn't. If not, if she allowed herself to be distracted by things that she couldn't control, by things that happened all too often over the course of a century or two, then she would probably get her head blown off sooner or later. Theo would just have to make sure that she didn't do something that got *his* head blown off. But he had a lot of experience with that sort of thing. This takeoff excluded, it wasn't often that he put himself in a situation where his ass was on the line if somebody else fucked up.

Maybe that was what had bothered him about the whole thing with Jan—not knowing about the spy, not knowing if that other end of the plan was covered or if all of Theo's own work was going to go for nothing. In a way, it wasn't that different from what Lydia faced—that had been stuff that Theo could only affect so much, so he'd gone on with his own job, done it well, and things had mostly worked out. So far.

Theo glanced at his watch. A few hours. They should arrive just after dawn. Pieterzoon would take care of them—this was the type of thing that Theo more or less trusted Jan with, that the Ventrue was well-practiced with: logistics, receiving four roughly human-sized crates, and getting them to a safe haven. And then the real fun would start.

Theo closed his eyes and looked forward to an hour or two of relaxation—not having to think about anything—before he needed to climb into one of the crates.

Lydia took it for as long as she could, but the droning, deafening hum of the engines didn't soothe her. If anything, the constant vibration served only to agitate her further. And there was Theo, sitting across the hold from her, ignoring her. He even closed his eyes and leaned his head back—like he was asleep, like he would ever sleep again…at night!

Almost before she realized, Lydia was on her feet, making her way across the hold. She was standing over Theo. This time, this one time, she was looking down at him. He knew she was there. She could feel that he did. But he didn't open his eyes, didn't do anything, didn't say anything.

Lydia stood there, looking down at him, feeling the engines through her feet and her legs. A few weeks ago, she'd been completely in awe of Theo—hell, she was still in awe of him. Even tonight, out there in the park, she'd seen what he could do, what he was capable of. But something had changed. Over those weeks of patrolling, of finding Sabbat vampires and blowing their fucking brains out, something had changed. It didn't seem to be Theo; he was as steady, as inflappable as ever. He never even had to raise his voice. He didn't have to shoot at Jasmine in some shithole bar. He didn't have to take crap from anybody. Maybe, Lydia decided, it was her that had changed.

She kicked Theo's foot. Hard.

Very slowly, he opened his eyes. He looked at her with that cool, not-pissed-but-not-happy-either look, his normal look, as if he'd just met her on the street, as if nobody had been shooting at them, as if she hadn't just kicked him. So she kicked him again.

"What?" was all he said. His voice was deep, barely audible above the engine noise, but that one word carried the obvious message: *Do that again and you'll wish you hadn't.*

So she did it again. She kicked him—kicked *at* him, at least. Theo caught her foot. Or Lydia, picking herself up after crashing against the far wall, figured he must have. She was back on her feet in a second—the ringing in her ears blended in with the engine noise quickly enough—ready for anything. Theo was still sitting in the same spot. He hadn't bothered to get up.

"Don't you do it!" she yelled at him. "Don't you pretend I'm not here, you fuckin' bastard! Don't you dare close your eyes again!"

Nearby, Frankie didn't stir from whatever he was experiencing in his own little world. Christoph, like a puzzled Houdini, looked on but didn't move. Theo, too, looked at her. He wasn't pissed, he wasn't amused. He was just...Theo. Grim, angry just below the surface. He was calm, and that enraged Lydia more than anything.

"Fuck you!" She spat in his direction. She was pacing now—she vaguely realized that she was—a few steps back and forth, like a caged animal. Her hands were shaking.

Theo watched her from where he sat. "What's on your mind?" he asked, his voice calm but not soothing, patient only in that he hadn't gotten up and bashed her head in.

What's on your mind? As if he didn't damned well know. It was a simple enough question…*seemed* like a simple enough question, but Lydia couldn't quite form the words to answer him. Her thoughts wouldn't hold still. She couldn't grab them; they were swirling, violent, like the rushing air that buffeted the plane.

"You know," she said finally. "You been pretendin' it didn't happen, but it did!"

Baldur. He'd met his Final Death, crumbled to dust as Lydia had watched, and for more than a week, Theo had said nothing about it, had pretended that nothing had happened, just like he'd been pretending a minute ago that Lydia wasn't there. There was a reason, Lydia knew. He'd told her, told all of them, but she wasn't buying it.

This never happened, Theo had said before they left the warehouse that night. *Vitel disappeared, faded away. Far as anybody knows, he probably slipped out of the city. Just wanted to save his own ass. None of this,* he'd said in the smoke- and body-filled warehouse, *ever happened.*

And that meant that Baldur had just disappeared. Faded away. Without a trace. And that didn't sit well with Lydia.

"Tell me about it," Theo said, the droning of the engines almost drowning out the sound of his voice.

"This once…" he said, pausing, leaving unsaid the last part of the sentence, *and then never again.* "Tell me."

Lydia stopped pacing. She was caught off guard. She hadn't been ready for that. She wasn't sure what she *was* ready for, but that wasn't it. Her thoughts were still churning, still angry, her every muscle, her blood, ready for conflict. She balled her fingers into fists to stop the shaking.

"I know we can't talk about Vitel," she started weakly. Words were so uncertain. They weren't what she'd wanted. What she'd wanted—and she knew it suddenly, saw it, now that the impulse crested, fell back—was blood. Her knees felt like they were going to give. She felt pale, cold, more aware of it than ever before. She felt more *dead* than she ever had, as if what she'd eventually accepted intellectually was finally coming home to her body.

"Jesus." She lowered herself to the floor, sat with her unsteady legs stretched out before her, black denim hiding cold, dead flesh.

"Baldur was always there for us," she said. "And now he's just gone, and we just let him go, like he never was here. I don't like it."

Theo crossed his arms. "What the hell d'you want me to do? Buy an ad in the paper?"

Lydia's anger started to rise again, tried to, but she was too tired. Her body seemed not to be hers; the cargo hold seemed very large and Theo very far away. Her thoughts, so violent and churning moments before, were dissipating, dissolving like a morning fog burned away by the sun. Maybe the sun was rising beyond the walls of the plane.

"Look," Theo said, "I'm not your momma, and I'm not your shrink. I'm not here to hold your hand. You don't pull your shit together, before long you won't be no good to me or to anybody else."

Lydia was sinking. Otherwise, she would've told him to fuck off. But Theo was very far away. Maybe it was the sun, but it felt different somehow, like it was her blood pulling her down for some other reason. She felt like she'd been climbing, climbing to the brink of...of something. She'd almost gone over, but now she was tumbling back down the hill.

"Baldur's gone," she heard Theo say. "It was his time. Some night it'll be yours, and some night it'll be mine. And maybe somebody'll cry, and maybe they won't, but I don't really give a shit. I got things to do while I'm here."

He might have said more. Lydia wasn't sure. Probably he hadn't, she decided. Theo wasn't one for speeches. Either way, Lydia was crawling into one of the long crates, forcing her body to go where she wanted it to go, pulling the top back on, not really feeling the splinters that dug into her fingers. She listened to the deep droning of the engines, felt the vibrations of her bones against wood, listened to the droning....

"He's right," said the voice. "He's right." A faint French accent. Christoph. Lydia didn't open her eyes. She wanted to, but not enough to force the issue. "We've all got things to do while we're here, or else we're not around very long. Fighting to be fighting isn't enough."

Lydia couldn't absorb what the voice was saying, what Christoph was saying. He had opened her crate. She could feel the cold air. Or was that just her skin?

"You've got to find a reason, Lydia."

What the hell was he talking about? She didn't want to hear, didn't want to think.

"Find a reason."

Yeah, whatever. Go the fuck away.

"Hook the latches on the lid," the voice said. The lid was back in place, the voice fainter. "Hook them!" A fierce pounding on the crate denied Lydia peace. She did what the voice said, fumbled at the latches, one at a time hooked them. The pounding was gone, and the voice. All that remained were, again, the plane's engines gently rattling her skull.

Thursday, 11 November 1999, 3:18 AM
Alfred Thayer House
Baltimore, Maryland

Temporarily Closed for Renovations read the sign on the front gate of the restored nineteenth-century house and former home of some local personage. No lights burned within the building. In the spacious parlor, Parmenides sat in darkness. Sat and waited. For what he was not exactly sure.

"Are you ready, my *philosophe?*" Vykos crooned from nearby. Her voice, though still pitched like that of a woman, was more nasal, almost mechanical, as if the larynx had been reshaped, only slightly, but in some strange manner. There remained no trace of the feminine about her words. "We are close now."

Parmenides waited in silence. He had given up trying to predict the actions or interpret the mutterings of this creature. She sat wrapped in darkness, her black robes indistinguishable from the shadows. All that was visible were her face, bone white, a vile beacon in the night, and one smooth, almost skeletal hand at her throat, as if she might at any moment choke herself.

"Are you ready, my *philosophe?*" she goaded him.

"I am ready." Whatever the task, the Assamite was prepared. This fiend, to whom his masters had delivered him, had over the past months required any number of deeds from her charge, deeds ranging from the dangerous to the mundane, from the perverse to the menial. He was Ravenna, prepared to serve the whim of this abomination that occupied his heart and mind; he was Parmenides, prepared also to carry out the terrible purpose of his masters.

"Excellent," said Vykos. Her eyes were not visible; they were hidden in the depths of hollowed sockets, beneath hairless and razor-sharp brows. "Then when my rivals assail me, you must strike me down."

The words hung in the darkness between them, between the Cainite and the child of Haqim. Parmenides doubted himself, doubted that he had heard correctly—the fiend supporting the terrible purpose of his masters, urging her own destruction.

"You are silent," Vykos said. "Have I not stimulated your mind as well as your body?"

"A thought unspoken is no less a thought," Parmenides said.

"Ah, there is my *philosophe*," said Vykos, but her words were cold, an emotionless mockery of her playful manner with him over many weeks, itself a mockery of true affection. Mockery of mockery. Just as the fiend was a mockery of all Cainites, themselves mockeries of frail humanity. "Good. I have not lost you. When my rivals assail me, you must strike me down," she said again.

"I…" Parmenides did not know how to respond, could not quickly enough unravel his tangled impulses.

"That is what you people do, is it not?" Now Vykos's words were not mocking, but measured, completely and utterly reasonable in their unreasonableness. "We will discover how much of the *philosophe* remains, will we not, Ravenna?"

Parmenides was distracted by the sound of several automobiles outside, not passing on the street, but stopping by the front gate.

"Soon," said Vykos. "Very soon."

A few more seconds passed. Parmenides could hear car doors slamming, the gate swinging open, footsteps climbing the stairs to the porch. The front door burst open, and in strode Cardinal Polonia. He was flanked, as was beginning to seem usual, by Costello on one side and Hardin on the other. Parmenides heard others, but they remained outside; they were spreading out, surrounding the house.

When my rivals assail me...

"You have betrayed us," Polonia's steely voice snaked through the darkness as forcefully as any of his shadow minions.

Little light from the open front door was able to make its way as far as the parlor. The gathered Cainites remained in darkness, as Polonia no doubt would have had it. Parmenides, however, was assaulted by lights. For him, lightning flashed, terrific bursts that left him leaning on his cane lest he collapse to the floor. Conflicting images assaulted him: There was Polonia confronting Vykos, the here and now. But there was also the image of himself on hands and knees, vomiting forth black liquid that he had suckled from Vykos's foul breast.

You must strike me down.

What is your passion? Vykos had asked him. Death. He was bred and trained for it. Destruction. *Who would you destroy?* He had told her Monçada, had misled her, kept from her his terrible purpose. But there was memory layered beneath memory, cloud upon cloud, lightning crossing lightning. Preceding the lie—the lie that was for *his* benefit, not hers—he had revealed all to her: his clandestine meeting with Fatima, the information he was seeking, his task once the knowledge was passed on.

Who would you destroy?

I would destroy you.

Ah, but the night was fated to come. It can be no different with your kind. When my rivals assail me, you must strike me down. You cannot betray your nature.

"Betray you, my Cardinal?" Vykos said. "But the city is yours…. If this is betrayal, then long reign the treachery of the Sabbat."

"We did not take the city," Polonia spat. "It was given to us, *handed* to us…and you knew. Your spy knew. Last night's resistance was for show, a token defense. We surrounded the city, cut off the airport. There was no mass exodus to the north or any other direction, not by land or sea, yet *they are not here*. They are not hiding in wait for us. They are not here!"

"Then the city is yours," Vykos said again, as if speaking to a slow child. "The last Camarilla city on the East Coast taken in a bloodless coup of your arranging. What more could you want?"

"I want to *crush* them," Polonia said through clenched teeth.

Parmenides, still reeling from the lightning of his own self-discovery, could sense the tension in the cardinal's muscles, could see the outline of the sword at his belt, even in the darkness.

"You have betrayed us," Polonia repeated. "Now you will come with me, and I will determine what else you have kept hidden."

"Ah," Vykos sighed. "This was bound to happen without Monçada to stand watch over you, eh? Tell me, did you wait to move against me out of fear of him, or merely so that I could first help you win your war?"

"Say what you like. We stand united against you, Archbishop."

Vykos laughed: the sound of bone grating against bone. "You may have your cities, Cardinal. I do not care for them. As for standing united against me, I have little doubt. You have spoken with Bolon then, who cannot fashion his own war ghouls to command. And good Gregorio, my clansman?"

"Gregorio is loyal, as much as any fiend can be," Polonia said. "Bolon has been dealt with." The cardinal gave a slight, mocking bow. "Now...you will come with me." Polonia's hand moved to the hilt of his sword, but he paused.

There were more footsteps now, a single set ascending the front steps, entering the house. A young aide to Polonia, a junior Lasombra whom Parmenides had seen before, came into the parlor. The aide hesitated, sensing the tension between the leaders, but he was driven by the task entrusted to him.

"Your Eminence," he said to the cardinal, "news from Bishop Mendes. There is trouble in New York."

Polonia, still not forgetting Vykos, regarded the messenger skeptically. "Trouble—what sort of trouble? What did Armando say?"

"The news is not from the bishop *directly*," the

younger Lasombra clarified somewhat sheepishly. "Apparently he is…occupied."

"Occupied? Yes?"

"Apparently New York is…well…under attack."

Parmenides imagined that Polonia did not care to appear surprised in front of his underlings, because his obvious shock transformed almost instantly to rage. His eyes, flaring wide for an instant, narrowed. His dark, handsome, Spanish face contorted violently. To the cardinal's credit, he didn't sputter and bluster about the impossibility of an attack, as Borges might have done in similar circumstances, but neither could Polonia seem to accept that the oversight, the *fault*, could lie with him. Instead, he turned back to Vykos.

"You and your damnable spy arranged this!" Polonia bellowed, then his sword was unsheathed and in motion. The strike blurred toward Vykos's head— but was deflected at the last instant. The cane should have been shattered by the force of fine Toledo steel, would have been had not Parmenides's parry been timed and angled perfectly.

In the same motion that he blocked Polonia's sword with the spiked cane, Parmenides lashed out with another blade. Two quick slashes at Costello's eyes. The Lasombra stumbled backward screaming, hands over his face, blood streaming between his fingers.

Polonia recovered quickly and struck again— where Vykos had been standing but an instant before. The cardinal's sword found only air. Vykos had skillfully shifted to interpose her assassin-ghoul directly between herself and her assailants.

When my rivals assail me, you must strike me down.

Parmenides stood between archbishop and cardinal, Vykos's words, lightning, flashing through his mind. This was undeniably the moment—the moment to act upon his mistress's command, the moment to fulfill the terrible purpose given him by his masters from Alamut. This was the moment to turn and strike down the Tzimisce fiend that had violated him body and soul.

But the assassin could not strike, could not raise blade or hand against his torturer…his love, she who had made him what he was. *We will discover how much of the* philosophe *remains, will we not, Ravenna?* And in that instant of impotence, the question was answered. Not enough of the *philosophe*, not enough of the assassin, the Assamite. He was Ravenna. Created to serve his mistress. He passed one test only to fail another, his purpose for existence supplanted by this fiend! This, in the space of a human heartbeat.

Polonia's sword, raised again, fell. Ravenna blocked it not with the cane but with his own arm. Steel struck flesh, dug deeply, cut into bone—but did not pull free. Pain like fire coursed up Ravenna's arm, and he smiled. He smiled because, at the same time, with a flourish of black robes and one last alabaster sneer, Vykos was gone. Ravenna knew that she would be free, that he had served his purpose—her purpose for him.

The sword lodging in the ghoul's arm threw off Polonia's timing for a moment, and in that moment Ravenna plunged the ferrule spike of the cane through the cardinal's right hand, splintering bone, severing tendons and nerves. Polonia jerked his hand back. He managed, barely, to keep hold of the sword as it pulled free of Ravenna's arm.

Hardin rushed in with his falchion as the cardinal stepped back. The Lasombra messenger, too, had produced a weapon, a pistol that he was firing ineffectually above their heads. Ravenna, with his stiletto in his good hand, met Hardin's charge. The transformed assassin drew his blade along his useless arm, coating the blade with the toxin of Assamite blood. He brushed aside Hardin's awkward thrust and buried the stiletto deep in his attacker's gut. Hardin seized up almost at once, the poison taking hold. His falchion clattered to the floor. He raked frantically at the burning wound in his abdomen, but the poison spread, the fire shooting through his body.

Before Hardin hit the floor, Ravenna had flung his blade at the messenger. It sliced through his esophagus, coming to rest lodged in his spine. There was some poison still on the blade—enough, Ravenna suspected.

The guards from outside would rush in soon, he knew. But there was still time. As he reached for another hidden blade, however, the shadows closed in about him, slowing his movements. He tried to dive away, but the darkness was nearly solid; it held him in place—far too easy a target for Polonia to miss, even wielding a sword with his off hand.

The steel bit down through Ravenna's shoulder. Had the blow been a few inches farther from his neck, it would have severed his right arm. The next blow destroyed his right knee, and Ravenna collapsed to the floor slowly, the darkness cushioning his fall.

The enraged Polonia stood above him, and, as blow after blow fell, hacking Ravenna to pieces, Vykos's ghoul smiled.

Thursday, 11 November 1999, 3:51 AM
East 129th Street, Harlem
New York City, New York

The blood-splattered drywall sizzled. So did the clothing and flesh bordering the massive, charred hole in the chest of the man of the floor. A few sputtering flames lent ghostly shape to the wisps of smoke rising from the wound. The hallway was dark otherwise. No electricity. The tenement was abandoned except for a few squatters: homeless, down on their luck, drug-addicted, illegal immigrants, mentally ill, whatever. They were nothing more than food to the predators among them.

Theo slipped another dragonsbreath round into the shotgun's magazine. Full up. He'd need to be— had needed to be all night. He'd used more ammo tonight than in the fight with Vitel. And the night wasn't over yet. Not quite.

He stepped over the body. The phosphorous blast at close range probably would have been enough to finish this Sabbat nobody, but for good measure the corpse had a crushed skull as well, the deep indentation conspicuously shaped like the metal butt of Theo's Franchi SPAS. They were like cockroaches, these Sabbat flunkies. Individually they weren't much of a threat, at least not to Theo, but they carried disease. Sickness spread wherever they gained a foothold. Society crumbled. The poor and the weak suffered the most; the disadvantaged preyed upon one another. It happened other places too, but when the Sabbat vermin infested a neighborhood, a city, it was far worse. They didn't give a shit about the kine. Neither did most members of the Camarilla, Theo knew, but the order provided by the Masquerade at least gave the mortals half a chance to pull themselves up, to fight the prejudices of their own society rather than being consumed by the hunger of the shadow predators. The archon might not have approved of everything that had happened tonight, but progress was progress.

Theo paused, looked back at the corpse, spat on it. Then he opened the door to the basement and began down into the darkness.

Almost twenty-four hours earlier, the Eurofreight cargo jet had touched down at JFK International Airport. Theo had already secured himself inside one of the crates on board and surrendered to the oblivion of day, but he resurfaced enough to know that he was being unloaded. He was not cognizant to the point that he could worry—which he would have if he'd been able.

Pieterzoon had made the arrangements for this part of the trip. That was tolerable, as far as it went. But Jan had been forced to deal with representatives of Clan Giovanni. The smuggling of an individual Camarilla member into New York, especially through JFK, was nothing irregular. It happened often enough to have prompted Sabbat leadership—most notably, Francisco de Polonia, who reports indicated had assumed the mantle of cardinal of the Eastern United States—to send roving packs through the airport periodically. But the airport bureaucracy was riddled with Camarilla agents and sympathizers of one sort or another, and the smuggling continued.

In the past forty-eight hours, however, practically every member of the Camarilla that had escaped Baltimore, including most of the refugees from the rest of the East Coast, had been ferried through JFK and LaGuardia. A half-dozen obscure air-freight companies had directed flights to New York, many rerouted through various cities or with falsified itinerary and flight manifests, but all having passed through Baltimore. All of the companies were owned or controlled by one of three different holding companies, which in turn were subsidiaries of firms that, if someone wanted to spend the time and resources, could be traced back to Jan Pieterzoon. Not to Pieterzoon himself, of course, but to a dummy board to which he had no ostensible connection. If anyone *were* to dig that far, though, they would certainly attract the attention of Mr. Pieterzoon, and the investigation would be brought to a conclusion, by one means or another.

For an undertaking of this unprecedented scale, there was another faction which, through various mob and financial guises, had its fingers in almost as many union and bureaucratic pies as did the Ventrue, and could not be ignored: Clan Giovanni. Pieterzoon didn't need the necromancers' help, *per se*, as much as their acquiescence—and their silence. After abortive initial negotiations, a bit of hardball, Ventrue style, in the form of the Italian currency crisis, had convinced the relevant Giovanni that looking the other way in this case might not be such a bad thing. Thus the airlift had proceeded, and thus Theo found himself spending the day in a crate in a storage hangar at JFK.

The fact that the Brujah archon was too under the sway of the sun even to worry only made him that much more vulnerable. He'd known that that would be the case, and so he'd done his brooding ahead of time. Being among the very last to leave Baltimore as the Sabbat closed in, though dangerous, hadn't bothered him. That had been part of the plan—*his* part of the plan. This, he'd had to admit grudgingly, had been part of the plan too, but it was part where he had to depend on others, a Ventrue and—God help him—some faceless Giovanni who wasn't likely to be loyal to anybody who wasn't his cousin, if that. What did some greasy customs mole in the U.S. care if Italy's economy went in the tank? And it wasn't as if anything innately Italian spawned loyalty—Axis, Allies, Sabbat, Camarilla, whatever.

In the weeks leading up to the pullout from Baltimore, Theo had kept his mind on other parts of the plan, parts that were right then and there. There had always been the chance that they would never even get this far. But they had, and there he was, and when Theo climbed out of the crate that night, someone was there waiting for him.

"Right this way, sir," said Hans van Pel. Theo looked at Pieterzoon's ghoul and then at the other crates, those that contained Lydia, Frankie, and Christoph. Van Pel followed his glance. "They will be brought along separately."

Theo and van Pel got into the back of one of two unmarked delivery vans. Within thirty minutes, the van pulled onto the grounds of Aqueduct Racetrack. The smell of horses was unmistakable in the air: sweat, grain, manure. The odors took Theo back—back to what he didn't care to be reminded of, his mortal years in Mississippi, the plantation years, the years when humans were bought and bred like horse or cattle stock. Theo was a product of that world, but he had rebelled against it, risked his life to overturn it, and in the end outlasted it. Now, looking over the van driver's shoulder, the Brujah watched the track facilities, deserted except for a few cleaning crews, pass by. The place was eerily quiet at night, empty other than the familiar horse smells, and other smells that he noticed now: stale cigarettes and beer, human sweat too. The scents mingled and formed what Theo could think of only as the smell of desperation.

Those earthy, plebian odors retreated as van Pel led Theo into the track offices, to a suite that was ostensibly an auxiliary office for the New York Racing Association. This was the turf of the modern high-rollers, dealing in horse flesh.

"Ah, here is Archon Bell now," said Jan Pieterzoon warmly. He rose from his seat at a crowded conference table.

Van Pel took his place behind Jan, but Theo stopped in the doorway. He and Jan had carried their scheme this far, but looking at the other Kindred around the table, Theo wondered if all their planning had been shot to hell. Lucinde was there; that was no surprise—not this time. The Ventrue justicar had come from Baltimore with Jan. She'd helped him with convincing the Giovanni to cooperate; she'd done some kind of deal with Hesha; she'd consulted with Jan regarding the spy. Now she was here, in business suit and gloves, appearing deceptively young.

Neither was it a surprise to see Michaela, prince of New York. Jan had been in contact with her for some time. It was her city after all—at least nominally—that they were betting everything on. Michaela was very proud of having held on to the city for the Camarilla. She had long boasted of having kept the Sabbat out of Manhattan—mostly. To Theo, that meant that she had held on to the blue-blood financial district—like the Sabbat was going to try to waltz into the boardrooms anyway—and let everything else, the majority of the city, all the *real* parts of the city, go to hell. In addition to this limited—in his opinion—success, she'd managed to seriously piss off quite a few higher ups in the Camarilla by Embracing a considerable number of stuffed shirts—eight or nine by most counts. Even Lucinde had criticized her clanmate. What would happen, the justicar had asked, if Michaela came to an unfortunate end and left that many equally powerful childer behind, all of whom would certainly want their share of the inheritance? Internecine warfare, that's what. A civil war within the city that would claim much blood or, just as bad, balkanization. Either way, the "stronghold" that had been Manhattan would be compromised, and the Sabbat would be that much closer to traipsing in and taking over for real.

In recent years, though, the problem had begun to alleviate itself somewhat. Several of Michaela's progeny had themselves met unfortunate ends, some ambushed in the city by Sabbat packs who seemed to know where to find them, others simply disappeared. There were those in the Camarilla who argued that the Sabbat was making a determined effort to undercut Michaela's power base in preparation for storming Manhattan. Theo had other suspicions. He wasn't one to cast aspersions or make unfounded accusations, but surely there were those in their own sect who would be more than pleased to see Michaela out of the way. Those kind of sentiments, if shared by a large enough number of Kindred, and at high enough a level, tended to be acted upon.

Only three of Michaela's brood remained, and they were all seated at the table. Suit-and-tie business sort. They were, in Theo's opinion, being treated above their station. Sure this was their home turf, but what the fuck did they all need to be here for? After all, Lladislas wasn't here, neither was Goldwin, and he'd been a prince, in title at least, before they'd ditched Baltimore. Gainesmil wasn't here. Hell, there weren't *any* Toreador in the room. This was the kind of stunt—thumbing her nose at the other clans—that got Michaela in trouble.

There were two more Kindred at the crowded table. One was ruggedly handsome and wearing clothes that Theo considered dressy but the high-society types would call casual. This Kindred looked like the cover off a catalogue come to life—he might as well be. Theo had met Federico diPadua before and knew that the square chin and strong brow hid that bone-ugly that could only be Nosferatu. Federico was a decent sort, as far as Kindred went.

The other man at the table wore a suit, but he wasn't one of Michaela's stuffed shirts. A white orchid graced his lapel. "Archon Bell," said Jaroslav Pascek briskly, "we've been waiting."

Sucks to be you, Theo thought, but held his tongue. Taunting a justicar was generally not a bright idea. Besides, something big was going on here, something big enough to attract two justicars, whether Theo liked it or not. He glanced at Jan, but the Ventrue didn't meet his eyes. Still something about Jan's manner—the perfect, *practiced* normalcy of his manner—made Theo think that some of this, at least, was news to him as well. *Shit*, Theo thought, holding down his aggravation with the secrecy and fuck-you politics of the Camarilla higher-ups. *It could be worse*, he reminded himself.

Pascek watched Theo impatiently. The green specks in the justicar's hazel eyes seemed to glow with an inner fire. "You and Mr. Pieterzoon have devised a passable plan," he said to Theo. "We've made some changes."

That was when Theo knew that it *was* worse. And he had a feeling in his gut that it always would be.

In the basement of the tenement in Harlem, they were waiting for Theo. Firing his shotgun upstairs a few minutes before hadn't exactly left a lot of room for sneaking, so he was expecting them too. At times like these, Theo took pride in the fact that he always seemed better able to predict what his enemies would do than what his allies would do. As he went down the stairs, the darkness deepening with each step, he felt the tendril of shadow snaking around his feet before it was able to trip him. He ducked so he wouldn't hit the ceiling, and jumped the tendril and the last few steps.

As soon as his feet touched the floor, he whirled and fired into the room. The muzzle flash and the exploding phosphorous shell lit the room like a streak of lightning at midnight. For that split second, Theo could see them clearly. Two were within a few feet of him, one with a baseball bat, one pointing a revolver at him. A third was not far. The Lasombra maybe. A fourth—wide-eyed, deformed monstrosity; a Nosferatu that had lost its concentration, not a Tzimisce creation—was in the corner.

After the flashes, the room plunged into total darkness. Theo stepped toward the Sabbat with the bat, stepped into the swing that had to be coming. The attacker thought he was hitting something two feet farther away. The handle of the bat and the Sabbat's hand pounded Theo's shoulder.

At the same time, the revolver fired. Theo had moved enough that the bullet struck him a glancing blow, didn't make it through his reinforced jacket. Theo fired his shotgun again—at the corner. The Nosferatu was the most likely to get away. Theo didn't plan on anybody getting away. The misshapen thing was lit up by phosphorous fireworks and slammed back into the wall, screaming, squealing.

Another blast from the revolver—this time square in the back. The Sabbat had a better idea again where Theo was standing after the veritable flare from the shotgun. The jacket helped, but the bullet penetrated, and stung like hell.

By feel, Theo clicked the SPAS from single shot to burst, and fired. The Lasombra practically disintegrated in a fiery spray. The shot bathed an entire wall in chemical light. The angle, as luck would have it, was good enough to send the revolver-wielding Sabbat down screaming too.

Sputtering phosphorous and flaming shreds of clothing cast an uneven pall across the room, which was quickly filling with smoke and the pungent smell of burning flesh. Theo looked for the Nosferatu—saw him dragging himself toward the stairs, going nowhere fast with wounds he couldn't heal and too shaken up to concentrate and disappear.

The Sabbat with the bat, a bruiser almost as large as Theo, was more reckless, or maybe frenzied, than smart. He charged, swinging. Theo blocked the bat with his forearm. The wood splintered, the barrel flying over Theo's shoulder. Theo smashed the stock of the SPAS into the Sabbat's face. The nose and left cheek bone gave way. The bloodied slugger crumpled to the floor. Back to single shot. One more white-hot blast and it was over.

Except for the mopping up. The Sabbat who had shot Theo was still moving. Theo replaced the couple of dragonsbreath rounds that were still in the magazine with conventional cartridges and blew the Sabbat's head off.

Then Theo walked over to the Nosferatu—the Nosferatu *antitribu*—who had pulled himself up to the fifth step. "I was spying on them," he pleaded through yellowed teeth clenched in pain.

I don't think so, Theo thought. The loyal Nosferatu knew what was going on. Federico's few words at the track had made that clear enough. If this was a Cam Nossie, it wouldn't have been here. Not tonight. Theo had no use for *antitribu*. Lasombra and Tzimisce were bad enough, but if it weren't for defectors from the Camarilla, the Sabbat wouldn't have the numbers to thrive. Probably one of the other fuckers on the floor was—had been—*antitribu*. It was a seductive call for somebody who was sick of taking orders, sick of being told what to do and pushed around. But it was just trading masters.

Theo sometimes wondered what would have happened to him if Don Cerro hadn't found him, if he hadn't been Embraced. He had achieved his freedom as a mortal. Probably he would have been shot eventually, while helping other slaves escape. Or he would have been captured and hanged. But he would have died a free man. Instead, he'd agreed to a deal with the devil. He'd received the power to avenge himself, to avenge his people, and while he wasn't exactly a slave to his masters in the Camarilla, he sure as hell wasn't free. How much more plainly could that point have been driven home tonight?

"Please…" the Nosferatu pleaded.

Theo cocked his shotgun. Finished it. Then he climbed the rest of the steps to find the others.

Earlier, around the conference table at Aqueduct Racetrack, nobody had minced words. Theo hadn't even sat down. The Ventrue present didn't say much. Maybe that was what made the briefing seem unusual, surreal. Jan, even Lucinde, listened attentively. Pascek did most of the talking, and as the Brujah justicar spoke, Theo became even more convinced that much of what was happening had been sprung on Jan at the last moment too.

"You and Mr. Pieterzoon have devised a passable plan. We've made some changes," Jaroslav started.

"There have been certain preparations that allow us a more aggressive stance, and the strike teams you've coordinated have been altered somewhat. Archon diPadua will be leading one, as will Prince Michaela, as will myself, in addition to you and those others you selected, such as Lladislas, et cetera, et cetera." Though he spoke with a Slavic accent, Pascek's words were crisp, terse. He was giving instructions, not seeking advice. "Today's activities have been singularly successful," he said, "and I trust tonight will be no different."

"Today's activities…" Theo repeated.

"Yes. Our ghouls have been quite effective," Pascek said quickly. "Law enforcement and city services have served us in good stead: known Sabbat ghouls arrested or executed; widespread destruction of Sabbat lairs. Our contacts among the local media are focusing attention nicely on the heroism of emergency workers. No one will have a chance to explore the possible relation among fires, industrial accidents, burst gas mains, demolitions, et cetera, et cetera, for several days, if at all—that 'support our boys in the field' mentality. Quite helpful of you Americans."

There was no laughter, if indeed Pascek's last comment had been an attempt at wry humor. The justicar was not known for his joviality. Next he launched into a machine-gun recitation of the strike teams: "Prince Michaela, you and yours will lead four teams and cover the Bronx. Here's a list of addresses; those crossed off were seen to today. Archon Bell, you are familiar with Harlem. Three teams. Your list…"

Theo was not surprised to see those assembled defer to Pascek, even Lucinde and Michaela—although Michaela seemed particularly sullen, which made Theo suspect that she had been as much out of the loop for the overall plan as he and Jan. Pascek gave decisive orders—this was his element, search and destroy, rooting out evil, in this case the Sabbat. To say that his arrangements were "more aggressive" was a phenomenal understatement. He had about the same number of Kindred to work with that Theo and Jan had—utilizing the mass exodus from Baltimore—but it was amazing the difference a few battle-tested elders could make.

And an extra archon and two justicars, for Christ's sake, Theo thought. That still rankled. In fact, he resented it more and more as Jaroslav talked. He and Jan had been left to slap together what they could, to get by on their own when these other resources had been available—not only available but committed to a parallel plan to the one they had come up with. The two had made the hard decisions—to sacrifice Buffalo and Hartford for the dual purposes of concentrating forces and smoking out the spy. Then, by slowly drawing their defenders back into Baltimore, they'd suckered the Sabbat into using everything it could muster for a *coup de grâce*, into attacking just as the Camarilla was striking elsewhere, where many of the invaders of Baltimore had just been taken from—New York. Jan and Theo's plan had been necessarily more modest: Shore up Manhattan, press into the Bronx, establish a beachhead in Brooklyn. They had negotiated and worked it out with Michaela, who was pleased to accept the influx of manpower but was not excited about possible rivals to her authority. They'd set it all in motion—held off the Sabbat, suckered them in, dealt with the spy, abandoned Baltimore, arrived in New York to find...

That others had taken over, and that their own efforts had been a screen, a diversion, for what had been going on behind the scenes all along. Because from what Pascek was saying, it was obvious that the preparations had been underway for months, perhaps years. The ghoul attacks, as Theo saw reading over some of the lists, were too surgical, the intelligence gathered too complete for this to have been hastily arranged. From what he could tell, as much as a quarter to a third of the Sabbat strength in the city, mostly ghouls and lower-echelon types—Theo didn't recognize many of the names or pictures—had already been ass-fucked. Tonight would probably push that figure over half. Meanwhile, the Sabbat was partying in Baltimore and maybe starting to figure out what had happened.

The whole thing smelled of Lucinde. It had been so invisible until the last second. Theo wouldn't have been surprised if Michaela had been involved, if she'd led him and Jan on, knowing what was coming, setting them up. But no, she was the type who would gloat. She was too pissed off right now. She was out of the loop, and that didn't bode well for a prince trying to hold her own against a justicar.

Against two justicars, damn it all, Theo thought.

"Mr. Pieterzoon," Pascek was saying, "you will coordinate strike-force activities with support from the Tremere. Regent Sturbridge will be arriving shortly."

Jan nodded. He wasn't looking too chipper either, Theo noted. But like the Brujah archon, Pieterzoon did a better job hiding his resentment than did Michaela hers.

As long as we fuck the Sabbat, Theo kept telling himself. That would make it all worth it. He may have been hung out by Pascek—justicar, fanatic, asshole—but if it worked, that was what mattered. Like so much Theo did as archon, the end justified the means. It had to.

"Damnedest thing I ever seen," Reggie said.

Eustace nodded and kept an even pace with his friend. "I think that white girl and that black girl was..." he searched for the right phrase, "you know...shacked up." Now he started shaking his head. "That's how you get them mongrel breeds."

"With two women?"

Eustace saw his partner's point. "Well, you know what I mean."

They walked in silence now—or without talking, at least. There was no real silence. Even at this time of the morning, a good number of people were out and about, staggering home late, or on the way to early work.

"The city that never sleeps," Reggie said to himself.

"Huh?"

"The city that never sleeps—that's what they call it. New York City."

"Oh. They ought to call it the city where don't nobody speak English. I swear, except for us, I don't think I've heard ten words of English all night. We *are* still in America, right?"

"Uh-huh."

"All three of them Sabbat fellas we caught were jabberin' something at us. You understand any of it?"

"Nope."

"Then again, I guess we weren't sent to stop by for tea with them."

"Nope."

Three jobs carried out successfully, now they just had to find the safehouse and hole up until tomorrow night.

"We on the right block yet?" Reggie asked.

Eustace took a scrap of paper from his pocket as they walked. He checked the address, checked a street sign. "Not yet."

One block looked pretty much like the next: row after row of brick tenements, shops and cafes on the ground floor, z-stacks of fire escapes. Only the accents changed.

"This a Jewish fella we're supposed to stay with?" Eustace asked. "I don't know Jewish. I hope he speaks English."

"Yiddish."

"Huh?"

"They talk Yiddish."

"Don't say."

"Uh-huh."

"Well, I still hope he…"

Reggie and Eustace both noticed the stranger at about the same time. It took a lot to stand out from the kind of folks they'd been seeing all night, but this was not a run-of-the-mill vagrant. He was dressed as shabbily as a lot of them, but what set him apart was the thick, yellowish discharge running down his chest from his face, from his eye.

Eustace stopped, grabbed Reggie's arm, pointed. "Je-*sus*. Look at all that pus. I guess that'd make him a…*pus*-sy." Eustace chuckled.

Reggie wasn't so sure this was a laughing matter. The closer he looked, the more he decided there was something seriously not right about the vagrant's eye, his left eye. "It don't fit right."

"What was that?" Eustace asked.

"Looking, yes?" the vagrant asked. He seemed to be talking to them. "Looking for…?" He started moving closer.

Eustace sniffed at the air. "Jesus, do you smell that? We must've walked out of Little Italy and right into Little Leper Colony."

"Looking for…? *Won't* find…" The vagrant was coming toward them still.

Reggie took a step back. He had a bad feeling, a feeling he hadn't gotten even from the inhuman Sabbat creatures he'd encountered over the past months. "Look, buddy, you keep your distance, or somebody's gonna get hurt."

The vagrant stopped, smiled, nodded emphatically. And then the sidewalk opened up beneath Reggie and Eustace. It just wasn't there, and they were falling. They landed hard at the bottom of a steep pit, but they didn't have time to worry about that. The walls of the pit were melting, and molten rock rushed down over them to fill the hole.

For agonizing seconds, Reggie could only see the eye gazing down at him, glowing….

She was straining against him with all her might, but somehow Hesha managed to keep his grip on her arm, to keep her from pulling away from him, to keep her from rushing to her doom. Ramona flashed him a glare of pure animal fury. He feared the Beast might take hold of her completely—it was so close to the surface, even at the best of times. She bared her fangs at him and growled, a feral, guttural rumble from deep in her throat.

"*Ramona!*" he hissed at her, forcefully enough to get her attention, not loudly enough for Leopold to discover them. Hesha's tongue flicked in and out of his mouth. Despite his years and years of practiced calm, the girl's near-frenzy was almost contagious.

She raised a hand to strike at him, claws glinting in the moonlight. Hesha did not flinch or turn away. He met her wild gaze, held it, would not let her look away.

"Ramona!" he whispered harshly. "If you do not stop, you will *fail your elders*. Their blood will remain on your hands."

She cringed at that. She drew back her hand but did not strike. Still Hesha held her gaze; he willed her return to sanity. And slowly, he saw the red fury fade from her eyes. She looked away from him now, quizzically, up at her own raised hand, at the claws that were no longer extended. Ramona lowered her arm.

Hesha let go of her other arm. "That was him," he said.

"Fuck, yes, that was him," Ramona snarled. Her words dripped bitterness. They had seen Leopold, had watched him kill, *again*, and had done nothing.

"You must be patient," Hesha said, "Or you'll end up like…"

"I know, I know." She smoothed her hair back, stretched her fingers against her legs as a cat stretches its claws. "But we just let him go…"

"We can find him again. Whatever was shielding him from me, is no longer. The gem I showed you—I can track him."

Ramona sneered. "Yeah, well, that didn't work so damn hot before tonight. What if it goes on the blink again?"

She was right. It was an infuriating habit she had. "I will find him," Hesha assured her. Let her argue. Frustrating as she might be, he needed her lucid; he needed to know what she could see. "Was it the same as before?" he asked.

"The Eye," she nodded, "yeah. He held it in his hand…and the nerve, bloody, hanging down from it, goin' into the ground."

Hesha watched her closely. That was not what he'd seen. Not what he'd seen at all. But he had reason to believe her. In fact, Ramona, and what she claimed to see, was his reason for hope.

"Come on," Hesha urged her, taking her by the arm and this time gently leading her away. "We'll find him again. You'll have your chance."

Ramona didn't resist him, but neither was she comforted. Her blood was up. And blood must answer blood.

Christoph had finished cleaning the blood from his sword; it was strapped on his back again, hidden beneath his trenchcoat. Frankie waited…patiently? The shoulder twitch he'd developed recently didn't seem to be a sign of impatience. It just was there sometimes, and this was one of those times. Lydia had a smudge of blood on her cheek. Theo licked his thumb, wiped her face hard.

"What the fuck?" Lydia pulled away.

"The Avon lady you ain't," Theo said; then, "Let's go." They had time to get back to the track but not a lot of time to spare.

"Shouldn't we check back over some of the places we hit?" Lydia asked. "Make sure nobody's crawling out now that we're gone?"

"Nope," Theo said. They *could* do what she suggested. It wasn't a bad idea. They could find a place to spend the day in this part of town without too much trouble, but they'd had a full night already, and Theo had personal business he wanted to attend to. He didn't have personal business very often. Usually there was business, and that was it. Theo didn't take too much personally. But when he did, like tonight, he wasn't about to be kept from it just because Lydia had gotten herself a taste for killing.

She stared at him but didn't say anything, didn't give him any shit like she'd started to on the airplane. Could be that she was just tired. A long night of tracking down Sabbat cronies and blasting their fucking heads off could do that to a person. God knew that Lydia had done more than her fair share of patrolling and fighting in Baltimore, but tonight had been one long string of rooting out the bastards and tearing them apart. Then again, maybe she wasn't tired. Maybe she just had a handle on the fire in her belly—like she hadn't on the plane. Theo gave her a hard stare, held her gaze until she looked away. He wished he knew. She was a good kid, mostly. Better than a lot of others. He'd come to depend on her over the past weeks. It'd be too bad if she gave in to the fire, if the Beast clawed its way out.

But Theo had lost other people he'd depended on. Depending on somebody was a luxury, not a necessity. Losing people, that was a reality. He'd gotten over it before; if it came to that, he could get over it again.

Theo trudged down the plain corridor that only ever saw fluorescent light. He had on his steel-toe-capped shit-kicking boots. Anybody looking closely would see dried blood—very recently dried—on the toes and heels. It had been a long night, longer than most, and it was late. He wouldn't be up for much longer—wouldn't be able to stay up much longer. Lydia and the others had already turned in. Most of the strike teams weren't being housed here at the track facilities. They were spread among various safe locations in secure portions of the city. But apparently Pascek wanted Theo nearby. For the moment, that suited Theo just fine.

He came to a particularly solid metal door, stopped, knocked.

"Enter," Jaroslav Pascek said from the other side.

Theo opened the door and went in. Despite his dislike for his boss, Theo was impressed that Pascek hadn't used his position to secure extravagant lodgings for himself. No perks—hell, very few basic comforts, for that matter. The room was small, cinderblock walls painted dingy white, uncovered cement floor. There was a metal-frame folding bed that had been made up neatly, sheet, blanket, pillow, no wrinkles. A closed suitcase rested, exactly centered, at the foot of the bed. The only other pieces of furniture were a metal chair, which Pascek sat in, a free-standing metal closet, doors closed, and a metal table against one wall. On the table lay a mace. Not a can of Mace. An honest-to-God, crack-your-skull-fucking-open mace. The knobby steel head was clean, almost polished, but Theo knew that tonight, like his boots and his shotgun, it had seen use. Pascek himself, in the chair, wore a loose robe tied at the waist. He was bare-chested and didn't seem displeased to see Theo. There was not another chair. Theo did not sit on the perfectly wrinkle-free bed. The room was indeed too small for him to want to move in beyond the doorway. He towered over the seated justicar, but even had Jaroslav stood, Theo would have towered over him almost as much. The archon folded his arms.

"Theo," Pascek said curtly, "successful night?"

Theo nodded.

"Good. Tomorrow the Tremere help us track the survivors, but we won't have the element of surprise like today and tonight. It was imperative that tonight go well. We already have a bead on Armando Mendes, by the way. Polonia's second-in-command." Pascek watched Theo for a moment. The justicar's expression took on a slightly curious aspect. He'd said what he had to say, and he didn't recall asking his archon for anything. "What do you want?"

That's a loaded fucking question, Theo thought, thinking also some of the many things that he could but wouldn't say. It wasn't a good idea to push a justicar, especially Pascek, too far. It wasn't a good idea to push him *at all*. It was bad from the start and just got worse and worse. Theo knew it was a bad idea for him to be here in the first place. But he could feel the fire. Fire and hunger, his twin curses. All

Kindred felt the hunger, but only Brujah truly knew the fire, the unrelenting *anger*. The hunger had been sated by blood tonight, and the fire had been assuaged through most of the night by the bloodletting, but as soon as Theo had started thinking about Pascek, the fire had been back. It was back now, growing.

"I wanna know why I didn't know what was goin' on," Theo said.

Pascek's face did not change at all, but instantly his gaze was hot, hard, as if he thought he could, from where he was sitting, crumble the cinderblock walls, collapse Theo's massive chest. "There is no middle ground," Pascek said quietly. "Are you challenging me on this?"

No middle ground. With us or against us. Your Camarilla, love it or leave it. Theo had heard all this before. "I did my job, didn't I?" he said. But he knew that the justicar, even without provocation, often saw treachery where others did not. And Theo was provoking Pascek, counting on his actions to account for himself. But motives could *always* be suspect.

Pascek regarded Theo a moment longer, then smiled. It was not a warm smile. It was the smile of someone who sets you on fire and then, very calmly, asks you to repent. The justicar abruptly moved on to other matters. "This Prince Goldwin from Baltimore, what can you tell me about him?"

Theo shrugged. "Not worth a shit."

Pascek actually laughed at that. "I see. And Gainesmil. Could he run a city?"

"Probably."

"And Lladislas?"

"He's done it. I hear he's in the market."

Pascek thought about that, then sighed. "Ah, but we could never replace a Ventrue with one of our own," he said.

Theo wasn't impressed by what Pascek was, in oh-so-general terms, hinting at. Was this the justicar's way of trying to convince Theo that the archon really was in his confidence, by suggesting that Michaela's position might be usurped, as if Theo couldn't have guessed that on his own? Or was Pascek more pointedly reminding his underling of the influence, the *power*, that was entrusted to a justicar? That wasn't news to Theo, but neither did it do anything to calm his fire.

"You didn't answer my question," Theo said.

Now Pascek's expression did harden. He rose slowly from his seat. Normal physical standards, Theo knew, didn't necessarily apply to Kindred, as with Lucinde's apparent youth. Pascek stood barely five feet tall, but his countenance was that of an avenging god. Theo wondered for an instant if he'd pushed too far. It would be a close thing if he and the justicar ever came to blows.

"This assault," Pascek said coolly, "has been under consideration for quite some time. Myself, Lucinde, Lady Anne, Prelate Ulfila...we were awaiting an opportunity...."

"And the Sabbat gave you an opportunity," Theo said. *An opportunity to take the city or to fuck Michaela?* He suspected capturing the city was merely a pleasant bonus.

"Precisely," Pascek said, not elaborating on the specific nature of the opportunity.

"Just like you had an opportunity to test me," Theo growled.

Pascek sighed again. He glanced at his watch. "A test that you passed with flying colors, as I knew you would. All the better for Lucinde to see first-hand how trustworthy my archons are."

Bullshit, Theo thought. *You're a paranoid fucking bastard, and you woulda loved catching me at something.*

Pascek could see that Theo was not convinced, but the justicar's patience was at an end. "If you fear a test of your loyalty, there must be a reason."

"I don't 'fear' shit."

"Very eloquent, Archon. As for your not knowing everything that you would like to have known," Pascek waved a hand, dismissing the complaint, "there are numerous explanations: You were on the front line. How many soldiers on the front line know what their general is planning? More importantly," and now he took a step closer; the justicar came up to Theo's chest but narrowed his eyes and glared menacingly nonetheless, "*that is how I wanted it.*"

The two Brujah faced one another from just a few feet apart, Theo not going quite far enough to be disloyal, Pascek not going quite far enough to dismiss his archon.

I guess you got what you wanted, then, Theo thought. The fire still burned in his belly, but it was low and hot like red-orange coals. It was a foundation to rival a furnace, but it did not burn out of control. He could have let it get beyond control. Easily. But standing there across from Pascek, Theo was reminded of Lydia on the plane, how pissy she was, out of control. Except this time *he* was Lydia, bitching about what his boss had decided was best. Maybe she was right then, maybe he was right now. Or maybe he'd been right then, and Pascek was right now.

Or maybe I'll just have to kick everybody's fucking ass, Theo thought.

Jaroslav Pascek didn't know quite what to make of the half-smile that came across Theo's face just before the archon turned and left. He trudged back down the hallway in his shit-kicker boots. No point in polishing them tonight. It was too late. Besides, they'd just get dirty again tomorrow night.

The others followed at a distance, ankle deep in putrid liquid and fecal matter. They didn't speak to their leader. His silence was contagious, oppressive. They didn't dare speak even to one another. The sewers themselves seemed to fall silent before the leader. The inevitable *plink plink* of water was absent. Squeaking rats fell silent and watched the procession of deformed corpses like some type of macabre parade.

Above ground—*in the world*, as the leader called it when he did rarely speak—the war was beginning anew. Let them have their war. There was enough to be done in aiding them. The *antitribu* were fair game, as well as a suitable alibi. However, *the underneath*, as he called these tunnels and caverns and crevices that were his lot, the lot of all of them, hid bigger game.

He stopped, observed the silence, swished his foot slowly so that the ripples would obscure the reflection of his visage. *We will find you*, he thought. *Yes, we will find you.*

Above ground, in the world, several hundred feet above and a few miles away, Theo Bell was again tracking Sabbat through Harlem. The Brujah archon could not know of these people, the third justicar in the city, and the hatred that raged in his heart.

About the author

Gherbod Fleming has recurring nightmares about that famous film clip of the javelin accident. He is only slightly disturbed by the "agony of defeat" ski wreck. Fleming is the author of **Clan Novel: Gangrel, Clan Novel: Ventrue,** and **Clan Novel: Assamite,** as well as the **Vampire: The Masquerade** Trilogy of the Blood Curse—**The Devil's Advocate, The Winnowing,** and **Dark Prophecy.**

The Vampire Clan Novel Series

Clan Novel: Toreador
These artists are the most sophisticated of the Kindred.

Clan Novel: Tzimisce
Fleshcrafters, experts of the arcane, and the most cruel of Sabbat vampires.

Clan Novel: Gangrel
Feral shapeshifters distanced from the society of the Kindred.

Clan Novel: Setite
The much-loathed serpentine masters of moral and spiritual corruption.

Clan Novel: Ventrue
The most political of vampires, they lead the Camarilla.

Clan Novel: Lasombra
The leaders of the Sabbat and the most Machiavellian of all Kindred.

Clan Novel: Assamite
The most feared clan, for they are assassins of both vampires and mortals.

Clan Novel: Ravnos
These devilish gypsies are not welcomed by the Camarilla, nor tolerated by the Sabbat.

Clan Novel: Malkavian
Thought insane by other Kindred, they know that within madness lies wisdom.

Clan Novel: Giovanni
Still a respected part of the mortal world, this mercantile clan is also home to necromancers.

Clan Novel: Brujah
Street-punks and rebels, they are aggressive and vengeful in defense of their beliefs.

Clan Novel: Tremere
The most magical of the clans and the most tightly organized.

Clan Novel: Nosferatu
Horrific to behold, these sneaks know more secrets than the other clans—secrets that will only be revealed in this, the last of the **Vampire Clan Novels**.

......................continues.

The American Camarilla is reeling. Can they take advantage of the death of Cardinal Monçada to turn the tide back against the Sabbat, who have grabbed vast tracts of the Eastern United States? Despite the apparent efforts of Hazimel himself, the Eye of Hazimel is again in the hands of a once-pitiful Toreador named Leopold. Whose influence could be greater than that of the Methuselah from whom the Eye originated?

Some characters have yet to be introduced, while the stars of previous books will still return. Victoria, Hesha, Ramona, Jan, Vykos and others have ambitions and goals to realize.

The end date of each book continues to press the timeline forward, and the plot only thickens as you learn more. The series chronologically continues in **Clan Novel: Tremere**. Excerpts of this exciting novel are on the following pages.

CLAN NOVEL: TREMERE
ISBN 1-56504-827-X
WW#11111
$5.99 U.S.

Saturday, 19 June 1999, 11:00 PM
Suburban Lodge
Cincinnati, Ohio

Nickolai awoke bathed in blood-sweat. A thin red film coated every inch of his body and had already soaked through the silk bedclothes. Ruined.

He peeled away the clinging topsheet and, holding it at arm's length, let it slump to the floor. Blood puddled and lapped over his hands as he pushed himself to his feet. A trail of sticky red footprints followed him down the hall and into the bathroom.

In a matter of days, no doubt, the authorities would discover these macabre signs and begin the search for a corpse that they would never find. But that was nothing to Nickolai. This particular ambulatory corpse would be far away from here long before daybreak.

The shower hissed to life. Nickolai's hand shook as he fumbled with the dial. *Running water*, he thought. *Just what the doctor ordered.*

For the first time this evening, he smiled. Running water was the usual folktale prescription for these situations. *Interpose running water between self and pursuing nightmare. Take once per night as needed.*

His kind, however, were traditionally on the receiving end of this particular superstition.

Nonetheless, the scalding water worked as advertised. Its humble magic not only dispelled the physical signs of the previous night's struggle, but some of the terror as well—the terror of waking with the certainty that, while he slept, he had been observed.

It was always the same—the faces of the children, watching him, judging him. He could find no hint of accusation in their glassy, unblinking eyes, nor words of condemnation on their cold, bluish lips. But the very sight of them sufficed to fill Nickolai with a dread, a certainty of condemnation.

For the third night in a row, Nickolai had dreamt of the children down the well.

Nickolai closed his eyes. The faces were there still, awaiting him. Round and bright as moons, smiling up at him from just beneath the surface of the still water. Infinitely patient.

His gaze was arrested by the face of the nearest youth, a boy of no more than seven years. Nickolai traced the gentle curve of the youth's smooth, unblemished cheek. The boy's icy blue eyes were as large and perfectly round as saucers. His hair fanned out all around the bright face like a fishing net cast out upon the surface of the dark waters. Tangled strands lapped gently at the slick side of the well.

The faces neither moved nor spoke. They had been drowned and their bodies had apparently been some time now in the waters. Although the faces were calm, almost serene, Nickolai knew that their deaths were not the result of some misstep in the dark.

They had *been* drowned. He repeated the phrase a second time with a slight, but significant shift of emphasis. They had been willfully drowned, cast into the well, abandoned to panic, flounder, and sink beneath the chill waters. Lost to sight. Lost to memory.

Only they did not stay down (would not stay down!). They had performed that final and miraculous transformation.

by Eric Griffin

They were like the alchemists, struggling for decades in their damp cellars to work the Great Art—to transmute lead into gold—to free themselves from the burden of their leaden physical bodies and achieve the pure gold of spiritual transcendence. But it was the children who'd discovered how the trick was turned.

The waters of the well had swallowed them utterly and completely. But the children, they had worked the Great Reversal, swallowing in turn the waters of the well. They rose, ascending bodily, if not into the heavens, at least to the water's surface. There they hung, suspended like luminous moons, presiding over the benighted waters.

These were his silent accusers, his judges. The lapping waters whispered to him like a lover, promises and gentle reproaches.

Nickolai no longer railed against their rebuke. In a strange way, he had begun to look upon their nocturnal visits as something of a legacy, a birthright.

They were old certainly, those bright, youthful faces. Older by far than Nickolai or any wrong he might have committed. Still, he knew himself to be party to the crime against them—if not against this child who bobbed gently against the slick stones of the well, then certainly against hundreds like him. Souls he had cast suddenly and unprepared into the river of night.

Nickolai had always suspected (but did not know, could never know now) that the well was brimming full of youth, swarming with bright golden eyes, buoyed up ever nearer to the well's lip by the sheer mass of bodies beneath.

He imagined that some night soon (very soon now) he might awake to find that they had spilled out over the brink of the well.

He imagined the tide of the drowned washing out over the fields, running like a tangled river through the woodlands, crashing against the heel of the mountains.

Nickolai wondered what, if anything, might hope to stand against that great flood—whether any bulwark against the rising tide might hope to endure.

No, they would win in the end, these children. This flood of shining victims. They had the weight of numbers behind them. They had the advantage of age—of uncounted ages. And they were so very patient.

Nickolai knew that he was to be their victim as surely as they were his own. He had been specially sought out, chosen, marked. When that tide finally rose, when his dream lapped over into the waking world, he would be culled out.

Nickolai did not fear death. He had been there at least once already. Nor did he fear oblivion. But he very keenly felt it his duty to remain among the living. This desire did not arise from any overdeveloped sense of self-preservation, nor even of self-interest, nor certainly of self-importance. Nickolai had a very acute sense of what he was. He was the last of his kind. And that was a great and terrible responsibility.

He had witnessed what no one should be forced to witness—his brothers, his order, his entire bloodline, being slaughtered to a man.

by eric Griffin

When Nickolai's death came for him at last, it would obliterate not only his physical form—a debt which was, admittedly, long overdue—but it would also erase forever certain memories, ideas, ideals, of which this physical form was the final repository.

With Nickolai's death would pass forever the sight of that ill-fated ritual enacted beneath the streets of Mexico City—the massacre that had destroyed his brethren. With his death would pass the memory of the multiform and varied wonders, the arcana, the passwords, the miracles, the secret sigils, the hidden names of God—the hard-won treasures of centuries. The legacy and birthright of his people.

And with his death would also pass the last living memory of those unforgettable eyes, their terrible brightness undimmed by the weight of death and dark water upon them. In victory, the children must necessarily die with him and the night tremors—*les tremeres*—at last come to an end.

Nickolai killed the spray of water and walked dripping from the tub, painfully aware that he was one evening closer to that end, and not knowing how to arrest or even delay its coming.

by Eric Griffin

next:TREMERE